CONTEMPORARY AMERICAN FICTION

LITHIUM FOR MEDEA

Kate Braverman is a novelist and poet living in Los Angeles. Her second novel, *Palm Latitudes*, is also available from Penguin.

CRITICAL ACCLAIM FOR *LITHIUM FOR MEDEA*

"To call *Lithium for Medea* a superb first novel is to do it a disfavor; it is a superb novel, period. . . . To tell her erotic, moving story, Ms. Braverman has chosen a style which makes one wish to resurrect freshness into that overused adjective 'brilliant.' Ms. Braverman is a powerful writer."

—John Rechy

"This first novel is a contemporary horror story, horrible enough to confound the distinction between the hallucinatory and the real. . . . The book intensifies our current sense of existing evils manifesting an intolerable past."

—*Chicago Tribune Book World*

"Highly charged and deeply moving . . . ambitious and impulsive . . . It's a book that lingers in the mind like a species of mutant flower."

—*Los Angeles Herald Examiner*

"Braverman's dialogue is cruelly brilliant, her style a pounding, jumpy staccato of accuracy, fierce and glittering and relentless."

—*Arkansas Gazette*

"Has the power and intensity you don't see much outside of rock and roll."

—*New West*

"Some of the best writing of the decade"

—*Fort Worth Star-Telegram*

"The prose is vital and original, the characters are haunting, and the structure is rich and subtle. . . . with *Lithium* as her first novel, one can only imagine that Braverman will become a major voice."

—*L.A. Weekly*

"Kate Braverman has the ability to write a great tragedy."

—*New York*

"Lays bear the dark side of the family while ironically affirming the primacy of familial allegiance. . . . Braverman is a poet, and in this first novel, the vividness of poetic image is present from the first page."

—*Miami Herald*

Lithium for Medea

❧ ❧ ❧

a novel by
Kate Braverman

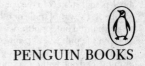

PENGUIN BOOKS

For my father

PENGUIN BOOKS
Published by the Penguin Group
Viking Penguin, a division of Penguin Books USA Inc.,
40 West 23rd Street, New York, New York 10010, U.S.A.
Penguin Books Ltd, 27 Wrights Lane,
London W8 5TZ, England
Penguin Books Australia Ltd, Ringwood,
Victoria, Australia
Penguin Books Canada Ltd, 2801 John Street,
Markham, Ontario, Canada L3R 1B4
Penguin Books (N.Z.) Ltd, 182–190 Wairau Road,
Auckland 10, New Zealand

Penguin Books Ltd, Registered Offices:
Harmondsworth, Middlesex, England

First published in the United States of America by
Harper & Row, Publishers, Inc., 1979
Published in Penguin Books 1989

10 9 8 7 6 5 4 3 2 1

This is a work of fiction. The characters and setting are the
result of the author's imagination. Any resemblances to per-
sons living or dead are coincidental.

Portions of this novel have appeared in somewhat different
form in a previous book of poetry, *Milk Run* (Momentum
Press, Calif.), and in *Cameos: New Small Press Women Poets*
(Crossing Press, N.Y.).

LIBRARY OF CONGRESS CATALOGING IN PUBLICATION DATA
Braverman, Kate.
Lithium for Medea : a novel / by Kate Braverman.
p.   cm.—(Contemporary American fiction)
ISBN 0 14 01.2641 4
I. Title.   II. Series.
PS3552.R3555L58   1989
813'.54—dc20   89–31759

Printed in the United States of America
Set in Caledonia

❧1❧

Everything requires an explanation: Name. Age. Sexual persuasion. Occupation. Incarnation. Marital status. Addictions. Past arrests (note convictions).

There was a sound.

Water.

I was running a bath. It was good to be liquid. I didn't have skin at all. I had the gleam of a fish, the fine etched scales and gills. I knew the soft channel down. I could burrow into the blue weight. I could wear whitecaps embossed across my back, a kind of spine. I could eat anything and breathe under water.

My paraphernalia was neatly arranged on the floor. I had the cotton and alcohol ready. I had ground the cocaine into a fine white powder. My spoon was balanced on the bathtub ledge, next to my syringe, when the telephone rang.

"I have to talk to you."

The voice was cold, sharp and precise. I tried to place it. Usually my mother will have her secretary call me. And of course Francine has so many voices, now plaintive and aloof, now cooing and abused. There's her voice of exhaustion, throat raspy from too many cigarettes and too much coffee at the end of budget conferences. And there's the whispery tone of caution she uses when she isn't alone.

"What is it?" My heart jumped.

My life was a set of parallel worlds. Each world had distinct rules and personalities. The chemistry, mathematics and history were different. The basic elements, evolution and development were all as intricate and absolutely different as the life on a carbon-based world might differ from a world built on methane. My parallel worlds were wide and smooth and clearly marked. The atmospheres were mutually lethal. There could be no collision course.

"It's your father," Francine said. She let it sit there a long time. "He's sick." She paused again. "He's going to the hospital in the morning."

"Cancer?" I had been holding the syringe. I put the needle down.

"Bingo," Francine said. "And bad."

My wet feet touched the floor. I took the syringe apart and put it on the bottom of my purse. I had a feeling I was going to need it.

I drove east toward Beverly Hills and wound north off Sunset Boulevard. I was filled with something suffocating, painful and dry. The whole world looked as if it had been washed in white paint.

My mother's house is very white. It is in the authentic Spanish tradition, built around an orange tiled courtyard. The house is nestled on the side of a hill, its long back red-brick terrace flush with the mountain. Francine bought the house the year she divorced my father.

"See what I've done?" she demanded.

It was the first time I had come to see her new house, to take the grand tour. Francine was wearing a peach-colored silk dressing gown. She rustled as she walked, now pausing, now pointing to each special feature in the house one by one. My mother has always had an enormous capacity and appreciation for details. She also has an excellent memory. I followed her silently through the thickly carpeted rooms.

"Notice the floor plan, the creative use of space. Only one bedroom." Francine stared at me. The other bedrooms had been converted to a study, a sunroom and a wood-paneled room housing a pool table.

I understood. In her way, Francine was saying it wasn't a family house. There wasn't a family anymore. The only overnight guests Francine planned on would be sleeping in her bed.

"I did it all myself." Her voice was rising higher, edging into her private danger zone.

Francine indicated the gently arched doorways, the rounded windows which a special crew would come and scrub once each week. I stared at the windows. They were large and sparkling clean. The air beyond was a pale undemanding blue.

"I did this all by myself. You know who's lived here? Zsa Zsa Gabor. Elliot Gould. Howard Hughes used to keep his starlets here." Francine grabbed my wrist. She put her face very close to mine. Her eyes were amber, enormous and fixed.

"Why do I tell you this? I want you to be proud of me."

Francine pointed to the twenty-two-foot-high ceilings. She showed me the fireplace in the bedroom and the mirrors along the far wall. She pointed to the wood ("genuine redwood—I had it tested") beams in the ceilings. She showed me the dining room with its three glass sides all looking down on the city.

"I was an orphan," Francine said. Her tone was hushed, conspiratorial, as if she had never before revealed this information to me or anyone. She leaned closer. "I was abandoned. Deserted during the Depression."

Francine was showing me the bar she had just installed. It had an imported black marble surface and water taps adjusted to accommodate bourbon, Scotch and gin.

"I had no education, no resources." She looked at me, hard.

I didn't miss the implications. She was saying I hadn't suffered gross deprivations as she had. I had been given an education, that nebulous thing she called resources and even the semblance of a family. And I had failed.

"I was sixteen when I married him," Francine said.

We were leaning against the bar. My mother poured herself a small glass of Scotch.

"Then he got cancer. Cancer!" my mother cried. She drank the Scotch.

"There we were. Bankrupt. Him in bed five years, an invalid. Me alone with a six-year-old kid to support."

Francine permitted her lower lip to slowly curl with disgust. As far as my mother is concerned, I am still that six-year-old child, helpless, overweight, needing eyeglasses and orthodontia, a terrible burden, a girl with nightmares and bad posture and an inability to make friends, to even say hello to strangers.

Of course, it got worse. And Francine does have her evidence. It's been dug up. It's been dropped in her lap. It's all there, polished and labeled under glass. I failed to graduate from college. I failed in my marriage. I failed with Jason repeatedly. I failed to find a man who wanted me, permanently and legally. A man to install me like a sparkling new appliance in the center of some streamlined kitchen with built-in self-cleaning oven. A man to give me children and Saks charge accounts, security and a future.

For Francine the world is simple. If one has the stuff, the talent, intelligence and persistence, one automatically succeeds. One literally soars above the huddled peasant masses, flies to the peaks of canyons to live on stilts and taunt the elements. Let San Andreas yawn down there in the butchered plateau. I am above it. I have ascended like the angels. If one had the stuff, it was simply a matter of reaching out and plucking one perfect sweet ripe peach after another.

Or else one compensated. One taught blind children or passed out government checks in the ghetto. One played the game right and became invisible. I couldn't even get off the playing field gracefully. I chose to study the special seasons of the canals and make love with Jason.

"Twenty-seven when my husband got cancer," Francine told me. She poured another small glass of Scotch.

I could remember what? There were sudden inexplicable absences. The house empty. A note left on the table. My first grade teacher gave me her home phone number. She said I could call her. Why would I call her? There were peripheral people, neighbors I barely knew taking me to sleep one or two nights at their houses. Their houses were filled with odd smells and the spices of alien foods. No one answered my questions.

I would sit in the rooms assigned me by one strange smiling woman after another and wonder how many people lived in each house. Who were they? When would my mother come back? Where was my father? Why was everybody lighting candles? Was it some kind of birthday? I would sit alone and wonder what these people wanted.

Later my mother canceled my piano lessons. My father spent entire days in bed. She brought him lunch on a tray. A terrible transformation was taking place, as if the big man who was my father was becoming a boy. Then a stream of strangers wandered through our house. They left with my mother's brass lamps. They took her new china plates. They carted out the living room sofa and chairs. I watched the truck drive away. By then I knew the world had collapsed.

"You have no idea what it was like," Francine assured me.

"You were a baby. I shielded you, protected you. I went out to work." She brought her face very close to mine. I could smell her perfume, her liquor and something hot and damp and sweet, overripe, overwhelming, her skin.

"I went out in secondhand clothes. I didn't even know how to drive or type. I went to work like that, in Hollywood, no less." Francine finished her Scotch. There were more implications, things black and darting, dangerous things with claws and teeth, perhaps.

"Do you understand?" Her lips trembled. Tears seemed to leap out of her eyes.

"I never even finished high school. Look." Francine gestured at the high ceilings, the arches, the sparkling clean windows, the genuine redwood beams, the whole city spread out flat and totally conquered below.

Francine sighed. There were implications, sharp, heavy, like metal splinters. My mother had done incredibly well. She had tested her wings against the airless, cloudless pale blue L.A. skies and soared, ascended. She began as a receptionist, answering telephones and bringing the boss coffee and yes, sir, sure thing, boss, I can do it. Do it better than you ever believed, ever dreamed. Now she was the producer of a television program syndicated by seventy-one stations across the nation.

"You've always hated me, resented me," Francine added. She was staring at the imported black marble bar surface. She sighed again.

What had I done? I had married a neurasthenic borderline psychotic and suffered the added indignity of having him leave me. My God, I had married a Trekie. I had not graduated from any organized, coherent course of study, certified and stamped by diploma.

Instead I had viewed slides of artifacts, bone chips, two-million-year-old skulls and shelves of ancient molars. The flesh shreds, the eyes disappear, the delicate printed wings of flying and hopping things dry to dust. Only the hard bones and teeth remain. The hard evidence.

Once I thought the hard evidence important and that a record of explanation must be left intact. Something undeniable, like trilobites, a kind of permanent fetus etched in the center of paleozoic rocks. The seas in which they lived disappeared before collective human memory. But the seas still exist now, still race their shadows toward some long-eroded shore. There is proof. Salt deposits lie at the bottom of oceans. The seas have dried and returned, again and again. The salt remains. It's something.

Without the hard evidence the past becomes infinitely malleable. The past can lose solidity, flow and rush the old banks, erasing and drowning. The past can take the road stones, one by one. And the memory of roads. It occurred to me that even hard evidence might not be anchor enough, not sturdy enough to withstand the flow.

I stood on the street in front of my mother's house for a long time. I looked directly up at the sky, which was an undamaged blue, plain blue, absolutely blue, blue as a piece of roof slate. I wanted some strange parting, an inexplicable red streak, an omen, however peripheral or at the mercy of that monster, interpretation. I wanted something to shake itself loose and take a position, any position at all. Nothing drifted in the sky, not even one spent cloud.

I knocked against the door, sensing, right at that moment as my fist hit the wood, that something was changing. Behind me lay the familiar convenient grooves of my parallel worlds. And I suddenly thought, perhaps it isn't all random. Perhaps there are patterns. Cause and effect. One thing was certain. The dropped brick lands.

❧ 2 ❧

I walked into my mother's house, wingless, hopeless. Francine still sees me as that six-year-old, pale and puffy. By ten, I was a marshmallow woman, pasty and white, almost as tall as I am now and afraid of everything. I did not accept easily. The sky was never simply a matter of air and space and color. The flametips of stars seemed to burn. My skin felt scarred from the constant abuse of a stalled white noon or a night black as a sea of rats. Summers wounded me, too yellow and hot, too molten and unmoving. Winters were bitterly short, a brief sharp bristle above singed lawns pushing stiff lilies with fat gaping toothless white mouths.

I was a brooder, caressing demons in my nine-year-old dark-ness, making pacts and spinning into sleep reciting my long lists of resentments. I could not forgive. I was sly, listening at locked doors and frowning at my mother pointing a camera, making certain she would remember and later, sifting drawers, discover a girl staring at her with twisted lips and mouth snarled. I was listless, always refusing, my mouth forming an iron no while I stored invisible scars from air torn by slammed doors. I wandered alone and practiced abandonment in parks of low drained hills. I was the one wearing childhood like a rare disease, already bored by fairy tales, already knowing better. I was the one with straight A's and secrets, the one who moved slow and said no and meant it. I was cold, closed, never learning to charm or beg. I was the one who spun webs and made night a contagion.

"You look terrible," Francine observed. It's a standard greeting between us.

"What are the odds?" I asked.

I knew Francine would compute the possibilities into odds. My mother and father had spent their first three years together on the road. My father was a gambler. The thoroughbreds were his passion. My mother and father rode trains and slept in hotels while following the thoroughbred horses from New York to Florida and back again. Their map was not cities or states, but race tracks. Tropical, Hialeah and Gulfstream, Havre de Grace, Monmouth and Garden State, Aqueduct, Jamaica, Belmont and Saratoga. That was before I was born. That was before the first cancer.

"Even money says he'll make it through the surgery. But there's more involved." Francine lowered her voice. "You know those bastards." She meant the doctors. "There's always more involved."

I was staring across the living room at my mother. Francine and I are always studying one another across a savage gulf of space neither of us wants or understands. It is dark. Things stir, rustle and peck. The path sinks. There are thorns. A dull wind thick with debris settles over the surfaces, the edges blur.

"Are you going to have a nervous breakdown?" Francine asked.

She walked to the bar. She sat on a stool with narrow cane legs. A mirror, round and the size of a child's globe, was perched near her elbow. The mirror was framed by small bright bulbs, pinkish and looking hot. Francine was rubbing a bluish cream into her eyelids. From time to time, she sucked in her cheeks and tilted her head, studying her reflection from various angles.

"Well? Are you going to break down?"

Francine made it sound like a race horse breaking a fragile leg. A horse that would have to be shot.

"I want to know what this is going to cost me. How many hospital tabs do I have to pick up? Just his? Or both of you?"

Francine held a small black brush in her hand. She was putting on mascara. Her cheekbones were high, rouged. They looked as if an electric current ran through them. Her neck was thin. Her mouth was full, expressive. I could see her thoughts float across her lips. Her hair had been arranged into a perfect auburn swirl. The telephone rang.

"No way," Francine said, holding the receiver lightly and opening a tube of brownish lipstick. "My husband's got cancer." Francine always calls my father her husband, despite their divorce. "I don't care if they're giving it away free. I can't get to New York now. Screw Barbara Walters." Francine hung up the telephone.

Francine's house is large and cool, elegant in an antiseptic way. Her house is a series of tans and beiges, caramels, browns, bones, oysters, bronzes, coppers and creams. Nothing of an earlier Francine remains. Here the past has been completely eradicated. There is not one single chair or table, not even a small lamp or vase, recognizable from childhood. The new tan sofas and light-brown rugs, the new suede chairs and camel-colored pillows came all at once. There was no birth. The house existed fully formed from the beginning, a house without mistakes, not even one tiny mismatched throw rug in a rarely used back room.

Over the years, Francine has been bleaching herself of the past and the invisible black scars it left embedded in her flesh. Francine has pronounced her past useless. Here, on the other side of the country, in the lap of the Pacific, in the land of always summer and peaches hanging big as melons on branches, Francine found her second chance. She was reborn. She ascended, white and pure, with the others, the elect, the white dazed, white bleached, white capped.

Despite her stiffness, and she is a stiff woman, Francine has a strange gaiety, a kind of unnerving optimism. I have observed her in lobbies and elevators, subtly alert, watching men out of the corner of her eye. She is waiting for the one who will take the sting out of darkness with a snap of his fingers. She is waiting for the one in particular to cross a crowded room and hold her close, hold her through everything—the childhood of orphanages, the lifetime of nightmares, hypochondria, chronic depression and the grinding tedium of endless budget meetings.

I have watched my mother straightening her shoulders when she feels a man glancing in her direction. Slowly, as if unconsciously (and perhaps it is unconscious), she rearranges the thin strands of gold necklaces at her throat. I feel her sucking in her breath, wondering, is this the one, is this him, has he finally come, at last?

In my mother's house, in the layers of tans and bronzes, brown-golds, creams and pale salamanders, I realize that this woman is not the same person I knew in childhood. Francine is something newly created, both inventor and invention. For her, the future is white and amorphous, flat and etched in something hard like stucco. The past never happened. It was savage and painful and now it is gone, over, finished, less than dust, less than the memory of dust.

"It's going to be a long haul. Months in the hospital, if he makes it. Months to recover, if he recovers. Are you going to collapse?" Francine asked me again.

"I'll try to hang on," I said finally. The ceiling looked dangerously low. The far side of the room had developed a slant.

"You'll do better than try, kid," Francine said. "We're in this one, this shit heap, together. I was twenty-seven years old the first time, alone, in a strange city. They said he wouldn't live through the winter. I had to beg the train ticket money. I didn't know a single person in this town. I had a child, an invalid husband, no education. You don't know. You couldn't know. I breathed life into him. He wanted to give up. He wanted to die and I wouldn't let him. It was August in Philadelphia, 102 degrees. He was lying under blankets, shivering. I bent down and breathed air into his mouth. Are you following me? I wiped him, washed him. I emptied bedpans. I changed bandages. I saw the blood, the scars, the horror. I went to work, paid the rent, put food on the table and clothes on everybody's back."

The phone rang. Francine held the receiver while blotting her lips with a Kleenex. "Sacramento?" She tilted her head. She lit a cigarette. "What kind of car?" Pause. "No, I'm not going to Sacramento for a goddamned Volkswagen."

Francine hung up the phone. She looked disgusted.

The phone rang again. Los Angeles is a city dedicated to the telephone. In part, everyone is constantly on the phone because they are continually making, breaking and changing their deals. They're constantly on the phone because here, in the City of the Angels, where the elect have ascended, they often find themselves perched on cliff tops, on canyon tops and hilltops, absolutely alone.

I sat down in my mother's den on a caramel-colored sofa with coral and tan stuffed pillows. For no particular reason, I began thinking about my ex-husband, Gerald. We were living in Berkeley, in a one-room attic apartment with a hot plate in the closet and a Murphy bed on the wall. The one window was small and permanently jammed shut. By April, the stiff air was unbearable. Heat dulled us into a terrible mindless lethargy.

Gerald had changed his college major for the fourth time. He had already lost his scholarship and his teaching assistant position. He said he needed entire days to ponder and reflect. A job, any job at all, would be degrading to the intellectual climate he lived in. When he spoke about his intellectual climate, I imagined he had a large fluffy white cloud inside his head.

We didn't have money for luxuries like soap and shampoo. We bathed at neighbors' houses. We ate Ritz crackers dipped in ketchup and salad dressing from the student cafeteria. I had completed one year of college. I was in the honors program, permitted to take special classes taught by visiting professors from Europe and the Orient, men and women who spent the semester dazed, in culture shock. When Gerald developed an inability to hold a job, any job, I dropped out of school.

I became a waitress in Giovanni's Italian Restaurant on Shattuck Avenue. The pasta sat steaming in big black pots and the smoke was hot against the thickening spring air. I had to wear my long reddish hair pinned up for work. I stuck the bobby pins in tight against my head each night. They felt like thorns. My feet ached continually. It didn't matter, I told myself. Wives often supported their husbands. Gerald would find himself, commit himself to some program of study, sooner or later. There would be grants and scholarships, a sense of progression. I wouldn't be working in Giovanni's forever.

Gerald and I hadn't made love in a year and a half. I was filled with an indescribable sense of futility. Gerald had gained weight. His flesh seemed oddly leaden, a heavy, awkward thing that had to be willed, jolted and forced into motion.

When Gerald wasn't reading, he was sitting in the lotus position on his straw mat in front of the television. Each night, at six o'clock, as if a gong had been struck summoning the faithful back to prayer, Gerald assumed the lotus position on his straw mat and turned on *Star Trek*. He sat there, barely breathing, rapt, as if in a religious communion.

The program was about a star ship, a gigantic machine holding a crew of four hundred human beings who seemed to be wearing flannel pajamas. The star ship *Enterprise* was one of only twelve such ships in the fleet. Its five-year mission was to roam through the galaxy seeking new worlds and new civilizations and boldly going where no man had gone before. After a while, I realized Gerald planned to watch the entire five-year mission.

Sometimes the *Enterprise* found parallel universes remarkably similar to earth, like planets patterned on mob-ruled Chicago of the thirties, or the Nazis, or ancient Rome with the added attraction of modern technology.

There were planets where the rulers lived in a cloud of magnificent splendor while the majority of the population suffered cruel exploitation below, in the mines, where a poisonous gas retarded their intellectual development. There were planets of aliens with antennae on their paper-thin white faces and the power to alter matter at will. There were green men, horned men, giants, dwarfs, blobs, monsters, Amazons and wayward telepathic children. There were decadent civilizations run by computers. There were witches, soldiers, merchants, kings, scholars, warriors, peasants and killers.

The *Enterprise* was run by Captain James T. Kirk. Gerald dismissed him as meaningless. Gerald was only concerned with Spock, the first officer, a scientist who was half human, half Vulcan. Vulcans had conquered their aggressive tendencies by severe mental discipline. Vulcans were freed of the scourge of unpredictability and emotion and love.

Gerald had a special appreciation for the forces and events that occasionally allowed Spock to have emotion. Once Spock was hit in the face by a kind of psychedelic plant that made him climb trees and laugh. And once Spock went back in time to an ice age generations before his people had conquered emotion. Spock reverted to barbarism, ate meat and had sex with a woman. Normally Spock had sex only once each seven years.

And then the sex consisted of something like an intense hand-shake. The rest of the time Spock amused himself with a special neck grip that made people instantly collapse, a more than genius IQ and a form of telepathy called the Vulcan Mind Meld. Spock also had gracefully arched pointed ears and greenish skin. Gerald seemed to love him.

"It's a metaphor," Gerald would say.

"But we've seen this one before. At least three times."

"Five times," Gerald corrected, sitting in the lotus position, transfixed.

Gerald claimed each new viewing revealed another aspect of the ship's functioning or Star Fleet Command. Gerald wasn't concerned with the plots. He was interested in the details at the edges.

"This is a poem about humanity," Gerald said, staring at the screen.

"But we've seen this show five times."

"The man of knowledge is a patient man," Gerald said, dismissing me.

I came back to Los Angeles to talk to Francine. I was nineteen and vomited all the time. I was seeking guidance. There were other problems. There was the revolution. Gerald had been in the library. He stopped to watch the demonstration in Spraul Plaza, the puffs of angry white smoke rising from the tear gas canisters. He had been listening to the explosions and the screaming. An Alameda police officer, tape covering his badge number and riot gear covering his face, hit Gerald from behind, across the back of his legs, with a billy club. Gerald collapsed on the cement.

"You look terrible," Francine told me.

I was sitting inside my parents' house, the house where I grew up, a modest pastel stucco in West Los Angeles with small square rooms and a sense of sturdiness and purpose. It is the house where my father still lives.

My mother and I were whispering. Francine and I whispered

together, as if my father were a foreign agent. He politely ignored us. He was standing outside in the small square strip of fenced backyard watering the avocado and peach trees, watering the perpetually balding ivy, the rubber trees and patch of wild black grapes growing up along the bamboo garden gate.

"You wanted him," Francine cried, trying to keep her voice down. We were sharing a marijuana cigarette, discreetly, a secret from my father. My father was watering the apricot tree. I could see him outside the window, his back turned, his hand directing the hose.

"I told you, no, hold out, you'll get something better. But you didn't listen. Oh, no, not you. You never listen." Francine inhaled marijuana deep into her lungs. "He's nothing. What was it? The Greek and Latin bit? Boy, oh, boy, did you sell yourself cheap. Cheap even for you," my mother added.

I began crying. There was a long period of my life when I cried and vomited almost continually.

"You've got to be tough," Francine explained. "Move out. Divorce him. Just go. He's nothing. Forget him. He's slime. Take a suitcase and don't look back. Maggots will do the rest."

Francine was getting dressed for a film premiere. She pulled a silk blouse over her head. Her arms looked like wings. She kept spraying herself with perfume. She was elated. Recently, she had crossed an invisible boundary whereby her name was now automatically included on special-invitations lists. She had joined a new, smaller, more elite inner circle. There were cocktail parties now before film premieres and dinner parties afterward. Francine showed me her new evening purse. It was made of round white beads that glistened like so many hard gouged-out eyes, or the backs of hard white insects. She sprayed more perfume on her neck. I couldn't bear her desperate optimism, her certainty of perfect ascension.

Los Angeles is like a white world, filled with ever smaller white circles, leading to some perfect white core. Los Angeles is where the angels, with their white capped teeth and their white tennis dresses, gradually edged closer to the pure center, ambrosia, the fountain of youth.

Francine swung her skirt in a peach swish against her legs. In her way she was saying, look at me, I'm not really an orphan. See the box they just hand-delivered, the big one with the fat round red ribbon? That's for me. I'm on a list with engraved invitations. I'm not alone.

"He isn't worth death by maggots," Francine said to the mirror. She was talking about Gerald. "You could probably get him committed, but why bother? He's got no assets, right? Christ, he's an embarrassment. He's garbage," she added.

My father wasn't going to the film premiere. He was going to watch a boxing match on television. My parents never went anywhere together. Once they had quarreled violently, kicked holes in doors and broken windows. Twice neighbors called the police. No one on the street spoke to us. They said our shouting made the dogs bark.

Now a strange calm had settled between them. They rarely spoke. There was a terrible sense of finality, of bitter ends beyond the possibility of synthesis or regeneration.

"We have nothing in common," my father explained. I stood near his shoulder while he picked avocados. "She has no sense of values. Her priorities are shallow." My father studied an avocado. He put it down gently in a rounded wicker basket. "She's been one hell of a disappointment."

"I'll call the lawyer for you," Francine said. She was walking down to her car. She was still talking about Gerald. "We'll nail that bastard. Maybe he doesn't have anything now, but when he does, we'll know about it."

I watched Francine get in her car. I watched my mother disappear down the street. I never seriously tried to talk to her again.

🐦3🐦

"Go see your father," Francine said to the mirror, making her eyes big, making her mouth red. "It's a bad night. The night before the hospital. I'll check him in tomorrow."

"You will?"

"Of course." Her tone was sharp and offended. She stared at me. "Do you actually think I'd let the old man die alone? After what he did for me?" My mother shook her head. "He took me off the streets. The bars with pimps and hookers. The hunger. The last foster family the state sent me to had three sons-in-law. It wasn't a family. It was two solid months at a gang bang."

My mother looked pale and tired. Her face was drawn tight and strained. Her skin seemed too thin. The proposed star of her new series had broken both legs in a car crash. He might never walk again. Her private secretary had eloped without giving two weeks notice. The calls were piled up, a stack of small square yellow slips. New York. Newspapers. San Francisco. London. Boston. Chicago. She tapped her fingers against the stack of paper.

"Kid, you don't know what bonds are," Francine pronounced. "I've loved that man for thirty years. He's been a father and a lover to me, a husband and a friend." Francine studied me as if I were oddly out of proportion, as if I had a scar or birthmark she had never seen before.

"You look terrible. Go clean yourself up before you see him."

In my mother's bathroom, with the special imported large round mirror bordered by fist-sized coral-colored sea shells, I improvised. I sat on the bathroom floor with my back against the bathtub, tied my arm off with my mother's bathrobe belt and shot up. I put the needle away. I stood up and the dull haze lifted. The room sparkled gold and radiant, seething and alive. The room was composed entirely of tiny orangy bulbs like brain cells. Each was distinct, each blinked open and closed. Within my body, a billion cells moaned, oh, thank you, thank you. I brushed my long hair. I ran the cold-water tap and patted cold water against my cheeks and forehead.

"You look much better," my mother observed.

The telephone rang. Francine was leaning on one elbow. She didn't seem to be looking at anything, not her face in the globe of mirror or even her tan and cream walls in the distance. She held the telephone receiver absently, running her fingertips across a stack of papers. She seemed exhausted. And part of me wanted to scream, Francine, Mother, abandoned, victorious, montage of babble, travel, swish of silk and hissing, the snake beneath the rock, absolved, holy asp, slow down, slow down.

"Yeah, I read the script." Pause. "You make the whole world sound like poison. Can't you find something pretty?" Pause. "How the fuck would I know? The Huntington Gardens? A new seal at Marineland? The goddamned sailboats?" my mother was saying as I closed her front door.

I drove to my father's house, the house where we had once lived together as a family. Once this house was my anchor, unchanging. Once my world was neatly contained between Pico, Olympic and Santa Monica boulevards. I knew the special seasons of West Los Angeles, seasons of white hot or stinging red at Christmas, lights strung on poles, glitter in the palms and the shopwindows brushed with machine frost. Dusks were a cold splinter at my back as I walked home from the school bus, the deformed sun dissolving above me and spitting sick orange blood on the pavement, the poinsettias, and the cats just fed and exiled to side streets with trimmed bushes.

Slowly I walked up the small hill, a hump struggling from the curb and covered with the thinning ivy my father planted. I glanced at the rounded sides of orange tiles on the low-domed garage roof. The roof was jammed with old newspapers, red rubber bands strangling their throats. They were tossed there by little boys on bicycles who knew better than to stop. Watch out for them, the neighbors cautioned, their midnight shouting, the sounds of things breaking. They're not our kind. Be careful.

I followed the narrow gorge of steep cement carved between house and ivy to the sliding glass back door. There had been long bad years, when my father was draped in a silence, when he sat alone, strangely fermenting. The years when he seemed to suck in all the air around him and give birth to vacuums, to cursing, my mother and father fighting, my father with the veins in his neck throbbing and his fist balled up tight and breaking a window.

There were the bad years, waiting for my mother to come home from work, the sound of her high heels on sun-baked cement, her arms wrapped around folders, free-lance assignments. She would pull the glass doors apart and sink into the closest chair, exhausted, pouring Scotch and eating scrambled eggs alone. My father would be watching baseball or hockey on television. My mother would run a hot bath. Basketball would become boxing. Francine would pull the covers over her bony shoulders.

I would wake to breaking and shrieking, my mother screaming and packing a suitcase at midnight. She was a pale shape by lamplight, crying, crumpled on the stubby wet grass in front of the house. A lone car passed near her head. My father would go down to the curb and bring her back.

I looked at the house. It seemed innocuous by dusk. The shame was covered with fresh pastel paint. The hate was covered with fresh pastel paint. My father would sit in his piece of fenced patio, silent and impossible as the banana plants along the back hedge.

This was the house my mother found. She collected the down payment and promised them anything, everything, after the orphanages, the cold stoops and red bricks of slums in winter. After the hospitals, this house, my mother and father together. And my father was master at last, with built-in barbecue, rainbirds and leaves to sweep. A man of property in a land of second chances.

I walked through the backyard. Absently, as if taking inventory, I noted the firm new branches on the peach tree. Lilies pushed up by the side gate. He had cut the apricot tree back. The branches looked blank and stripped, almost amputated.

I knocked against the sliding glass back door. I could see the whole back part of the house through the glass. After the divorce, after Francine moved herself to Beverly Hills, my father had redecorated. He took the collected sports paraphernalia from forty years out of boxes in closets and put them on view. Francine had always insisted on plain off-white walls. My father hadn't repainted. He'd simply tacked up an additional layer. The walls disappeared behind red and green and yellow pennants, framed ticket stubs from World Series games, Super Bowl games, basketball play-offs, horse charts from newspapers and photographs from magazines.

The room that had once been my bedroom was now my father's racing room. The walls were entirely covered with enlarged photographs of my father's favorite horses—Swaps, Omaha, Native Diver, Round Table and Secretariat. My father had bought a desk for the room. He sat there at night, studying his form sheet for the next day. He could still feel my presence there and I had always brought him luck. And it is true that when my father and I go to the race track together, to Santa Anita, Hollywood Park or Del Mar, we often win.

"I could of got a Ph.D. for the time I've spent studying this crap," my father once observed, puffing a cigar and glancing up from his form sheet.

"Some life," Francine used to accuse him. "You taught that kid to read a form sheet instead of fairy tales."

While I do know how to read a form sheet, to look for the horse's past performances, his works, the company he's raced with, if he's slipping in class or moving up, the distance of the race, the kind of track, the jockey, the horse's condition and breeding, I pick horses purely by intuition. I look for horses that have my initials or names that seem relevant to my life. I have never told this to my father because, after the serious training he gave me, it would disappoint him. My father's forte is middle-range horses. He's a master of six-to-one shots, eight-to-one shots. I pick them longer, twenty to one, twenty-five to one. My father doesn't know how I come up with them. He's afraid to ask.

Once at Del Mar, the summer my parents broke up, I won a three-thousand-dollar Exacta by picking Heartbreak and Mom's New Place.

I slid the glass door open. My father was lying on the kitchen floor. At first I thought he was already dead. He heard me and pushed himself up slowly on one elbow. The veins in his neck throbbed. He was breathless. He looked almost delirious.

"I'm going to die, I know it," my father said. He looked as if he were drowning. He had been crying. His eyes were the yellow of a cornered cat. His eyes were full and restless as a river moments before a flood.

"I'm dying. I can feel it." His hands were fists. He was a bird with a broken wing beating the heavy useless blank sides of a day.

"Don't quit, Daddy," I said. "Even money says you'll make it. Those are the best odds we've looked at in years. And you licked this same field before. Remember?"

Suddenly he seemed very small and old, bent, shriveled. I thought, you can't die. And something inside me was aching, was breaking. If you die, they'll call me a woman, not a girl. And I'm not ready, Daddy. I'm not ready for that at all.

"I'm cursed," my father said.

I nodded my head. Horse players are notoriously superstitious. They see omens. Even my father, who is strictly a form-sheet player and denigrates those who bet on the basis of names, numbers or colors, won't change his clothing when he's winning. When he's on a hot streak he will sit in precisely the same spot at the track and make his bets at the same window.

"I should have known. I was four grand up on the Santa Anita meet. I had a twenty-seven-to-one shot last week. Two sixteen-to-one shots. I should have known," my father said.

We were sitting on the sofa in the living room. My father was drinking bourbon. He had killed nearly half the bottle.

The first time my father got cancer I was six years old. Overnight the world changed. One day my father simply stopped going to work. His big brown toolbox sat unused in the narrow tile hallway. It just sat there day after day like a big brown sore. My father stopped eating dinner. He lay in bed. He whispered with my mother.

That was the year I was learning colors at school. On Monday we learned red. We drew apples and crayoned them in. Mother didn't have time to look at my apples.

"Apples?" My mother laughed. A strange harsh sound, not like her. "You want red. Red is blood. You'll see plenty of that soon." Could she have said that?

Friday we learned white and black. The neighbor boy across the street was vying for the gold star with me. We were throwing rocks down by the train station. He leaned over and whispered, "Your father's dying."

My father stopped driving his car. Now he sat in Mommy's seat, leaning against the window while she drove him away every afternoon. He was taking cobalt treatments at the hospital. He was only the second one in Philadelphia to get his throat blown up by a cobalt gun. And what was cobalt? It was a kind of blue, a kind of blue you wore inside. A blue that made my father push his plate of steaming food to the floor and rasp, "Everything tastes like garbage."

I watched my father fill his glass with bourbon. After what seemed like a long time I said, "Daddy, I need a philosophy for all this." I was aware, painfully, achingly aware, that my father and I might never speak to one another again.

"Life's a grab bag," my father said. "It's all a matter of chance. Take it off the top and don't look back. There are no guarantees. It's all a photo finish. You know what separates a hero from a bum? Inches. A nose under the wire."

Was he offering me his particular brand of Zen? I thought of all the years between the cancers, years my father spent content in his special solitude. He would stand at dusk watering the backyard, wrapped in his own personal communion with peach blossoms and twilight. He watched each sunset carefully, individually. For twenty years he lived waiting for the wild cells to come again, that black invasion. The ambush at the turn in the road.

"What are you thinking?" I would ask my father as he stood with his hose pointed at the roots of the apricot tree. Francine would be at a film premiere. Francine would be out of town on business or at a budget meeting.

"I'm thinking that shit always comes back. Sooner or later." My father would sometimes say.

Now my father looked at me. His face seemed to be slowly collapsing. Then he glanced at his watch. He turned on the television. The UCLA Bruins were playing the Washington Huskies. Dogs versus bears. Godzilla versus Mothra. God, it was all falling apart.

"I want to tell you something about your mother," my father said during the first commercial. Young men washed in the ecstasy of macho male companionship rode a jeep through barren country and embraced at a bar piled up with beer cans. "You only go around once," the announcer said. I thought, if this is a cosmic connection, I am grossly unprepared.

"I'm hip to Francine," my father said. "I knew it couldn't go on forever. I was thirty-five. She was some sixteen-year-old street kid. Crazy. Talking about poetry. Talking about communists. Running around in black tights, some kind of beatnik. Hanging out in the Village. I knew she wasn't playing with a full deck. And skinny. She had malnutrition. She was six months away from a whorehouse. But I don't blame her, dig?" My father looked at me hard.

"We were gamblers," my father said. "I got sick and it changed the whole balance. Your mother has a father thing. Some complex from being deserted. The welfare people were sending her to a Park Avenue psychiatrist when I met her." My father lit a cigar. He smoked it slowly, savoring it.

"She had talent. I always knew that. So she went out. She took a flier and won big. Still, for such a big winner she's really pathetic." My father puffed his cigar. "Tell her that for me, too. If I don't get off that operating table tomorrow, tell her. You got it?"

My father wasn't pouring bourbon anymore. He was drinking it straight from the bottle. "Look at that," my father said softly, with something like awe. "First Goodrich, then Alcindor, Walton, and now this." My father took another puff on his cigar. "This is a dynasty. This is poetry."

"Daddy," I began, reaching for something.

I remembered the last night in Philadelphia before the surgery for the first cancer. My father took me to see *The Ten Commandments.* He would get up every ten minutes to go to the men's room. Then he would return and hold my hand in the movie theater darkness. Years later I realized he was leaving to cough blood in the lobby. Cancer had pushed its special hard fabric, its whirlpool of black marbles, those wild cells, into a strange, strangling vegetation. Roots and claws planted themselves deep in his throat. Pieces grew in his cheek and tongue. Now it was happening again.

"Listen, kid. Don't plan on me for the play-offs."

I stayed with my father until he fell asleep on the sofa. I covered him with a blanket. I touched his hand in the darkness. It felt already bony and thin. The night was horrible. The whole world had started spinning in a fast silvery arc and I was being propelled out in a vast circle, absolutely blind.

4

I cut west and south down side streets, hardly seeing the road, running through stop signs and red lights to the ragged western fringe of Los Angeles called Venice, where I live. Here the city stops its white cement sprawl, its hunger to engulf the whole earth under tons of trucked-in concrete. Here in the lap of the blind blue-eyed Pacific, Los Angeles is stopped dead by the sheer liquid cliffs of the sea. Here the trail ends. After Death Valley and Donner Pass, there is only this last precarious oasis.

You must hang on here, inches from the sea. This is a land of strange personal mutations. There's a certain pull, an inexplicable force, some as yet uncharted form of gravity. The toes change, growing invisible sharp claws designed to dig in and fight against the slide into pale blue listless waves.

Once Venice was the summer resort of the first Los Angeles affluent, St. Louis and Chicago bankers and developers who pushed across the continent armed with the promise of an ever expanding manifest destiny of the soul. They built wood-slatted houses in a pocket of land facing the Pacific, ground webbed with canals. Perhaps the canals were filled with sea water then and the boulevards did not yet exist and one could simply swim home from the ocean. Perhaps there were families then and homes to return to at dusk.

Now the original houses of the Venice canals sag, paint peeling, reds a faded rust, yellows and blues bleached, a noncolor, not even suggesting pastel. There is a sense of abandonment. Deserted cars sit useless in weeds, looted, their vital organs gone. A shell of a canoe and a shell of a gutted speedboat stretch out like lovers in the field where two canals meet. Broken stuffed chairs rot under the sun. Old screens with the wire mesh ripped lie in random stacks between houses.

These are growing ruins. For decades the dirt has done as it pleases, pushing up what the winds brought, what a hand tossed. Here, where it is always some form of summer, everything grows swollen, enormous, oblivious to proportion. Early roses bloom in front yards on Carroll Canal. Honeysuckle spills over the wire fence of the house next door. Walls of red hibiscus hide windows. Lemon trees are opening up, stiff yellow. The sunflowers are higher than my shoulders, stalks thick as young trees. Soon the canals themselves will disappear, drained and filled to accommodate condominiums. As it is, few of the original dwellers remain. Jason and I are among the last.

Jason has lived on Grand Canal for twelve years. He owns his two-story red house. And he owns the house I live in on Eastern Canal, four city blocks away, four canals away from him.

Jason came to own these houses because he had a vision. He was living on the streets of Venice in the early sixties, living as it was easy to do then, sleeping on the beach and subsisting on peaches and oranges picked from trees. He didn't need to eat much. He was an amphetamine addict, a character known on the boardwalk, a too thin, small man with a nervous energy, talkative and curious, wandering the beach with a sketchbook, drawing faces and the ornate fronts of old buildings. One summer night on LSD with the sea at his back, Jason listened as a man spilled out enthusiasm for the new society. There would be great changes, a vast movement of people, social upheaval and revolution.

Jason was impressed by the stranger. There were new bodies on the beach now, long-haired men and women with sleeping bags and packs on their backs and a look of odyssey etched across their faces. Jason didn't know why they were coming to California. They could come to pan gold for all he cared. Still, they were coming. And, with his mind reeling and his eyes jammed wide open, he suddenly realized they would need somewhere to live. In the morning, Jason began looking at property.

He borrowed money. He began wheeling and dealing. By 1969, Jason owned a dozen houses and five apartment buildings on the streets closest to the sea.

My house is called the Woman's House. And for twelve years, all of Jason's women have lived here.

My house is set back from Eastern Canal behind twenty-foot-high hedges of pink and white oleander. From the poor rut of broken sidewalk a passer-by could see only a thin sliver of the second story. On the side of my house, two peach trees and a lemon tree sleep near the windows. Bougainvillaea hangs heavy across the front porch with its wood deck and one old rattan chair where I often sit and watch the canals, watch the lime-green algae near the bridge, the black-and-white ducks, the brown-speckled ducks with yellow beaks, push through the palm trees reflected in the water.

I study the canals because they have their own unique life cycle. In the early mornings when the sun is still pale and tentative, still wrapped in night haze, the canals are the color of a mirror, a delicate silver. As the sun anchors itself in the center of the sky for the long yellow noon, the canals thicken. This is the yellow of a mouth of sharp, pronged stained teeth, teeth yellow from grinding something unmentionable, something like bone. The water is coated then, somehow greasy and superimposed, not really like water at all.

In the later afternoons, when the sun is fatigued and indifferent, sensing loss and preparing for surrender, the water is clearly liquid again, but pitted with shadows. This is the season of sunset. The sun suddenly regathers itself for the final battle. It forms one perfect red ball and hangs smack above the ocean, a gouged eye, a beach ball dropped down into the slow stirring night waves of hungry fish mouths and darting crepe-thin fins.

At sunset the canals are streaked as the sky, fierce reds and oranges, thick, the color of lava. The canals assume a new texture then, something like boiling metal. I stand stock still in my garden, watching sunset across the surface of the water. I don't have to look at the sky at all. I sense the sun sucking in its last breath, preparing for the plunge. I know this sun. It sits above me, a monk in red robes, a suicide serene at the immolation.

Night rises imperceptibly. There is a slow darkening, an abundance of fast-darting shadows. This is the hour when shadows feed beneath the wooden bridges. Plants begin to sway and nod in some perfect agreement. They brush slatted leaves like tongues sucking at one another. They are plotting.

Someday they will find the sun's secret sleeping place. Vines will reach out and branches lock in an intricate embrace. The sun will be caught and bound to the ground. In time, a great new mountain will form. And only the trees and plants silently rustling and nodding their shadowy mongoloid heads will be able to see in the forever darkness to come.

There is night, the final season of the canals. The night is laced with sea salts. The air stings. The night is a terrible season, even when it is wrapped in a luminous grayish fog thick as the breath of condemned men.

Night is a kind of metal. Nothing stirs, not even shadows. The ducks grow quiet. One can't see the bottles that float in the water, the tossed-away pieces of old tires, the gray clutter of newspapers and plastic wrappers that stay on the surface for days like a species of mutant flower. Dogs begin to bark. It is time to wait for Jason.

Sometimes Jason will cross the Grand Canal bridge and then the bridge over Carroll Canal and Linnie Canal and Howland Canal and, finally, the bridge near my house on Eastern Canal. Sometimes I watch Jason zigzagging toward me, kicking beer cans from the eroded sidewalks into the blackening water. Sometimes Jason will come to me in his yellow paddle boat. I can hear him humming as he ties the boat to the wooden spoke he drove into the side of the canal in front of my house, the pillar he insists on calling a dock. Sometimes I will weave my way across the bridges to Jason's house. And sometimes we don't see each other at all.

I might wake up with Jason, at my house or his house. Sometimes I wake alone or with another man. The men are interchangeable and mean nothing. In Los Angeles no one is who he appears to be. Everyone will claim to be really something or someone else, aspiring, in transition, headed toward some all-encompassing vision. And they pass through my life like water, not even leaving an impression.

When I wake up it is the first or second season of the canals then, the pale mirrory unsubstantial silver of early morning or the thick yellow of noon.

My job consists of keeping Jason's books for him and collecting the rents from his various properties. Jason is too pure to do this himself. He must keep himself free from the tedium of ordinary reality, of calling plumbers and electricians, of keeping numbers in neat rows and making trivial decisions. Jason is too busy creating, planning his new canvases, sawing and nailing the boards together, sketching the canvases, arranging painting sessions with his models and sitting alone in dark rooms, thinking of women and their pink and yellow and peach-colored flesh.

Jason is also afraid to collect his rents. The pensioners with their gray streaked windows and canes, their cataracts and coughing, terrify him. The hippies call him a capitalist pig. The bikers threaten to beat him up and burn the house down if he bothers them again.

Oddly, no one threatens me. I step out of a fog bank, wave gray, a piece of the beach inching up to doors, peripheral. Ebb and flow and I am gone, shadow.

I lay down in my bedroom, the bedroom in the Woman's House, and waited for Jason to call me. Jason, making his eyes dazzle, dance and sparkle. Jason, making his eyes black tunnels, black torpedoes hurtling across rooms. Jason, making his voice a sea filled with small harbor waves. Jason, making his words promise, hard as spines. Jason making his words snap manic and red. Jason, my sorcerer.

I had enough cocaine for one more shot. I took it.

❧ 5 ❧

Jason and I live precisely nine hundred and twenty paces from each other; I've counted. But distance is always an illusion, relative. Jason and I live with an unspeakable gulf between us, a black space that might be filled with rows of stainless-steel spikes.

I think of my life with Jason in terms of eras, distinct blocks of time marked by unique characteristics. I look at our life the way geologists look at rocks. Still, a certain amount of dust settles, a fine layer of silt and sediment obscuring and graying. There is a loss of clarity. It becomes difficult to remember.

"I'll never get married," Jason said.

It was the beginning, the first era, when I lived in the Westwood duplex where Francine had installed me, wingless and hopeless. What was she going to do with me? I not only wasn't ascending; I looked as if I might be leaning in that other direction, toward burial. I had divorced Gerald. I had returned to flat Los Angeles planless and futile. It was the reign of Richard Nixon. I waxed my new floors. The war went on. I stared out windows, watching the tops of palm trees sway like greasy strips of confetti. I kept waiting for something to happen.

"I must be free," Jason informed me.

It was toward the end of my life in Westwood. I was edging into something new. He came to my apartment without calling. Sometimes he simply opened my refrigerator, made a sandwich and disappeared again for days. Sometimes he stayed for a week. I wandered through my apartment feeling like a guest, a newly arrived lodger waiting for my room key in a downstairs lobby.

"I'll make you walk on eggshells. I do it to everybody. I'll make the world a minefield for you. Help me," Jason implored.

I opened my arms and rocked him and cooed softly. Jason was like a skittish horse. I was afraid that the first time I looked him directly in the eye and said no he would bolt. I learned to take small noiseless steps. My mouth felt glued shut.

I wanted to nest with him, to cuddle him and cushion myself by lying secure in the warm dark center of his life. In his absence I was a somnambulist. I pressed the shirt he chanced to leave against my face and filled my lungs with his smell, his shaving lotion and sweat, sunlight and the undefinable, duck squawks and sunsets and honeysuckle coating a high wire fence. I rocked his shirt against my breast like a child. At this time, in that distant and blank era, I envisioned washing his morning breakfast dishes as a holy task, a profound purification ritual. I wanted to merge our lives.

"Swallow me, you mean," Jason has often accused. "You wanted to stuff and mount me, hang me on a wall."

Perhaps he is right. I know I longed for him, leaped and lunged for him, needed him as I needed to breathe. When Jason talked to me I thought cherries in summer, a slow swaying hammock, mint juleps and yes, you are master, take curry and just-baked bread and love me, love me.

If my words offend you now or ever, then forget them. They are lies, confusions. You know women. I was unwell. Does my body please? I'll change it for you. I'll thin down or fatten. Look, my skin will tan and firm simply by your command. I am yours, yours. I'll do anything. I'll grow new memories for you, cell by cell. I'll invent a new history with more laughter and more bells, more sunlight and sails. Watch me dream of drawers fat with socks that always match. I will be Scheherazade at 5 A.M. I am yours, yours.

"You're a romantic and I'm a sensualist," Jason explained. "That's the whole problem."

Jason had dropped by. I had been waiting all evening, sitting in a chair facing the front door, naked with a white feather boa draped around my neck and rings on my fingers, bracelets on my trembling arms, hands wrapped around the same melted-down Scotch in the same hot glass, waiting, waiting. We made love near the door standing up. We made love in bed. I was the shore and he was the ocean and I was eroding. My hidden parts opened glistening, a collection of starsides, a whirlpool, a phenomenon, girl, girl, girl.

At the end of our first year, after that initial period of probation, I moved into my house on Eastern Canal. Jason's second house. The Woman's House, he called it. The house where all Jason's women have lived during the past twelve years.

It would be almost like living together, Jason explained, but better. There would be no domestic quarrels, none of the trivia of an ordinary marriage, the dull predictable routines and all that goddamned bourgeois gray. We would stay viable human beings in our separate but equal ways, identities intact, free to come and go as we pleased.

I lived in a continual state of terror. Jason peered at me through eyes black from anger. He looked like a man slowly realizing he's been cheated of his estate, his birthright, his god-damned destiny. Every time Jason left my apartment in West-wood, every single time the door closed, I thought I would never see him again.

Then I moved into the Woman's House on Eastern Canal. From the top of the bridge in front of my house I could see his red roof.

"Nothing's changed," Jason cautioned, "but proximity."

He smiled, pleased with himself, as if he had invented that particular cliché. We both laughed. Jason laughed because he thought he was clever, witty and way ahead. He thought he was a silver bullet. I laughed because I felt superior. I smiled blankly while yelling and kicking and howling inside. I was encased in my private pretense of silence, a kind of form-fitting metal, my own brand of armor. I dedicated myself to becoming indispens-able, subtly, at the periphery. He began to need my intensity, my passion. Being loved excited him. Jason sensed the energy and power in it. It made him feel strong. He was anchored. I was there. He could drift.

"I'm with you almost every night," Jason said.

I nodded, not satisfied. We had driven north along the Pacific Coast Highway. We sat on rocks in the sun at the ocean's edge under a sky erased of depth. Sailboats slid slowly toward the Orient. I wanted to leap up and yell, let's get on a boat and eat rice and raw fish and sleep on straw mats all night holding hands.

"Let's get on a boat and sail away."

"I don't like boats," Jason said.

Jason's hair looked red in the sun. I wanted him to say he needed me. I wanted him to say, tell me everything, how you grew to your strange adulthood on streets of birches, streets of red fallen leaves clotting the wide lawns of gray stone houses. Tell me about your sled, I wanted Jason to beg. And the snow that fell, the fire with logs smelling of pine and clouds.

I wanted Jason to say, let it rise from ash, mysterious. I wanted him to press tight my swollen forehead and seal the dark and broken. I wanted Jason to say, let the gray shake apart like a shell. Come to me, darling. I will show you how to howl at nightfall and know the moon as our mother and dance the marble tides the sky provides for certain people.

"I need you."

"I know." Jason turned away. "It's tedious."

I reached out to touch his body bathed in sun. He stood up.

"I've got to paint now." He was already moving.

When I think of Jason, he is always in motion. Jason, pacing, restless. Jason, the mystery, the bastard, father unknown. Jason with his birth certificate stating that he arrived on the planet on the thirteenth day of May in Los Angeles. That year, the thirteenth day was a Friday. Jason often points to the date with its traditional aura of superstition and bad luck as if admitting his sense of stain. It exists within him, black and sharp, a kind of hard evidence.

Jason is a small man, two inches shorter than I am, even when I am barefoot. He is a man locked in a boy's body, a body he has exercised and pushed into abnormal strength in some endless rite of compensation, a rebellion, a kind of holding action against a buffoon fate. Jason's shoulders are broad as those of a man a full head taller. I have watched Jason build his enormous canvases and carry them over his head through his studio, dwarfed beneath his paintings and arrogant, balancing them easily.

"I'm a bastard," Jason often began, beguiling, voice soft, face opened, beckoning, smiling. It was one of his routines. Everyone in Los Angeles has an act, a polished five-minute cocktail-party or agent's-office version of his life. Jason had several.

"No, I really am a bastard," he would say, slyly, reciting his story of his unknown origins, the possibilities locked within him, past denied.

"I've always lived here, by the sea. I was a beach brat. I was born riding the peak of a crest of a wave. I was born with salt in my eyes. No, I mean it. I was conceived right down there on that beach. Six years old and surfing. It's all that sea in me. That's what makes my eyes change color. I've got waves inside. The ocean runs through me, man." Jason called everybody man, particularly women. Sooner or later, generally sooner, Jason would find his way into sex.

"We used to cruise the boardwalk when we were thirteen, fourteen. Let guys blow us under the pier for fifty bucks. I've made it with two chicks at once. Things happen when you're painting on the pier and boardwalk. You'd be surprised."

At some point in his routine, Jason would let his bombshell fall. "I've done everything. But the only thing I've ever cared about is painting."

It was a good line. He had been using it for years. The first time was when he was valedictorian of his class at Venice High. "This is all gratifying on some level," he said that day, in the high school auditorium, to a sea of white faces draped in black gowns, "but I'm just planning to paint."

Yes, painting. That was where Jason gave his image depth. He was an artist. He was permitted excesses, idiosyncrasies, lusts and addictions. He traveled to a different drum, all right. And if the woman he was talking to seemed receptive—and it was odd how Jason had the ability to find precisely the woman who would be open to him—he would ask her to pose for him.

"What do you think my painting is?" Jason demanded once. "Just some fancy way to get laid?" He was outraged.

Once I took Jason to Francine's house for dinner. It was a terrible mistake. They began badly and it got worse.

"I understand you're a painter," Francine began. This was the first man I had ever brought to her house, her new house, with the glass-sided dining room looking down on the city, the lights below an eruption of reds and ambers and violets.

"Yep."

"What do you paint?"

"Canvases."

"What is your subject matter? Your artistic concerns?" We were still on the hors d'oeuvres.

"Still lifes. Surfboards and rafts, tits and ass." Jason put another cracker in his mouth.

Pause.

"What do you think of the Impressionists? Monet? Degas? Cezanne?"

"They had their moments," Jason said. He was eating the last of the cracked crab.

"What about their statement?" Francine pushed.

"Getting out of bed in the morning is a statement."

Pause.

"Do you sell?" Francine's hands had begun trembling.

"Sell what?"

"Your paintings."

"Oh." Jason began working on his salad. "Nope. Not too often."

"What do you sell?" Francine was getting pale. It wasn't like talking to Gerald at all.

"What are you interested in?" Jason gave Francine his big smile. "I've sold a lot of things. Stolen surfboards when I was ten, eleven. Stolen bicycles. Later motorcycles, cars, property. I've sold grass from the ounce to moving three hundred fifty kilos a week. I've sold sex. Hey." Jason looked at me for the first time. "Did I tell you about the dudes I knew who were into white slavery? Stealing chicks and taking them across the border. They had camps down there in the mountains guarded by machine guns. Planes would come and fly the chicks out. They wanted me to go on a run with them. But I was doing the kilo trip then."

"What exactly are your plans for my daughter?" Francine demanded. "She's getting too old to pimp."

We had finished the salad. The roast beef was next.

"I got no plans for your daughter," Jason said. He looked offended. He forked a large piece of meat onto his plate.

It was becoming clear to Francine that Jason had not come to ask for my hand in holy matrimony. She was very pale. She was so angry she couldn't eat. "Are you telling me you're just going to use my daughter as you please?"

"She likes how I use her. And"—Jason forked another piece of meat onto his plate—"I'm not a humanitarian institution. I take care of myself. Period."

We didn't stay for the strawberry shortcake. "What a plastic cunt," Jason observed as we drove home. "Now I see why you're so sick," he said without sympathy.

"I never want to see that punk again," Francine told me the next day. "And I mean never. To think you let rancid garbage like that touch you. Don't you feel contaminated? Aren't you afraid of getting some kind of disease from someone like that?"

Perhaps that is when the schizophrenia set in. The night I sat at the dinner table with Jason and Francine, the night they spoke about me in the third person, as if I weren't there. And I wasn't. Who sat silently in the chair simply listening?

I thought there would be just two worlds then, the one with Francine and the one with Jason. I thought I could control the splitting and branching off, the places in me that seemed battered and ruined, the channels in my flesh that felt glued together, somehow bricked shut. I thought I could control Jason, myself, my passion and my contempt. I was trying to remember exactly how the splitting began, accelerated and took on a life of its own, when the telephone rang.

"He's going to die, I know it," Francine said, tearful and drunk.

"Even money says he'll make it."

"Don't jerk yourself off. Be prepared for the worst."

Francine believes in preparing for the worst. After all, she was deserted in childhood. After all, she was a foster child, taken in by Irish and Italian families who only wanted her for the forty extra dollars a month the state provided for her room and board. She spent her childhood among illiterates and drunks who starved her, beat her and never gave her a key to a house, not even in winter. And she didn't have the money for tampons and stuffed toilet paper between her too thin legs and thought she would never live until March, until the snow stopped and sun warmed the dull brown streets. After all, her right arm is permanently damaged, after the day she slipped on the ice, after the day and night she screamed and cried and begged before the foster parents took her to a doctor, before they set the compound fracture. To this day she cannot zip up the back of a dress by herself and the arm still hurts. And just when she thought she could take a rest, let her guard down, her husband got cancer and went broke.

She knows what it is all about. Let the world sift through the garbage and lies. She keeps her money in different banks. Her cupboards are stocked with canned goods and bottled water in case of earthquakes or wars, in case of depressions or invasions. Francine has a .38 revolver. She has detailed plans, with alternate and emergency subplans.

"Francine," I began, feeling weak, feeling the room start to spin. "I'm tired."

"You're tired? You don't even have a real job. I did two tapings today. I had a budget conference. I looked at film."

"I know." I tried again. I took a deep breath. "Your energy is astounding."

"I've got no fucking energy. I'm half dead." She began to cry. "He's going to die. Painfully, horribly. I can feel it in my bones. This is it, kid."

"Mother, calm down."

"It's a punishment. Him and you. My childhood wasn't enough. Heap it on me. Bury me in catastrophe."

"Why don't you get some sleep?" I glanced at the clock. It was ten-thirty.

"How can I sleep? Martin's coming in from Boston tonight. He's probably in a cab right now." Francine seemed to be regaining her control. "You know," she whispered, "Martin is very fond of me. He's a very important man. He's on the board of fourteen major companies." Francine named them, one by one. "Harvard Law School. The whole WASP bit. He thinks I'm exotic. That's what he told me last time I saw him, in Chicago. He said I was exotic in the best sense of the word. What do you think that means?"

"He wants to fuck you even though you're Jewish." And crazy, I added mentally.

"You're vulgar," Francine said, sobering up. "And so resentful. You can't stand it that men find me so attractive." Francine lowered her voice. "Men have always found me attractive. I have a special quality, a certain magnetism. I've always had it. Even in the foster homes, even wearing rags from strangers and hanging around street corners hustling guys for dinner. I just ate and disappeared. I had to do that to survive. Just food and then I disappeared. God, I was hungry, always hungry. I weighed ninety-three pounds when I married your father. I guess you blame me for it. You blame me for everything. Five foot eight and ninety-three pounds. Every winter, I thought I'd die."

"Mother—"

"Of course, you blame me for everything. That's the basis of your whole pathetic life, trying to stick it to me. That's why you live in a slum with that sick little maniac. It's all to punish me. Do you think I'm stupid?"

"Please." I noticed my hand was clenched so hard the blood had drained out. My fingers were sheet white.

"Of course, you think I'm stupid. Because I didn't get spoon-fed at some college? I'm in MENSA. You know what that is? It's a special society for geniuses. They verified my IQ at 168. Less than one percent of the population has an IQ that high."

"I've always been proud of your IQ," I said, digging my fingernails into the palms of my hand. The pain was intense. It helped distract me from the pain of talking to Francine.

"One day, you'll realize. One day, when I'm dead. And it's

going to happen sooner than you think. One day, at my desk, with the fucking telephones all ringing at the same time, I'll keel over, a heart attack. You go like that."

"I don't feel well."

"Your father's dying. He's the one who doesn't feel well. But then, that's typical. You never could face reality. Even as a kid. Why do I keep expecting anything from you? You've never given me one moment of love or solace. I jack myself off thinking you'll start now." Francine began to cry again. "You don't even think Martin cares for me."

I didn't say anything.

"You think I'm just a piece of ass for him? I got news for you. He's a very busy man. He's deliberately stopping in L.A. just to see me. He has to hold up a conference in Honolulu to do it. You think a guy from Harvard Law School with a Boston town house and an estate in Virginia has to hustle a piece of ass?"

Suddenly Francine's voice changed. "The bell!" she exclaimed, all at once thirty years younger, breathless, a teen-ager with a big, perfect lavender corsage on her way to the prom. She hung up without saying good-bye.

Somewhere, my father was curled up in a small ball, asleep on the sofa. I hoped the surgeon was getting a good night's sleep. I walked outside. I crossed the bridge near my house and zigzagged down Howland Canal. I stood on the broken sidewalk near Jason's house, on the opposite side of the canal, the water black and final between us. Jason's lights were on. I walked home quickly and telephoned him.

Jason answered cheerfully. Jason invariably answers the phone with rare optimism, as if continually prepared for the great moment, some ultimate offering. What is he expecting? A stranger's voice informing him that he's just won a prize in a painting festival? The big break? A new woman? An old woman?

"What do you want?" Jason asked, cold and flat.

I assumed Jason had a woman with him. He's always nervous

when he has a woman with him and I call, as if, after all this time, I'm going to rush across the bridges and broken sidewalks and storm through the front door hysterical, with a gun and a paternity suit, screaming he's the one, he's the one.

"Something terrible has happened," I began. It was very hard to talk.

"It's always terrible for you," Jason said, talking much too fast. "The sky's falling. The ground's cracking. The moon is sending you messages. Look." Jason decided to change his tack. "Could we take this from the top tomorrow?"

After a moment I said sure.

Outside, the sea breeze was rising, brisk and curled up like a wave. Everything felt black—the wind, the air, the inside of my body. I was cold. My bones ached. My bones felt chilled at their centers as if the blood was somehow leaking into them.

6

The operation took seven hours. The doctor, paunchy and opti-
mistic, smiled at us at noon. He looked like a man on his way
to a tennis court. When he pushed through the operating room
doors at 7 P.M. there was sweat on his forehead. His hands were
shaking.

Francine and I had waited together. We sat at a Formica
table in the hospital cafeteria while surgeons in green smocks
munched between cuttings. Delicate Filipino nurses scraped by
softly in their special padded shoes. The light was very white.

"I can't bear this," Francine kept saying, over and over. She
was slumped in her chair, her elbows pressing hard against the
hard Formica tabletop.

My mind wasn't working. My mind had shut down. I had gone

on vacation and left my shell behind, some hollow facsimile that slowly, dully kept dragging along.

Francine suddenly stiffened. She looked like someone who has just realized that what she is smelling is smoke. Her eyes went wide.

"He's hemorrhaging," she screamed. "His heart's stopped!" Francine leaped up. She rushed into the corridor.

Everything was moving too fast. The room seemed composed of separate pieces, like a shattered mural. I picked up my mother's coat and pocketbook. I ran into the corridor. I was riding on a train at night, hurtling past cities, harbors, junk-yards, graveyards. Buildings and bridges snaked and danced in the center of the train window. The landscape was smeared, a smoky magnetic ruin, part hallucination and mirage. Nothing was certain.

I found Francine in the doctors' lounge. "This is fascinating," she was saying. She glanced at me and smiled. "Dr. Harris plays chess, too." She indicated the dark-haired man on her left. He seemed to nod encouragement.

I walked out of the room, still holding her coat and pocket-book. I sat down on a curb in the hospital parking lot. A phrase began repeating itself in my head.

Fear is merely a condition of the mind, a condition of the mind. Isn't it? Fear is merely a condition of the mind, isn't it? Isn't it?

And the mind? The mind is a warm black pit. The mind is a kind of web, a nest where things hatch, things breed and grow, flutter, float and stab out with sharp impossible wings.

In the beginning, Gerald believed the mind could be de-scribed by the neurological model. I thought he was wrong, anchoring himself to an abstraction in flux. Every year the blackboard was erased clean and a new foundation laid. They called it the obsolescence of knowledge. They called it break-throughs and progress. They had an almost infinite number of labels and designations for their system, their process, all subject to revision and annihilation on a yearly basis. Why bother learning them at all?

Gerald thought it was a matter of mapping synapses. He thought it had something to do with placing pleasure electrodes in cat brains and shoving lights at glistening dazed worms. In his scheme of things, rats and mice running starved and terrified through mazes heralded a new era.

I knew the mind was soft and filled with waves like the ocean, dark at night, ebbing and flowing. The mind was connected to the moon, to currents and tides. It had nothing to do with the hard evidence.

"You're too whimsical," Gerald would say.

Were we arguing the nature of the mind? One point of view led to a commitment to technology. One side led to elitism and ultimately, unavoidably, fascism. One side denied, as true science mustn't, the evidence of alternative modes, the collective unconsciousness, the intangibles. It was a complicated argument with branching and forking side paths erupting everywhere. The whole world was like that then. Gerald was studying psychology in Berkeley. It was 1968.

Gerald's face was square, even and pale. It was the legacy left to him by generations of struggling shopkeepers and tavern owners, squinting over pennies by candlelight and voting without fail or principle for prosperity.

I would watch him walk toward me, up the steep path near my father's balding backyard ivy, and think, but he isn't yellow enough! Surely the one who will come to love me must be distinguished in some way. If it is to be this paleness, then let it be white, white as the side of a star, white as a sea-spit shell lying in sand, white belly up to a full white moon.

There was an unformed quality about Gerald. Later I would think he looked as if he had been created by a manufacturer of android astronauts. Not that Gerald looked like an astronaut. Rather, he was a reflection of that type. He was the stuff toy models were made from. He was like the perfectly detailed and nonfunctioning gadgetry attached to plastic ship decks, the miniature machine guns on glued-together airplanes. It looked fine but nothing worked, nothing.

Los Angeles spread out in all directions, a wound in soft flesh, impossible to contain. My world was bounded by the ocean, the slow arc of Santa Monica Bay gray and dying behind the break-water. To the north, flat dull hills arched like clubs. Somewhere the desert sat, hot and blank into Nevada.

What did I expect to emerge from the smog, the greasy numb boulevards? Gerald was a pale stain, August blond and blank as the sunbaked streets, a man like the anemic palm fronds and listless spokes of drained yellow day lilies.

I married him in Las Vegas, two days after we shared a mesca-line picnic in a Colorado blizzard. We climbed partway up a hill blanketed by new soft snow before the drug overwhelmed us and we collapsed laughing on the cold white ground. Snow fell like arrows shooting down, like meteors, gorged flowers, man-dalas with mirrory eyes. Our laughter shook the stiff mountain-side. Our footprints were like craters in the snow.

"I want to marry him," I had told my father.

My father was watering his peach tree in the backyard. He was smoking a cigar and evaluating something in the pastel distance. In the dusk the houses were simply pinkish and yel-lowish boxes. The strips of yard between them were pale green ribbons. And the pink-tinged dusk was draining, sickening. The whole world looked like papier-mâché stage sets, artificial, life-less and absurd.

"He's a jerk," my father said. He gave the hose a yank and wrapped it around the trunk of the apricot tree. "O.K.," he amended when I began crying, crying. I was always crying then. "He's a nice guy. But he's not for you. He's got no balls. He's a shy retiring professor type. He doesn't know shit about sports."

"Sports? Is that a criterion?" I screamed into the pastel patch of backyard surrounded by a twenty-foot-high bamboo fence, a yellowish wall in which stalks of banana and rubber plants and wild black grapes were imprisoned. And it was always pinkish, always summerish, and nothing seemed to change, nothing.

My father pulled the hose to the back of the yard. He sent a stream of water across the strawlike stalks that would open into bird-of-paradise, that stiff orange and purple flawed flower in the shape of a bird. And paradise was mindless and hard.

"You'd be surprised," my father said. "You think it's nothing?" He looked somewhere into the pinkish layer of night air above the tops of the pale yellow houses on the other side of the street. Houses on their own small mounds of green hill on a street where the neighbors never spoke to us and said our shouting made the dogs bark and twice they called police. And my mother and father were shouting at each other, were throwing glass ashtrays through the glass windowpanes, were packing suitcases at midnight, were fighting on the curb below the house in the soft white arc of a streetlamp and I was getting tired of it, tired of it.

"Sports is a clue, an indication. Take my word. You think I can't spot a stiff?" my father said.

But I hadn't taken my father's word. What were his reference points? New York City pool halls and horse rooms? The route of race tracks between Saratoga and Hialeah? The year he spent playing triple A ball for the Yankee farm club before his knees went bad? His manhood of trains and bookies and hotels, football and basketball games, boxing matches? What did that have to do with the issues?

Lyndon Baines Johnson came to Los Angeles. I went with Gerald to demonstrate against the war. LBJ was staying in Century City, a five-minute drive from the place where my father stood with his hose, inspecting his new crop of avocados.

I had witnessed a policeman beating a woman with a stick. She was trying to keep up with the flow of demonstrators circling the Century Plaza Hotel. She had a child with her. The little boy kept trying to jerk out of her grip. She was falling behind the others. The police were waiting. I watched them club her.

"The cops are beating up people," I told my father. He was watering his balding ivy. He was watering the bougainvillaea that snaked and danced purple across the roof of the built-in brick barbecue.

"We saw a policeman club a woman," Gerald said.

"Hippies?" My father wasn't looking at Gerald. He was dragging his hose toward the lemon tree. "They deserve it."

"Not just hippies," I shouted. And why should they be beaten, for that matter? "Ordinary people. Housewives with children. There was blood."

"You exaggerate," my father said. He was filling a rounded wicker basket with peaches. "Besides, the cops are all lowlifes, morons and sadists. Who else would be a cop?"

I watched my father wind up the hose into a neat green coil. I looked at Gerald. Gerald looked at me. We married four months later.

Suddenly we were living in Berkeley. And all at once, Gerald was a college boy with a desk and a Tensor lamp, yelling, "Quiet. Turn off that music. I'm thinking."

He began with physics, but it was wrong. Physics disappointed him. Physics did not make him feel complete. There were gaps big and wide as the black holes of space. There were limits strung everywhere like rows of barbwire.

Gerald decided to study mathematics and lost his scholarship. That's when I left school and went to work at Giovanni's Italian Restaurant. That's where the pasta sat in big black pots steaming and it was always hot, always dark, the secret tunnel down into the oily black center of hell.

Mathematics was closer, but still, Gerald sensed something missing. He conferred with more professors. A job was found for him in something called mathematical psychology. He was, after all, brilliant. He was on the ninety-ninth percentile in everything. Gerald dragged himself to his Monday, Wednesday and Friday teaching assignment as if he were living in a seeth-ing, form-fitting nightmare. He forbade me to come.

Once I went secretly. It was a small dark room in the base-ment of the Life Sciences building. The room was a permanent, windowless gray. Gerald was not wearing his glasses. I doubted that he could see me, hunched in shadows along the back wall of the room, squatting down, knees on the cold gray floor. Ger-ald was smearing chalk on the blackboard. It made a chilling sound like a rake scratching pavement. Gerald's mouth seemed oddly hard, as if the words he uttered were actually choking him and tearing his lips. They seemed to bubble from his lips and hang in the air all around him like gray stones. When they fell to the floor, there was a dull gray thud. I never mentioned this to him.

Gerald was settling into his thick silence. He stayed up late every night. He seemed disoriented in the morning, like a trav-eler, clothes crumpled, sickened by some subliminal, intermi-nable motion.

Psychology was the answer, he assured me. I nodded my head. Gerald was talking about the human mind, where all the possibilities were stored. When Gerald talked about the mind and the possibilities, my head filled with an image of long empty gray corridors lined with identical gray metal doors. The doors were locked.

Gerald began with physiological psychology. He reread his chemistry books and talked about blood groups, electrical charges and mapping the brain. He made it sound like an expe-dition into unknown territories. I thought of birds with emerald and purple plumes half hidden by jade green leaves.

Then the limiting factor appeared. Gerald decided that the system was rigged in favor of the experimentalists. He no longer believed rats were going to lead the way.

"Don't you see? The cosmos is infinite. It's man that's lim-ited."

"Of course," I immediately agreed. I felt as if I were taking

51

a holy communion. Gerald hadn't spoken to me for weeks.

The experimentalists were added to our list of enemies. Gerald was developing a social conscience. It was unavoidable. There were terrible events and forces all around us: the government, the war machine, the military-industrial complex, the Dow Chemical Company, the Pentagon, Nixon, the racist police, the FDA, the undeclared war in Vietnam, Laos and Cambodia, fragmentation bombs, napalm, the systematic annihilation of civilians, the rotting of stockpiled wheat while millions starved, the emerging American welfare caste system, the middle-class biases of IQ tests, the pollution of rivers and seas, strip mining, the destruction of bay seals and dolphins, the imminent extinction of most mammalian species, the draft, corruption at all levels of everything, anomie, ghettos, the oppression of women, the denial of civil liberties to just about everyone, the fascist AMA, the persecution of homosexuals, the plight of Indians, the threat of nuclear reactors built on top of earthquake fault lines, carcinogenic dyes and preservatives in virtually all foodstuffs, apartheid, urban decay, Detroit's planned obsolescence, the gun lobby, the exploited farm workers, Governor Reagan, the National Guard, the regents, the slum landlord we had, and now the experimentalists.

I tried to imagine the experimentalists. I thought they were identical men in identical white jackets. When I walked through the Life Sciences building and waited obediently for Gerald at one door or another, in one corridor or another, like a trained dog not even needing a leash, I watched the white-coated men pass near me. I imagined their identical cocks severed and placed in bottles of formaldehyde. The identical bottles sat on a neat row in a shelf at the bottom of my mind.

The experimentalists wanted to ring one universal bell and have the whole planet rise up en masse and salivate on cue. In time they would press one single buzzer and the world's population would march mindlessly out into the fields, harvesting the land past the point of calluses, smiles on their stripped and blank mouths, blood on their fingers.

"Don't complain to me," Francine said over the phone. "You want to live that stinking hippie life style, so be it. You want to be a big girl, all married, living in another city, then be a big girl. You don't know what hardship is, kid."

I was expected at work in ten minutes. I leaned over the toilet bowl and vomited my dinner.

On the television, Kirk said, "What do you make of it?"

"Most unusual," Spock answered. "Our data banks show no such culture on Gamma Four."

"But it's there, isn't it?" Kirk sounded as if he was thinking about what he planned to eat for dinner, after the taping.

Gerald was sitting on the couch. Buckminster Fuller's book was opened on his lap. It was a brown Naugahyde sofa I had bought for six dollars in a thrift shop. I called Gerald to help me. He was outraged. He complained. He had been reading Marcuse. We didn't need a sofa, anyway. We already had the three oversized pillows I'd insisted on buying. What was wrong with me? Had I no historical perspective at all? Most cultures had existed throughout time without any furniture at all. There were numerous examples of elegant, productive societies with nothing more than straw mats. I was too Western, too hopelessly middle class.

Gerald read Freud. He cut out a picture from a book. The photograph showed five men in stiff black suits staring straight ahead at the camera, unsmiling. They seemed to have a secret sneer on their lips as if they were silently thinking, there, assholes, see how right we were? Gerald tacked the picture to the wall near the brown sofa. I didn't know who the men were. I waited for Gerald to tell me. He didn't.

Whenever I remember Berkeley it is, in my mind, always autumn, always punched open, stinging and alive. It is the last apartment Gerald and I lived in, with the small asymmetrical bedroom opening into a dark hallway and the miniature living room with the three oversized pillows I'd insisted on even though we really didn't need them. Gerald was right. No one came to visit. We had no friends. It would be sunset. Below, the traffic was still and hushed. It might have been the rushing of small animals, gray scurrying rodents, perhaps.

Gerald was memorizing theories of primate social behavior. He talked about langurs, gibbons and howler monkeys. He was struck by the implications of sexual dimorphism and dominance hierarchies in *hamadryas* baboons. He said he was getting back to the essentials. The pieces were beginning to fit.

Jung appeared in our life. Now Gerald talked about dreams, trances, tarot cards, flying saucers, astrology and visionary states.

"What are you dreaming?" he demanded. He had flicked on the light.

I stared at him, rubbing my eyes, trying to wake up. Gerald and I no longer slept in the same room.

"You've got to remember. Tell me," Gerald screamed.

I couldn't remember. There was a red cast to everything. Red and black, like a fire at night when the black smoke burns into the black air and night itself smells singed. I clutched the blankets against my chest.

"Don't pretend," Gerald said darkly. I had never seen him so angry. "I'm warning you. Blue magic has the greatest spatial complexity. But green magic has the eternal power."

"Yes." I tried not to stare at him. "Of course."

"You're good, real good," he said. "You're not like the others. Sea traps over their holes. Weeds that smell." He made a kind of sucking sound. "You're not like the others. You keep yourself covered. Thank you. God will bless you."

"Of course he's crazy," Francine said over the telephone. "I told you that two years ago."

"I can feel them," Gerald exclaimed. He stretched his arms wide. He flexed his fingers. "My cells, my cells," he cried, rapturously.

His cells were ancient, he explained. Within him the first amoeba stirred. A fish struggled to grow lungs. An amphibian was washed upon a primeval shore and squatted in the sun, blinded and gasping for air. The climate changed. Mammals scurried out into a new world. A beast gambled, climbed down from the trees and left the dwindling forests. The beast was neither fast nor well-armed. It scavenged. It ate what other animals left behind. It was, from the beginning, an unspeakable creature. In time it realized its full potential and became man.

Gerald said he could sense the truth of it in his blood. He, Gerald Campbell, was a microcosm of the entire evolutionary life process on the planet earth.

I never doubted him. I simply never cared. Gerald was the scientist. He wanted me to understand. It was vital for my development as a human being that I become aware of the great events that shaped my destiny.

"You're not applying yourself," Gerald told me. He sounded disappointed.

Give him the black holes of space, I would think, slowly pulling on my short black skirt and pinning up my long hair for work, sticking the bobby pins in and jamming them hard against my scalp. Give him quasars and pulsars, African folk tales, the books with diagrams on how to build wigwams and canoes. Anything to keep him talking, anything to feel that we were still connected to some outside reality beyond the three rooms of our apartment. I put on the white cotton blouse of my waitress uniform, the blouse that denied the existence of my breasts. Then I leaned over the toilet bowl and vomited.

We had lived in the apartment two years. Previous tenants had painted the half-sized bathroom an enamel red. I would sit in the small tub after work, water hot, trying to empty my mind of everything while my legs and thighs turned lobster red. Above the tub, the walls felt sticky like blood, like some hidden and unforgivable wound in the building itself.

The bedroom walls had been painted a pale lavender. I slept

in that room alone. Gerald slept on a straw mat on the living room floor. I would lie in bed after my bath and watch the car lights on the boulevard below. I would watch the sunset. The sun was a thick ruby. It looked close enough to pluck and swallow. Then one could grow red eels inside. One could fill the bloodstream with red moths trying to push out.

Gerald was talking about the hard evidence. I turned away. Hard evidence had nothing to do with my life. Everything in my life was soft. Gerald was soft, as if his baby fat had returned. He held his blue jeans together with a safety pin, refusing to accept or deny his new white belly. And Gerald was soft, soft in the sharp darkness, the darkness that fell down on me like a huge clawed bird.

Heat clamped a lid over the city. Berkeley was sealed shut, air thick and hopeless. Not even the bay breeze stirred.

Slowly, stretched out on my bed, on the cool sheets, I pinched my nipple. I felt my breasts rise hard and red like the enamel walls. My breasts had stony eyes in the center, eyes straining to see something.

"You want it, don't you?" Gerald said.

He had appeared in the doorway. From habit, I immediately pulled my legs up and shielded my breasts with my arms. I was never naked in front of Gerald.

"I can tell you want it," Gerald said.

He sat down on the far edge of the bed. The it, I supposed, was sex. The it was Gerald on top of me, a paler layer of night, doing something to me, pushing some small splinter of night into me and collapsing near my shoulder, asleep. It was becoming difficult to remember exactly what the it was or why it had ever mattered.

"Why don't you admit it? I know you want it." Gerald's voice was hard. He seemed to be talking to a third party.

"Yeah, I want it," I said. I looked at Gerald. A stiff smile was positioned on his lips.

"If you want it so bad, go pick it up on the streets," he said.

I stared at him, startled. It sounded like the line from a movie. A nasty line, right before someone gets slapped. I didn't remember seeing that film with him.

"Go on," Gerald said from the hallway. "Whore. I've seen the devil. Big deal. He opened an import shop on Telegraph Avenue. He's got a backpack and smokes hash. Go on, whore."

Then night exploded, a tunnel collapsing in. And I was running into the night barefoot with the car keys.

I had rarely driven the car. Gerald said my manual dexterity and peripheral vision were inadequate. Now I pushed the car into darkness and let the night swallow me. I crossed the bridge into San Francisco feeling heady, letting myself glide down to the coves of flickering light. I parked the car in North Beach and began walking down Broadway.

The streets were crowded with summer night life. I walked quickly, as if I were meeting someone. I walked so fast I did not see the posters of naked women on the walls and doors of burlesque clubs. I felt the jostle of shirt-sleeved men and women, felt the imprint of their arms and legs as they passed. I felt the obsidian I had swallowed. I felt it turn inside, cutting new blood grooves. Something was moving through the empty corridors I imagined myself to be. Something was growing legs and a spine. Something was breathing. Soon it would start kicking down all the fine identical rows of pale gray locked doors.

I went with the first man who asked me. I was asked more than once, but in the beginning I didn't quite understand, didn't hear. Now I said yes, said yes before I clearly noted the man's features. I had walked nearly a block with him before I realized he was a sailor and young, maybe younger than I. He was chewing gum.

"Where's your place?" He had a Southern accent.

"Place?" I repeated, looking carefully at him for the first time.

"Room? Hotel?" He stared at me.

I was speechless. Perhaps I was not satisfactory. Perhaps he would not want me when he saw me, saw me as Gerald did.

Maybe it wasn't Gerald at all. Maybe I was the source of the terrible lack. It was my failure. I looked down at my legs. They were clearly outlined under the thin cotton skirt. Perhaps even the dark hairs showed, a blacker smudge in the night.

"I've got a car," I suddenly remembered. We were walking slower now, retracing my route, wandering parallel to Broadway, looking for the car.

"I haven't done it in a car since I left home," the man said.

I handed him the car keys. I leaned back against the seat, into the seat, and let the city reach out silvery neon spokes at my face.

We were winding down along the bay, down a long cliff. He parked the car on a cement strip above the ocean. I could see the white line of the curling breakers below us.

"You ain't what I planned on," the man said.

I had let the skirt bunch up around my knees. My legs looked long and white. I turned my ankle toward the light, slowly.

"I can be what you want," I said. The words seemed odd to my ears. I had no idea where they came from. I felt my nipples stiffen.

"You ain't Chinese." The man laughed. "Come to Frisco, I want a real Chinese whore." The man looked down at the water. "Or a real secretary. High-heeled shoes and all kinds of leg."

I flexed my ankle in the darkness. I was disappointing this man, this stranger. I was filled with a sense of failure.

"You shy?"

He was pulling me across the seat toward him. I let myself be pulled. My head rested on his lap. I felt him stir under me. Not certain what to do, I patted him gently, the way one does when reassuring a child.

The man arched himself toward me, toward my mouth. He had unbuttoned himself. He steered his hard cock toward my face. I opened my mouth. I could taste the man as I drove back across the bridge alone, could still feel his thick white fluid filling my tongue and lungs. It was like clams and sawdust, some kind of white glue. I shivered.

Gerald was sitting in his same position at the kitchen table. He was reading Rollo May. He did not look at me.

Heat burned the city. The day felt thick and old even early in the morning. June struggled to become July. Everything seemed out of focus, too liquid and burdensome.

Gerald began playing the guitar. He only played scales. He played the same scales over and over. He had been playing the same scales since May.

Gerald realized that the mind contained a musical component. The parallels between music and mathematics staggered him. Notes and numbers. Harmonies and equations. Language and sound. I had already slept with the bartender at work by then. That had been different. He had an apartment. I had lain in bed with him. He had kissed me. He had not seemed disappointed.

"You hate my guitar, don't you?" Gerald asked, not looking at me. His fingers kept moving on the strings. His fingers had become calloused, cut with deep black grooves at the tips.

"Don't you understand?" Gerald was staring at me now. "Pulsars are simply another type of flute. The universe is an orchestra."

It was late afternnoon. Gerald had sat on his straw mat in front of the television since early morning. Now he watched old black-and-white movies, grainy from age, about radiation monsters and magnetic monsters that looked like vacuum cleaners. Giant reptiles stepped over miniature cardboard Londons and Tokyos, breathing fire like mythological dragons. An American town was held in the hypnotic grip of aliens, things hatched from eggs or born from large seed pods.

"It's a metaphor," Gerald said. "Science fiction is our modern mythology. It's industrial man's creation myth."

I would lie in the thick heat half listening to the birth and death of monsters in the living room. The voices seemed muted and scratchy, like the poor old grainy prints. Always, in the end, a gleeful but subdued and momentarily humbled population smiled from the ruins of London or Chicago while the monster burned, while the monster was reduced to a big puddle of ash, while the monster was chained or hacked or drowned.

"It's an allegory about human nature," Gerald said. "Don't you understand the importance of this?"

It was Freudian, of course. It was Jungian. It had to do with the musical scales he was playing. It was night. I wasn't working. I had already slept with the history graduate student who lived in the apartment directly below ours.

Somewhere, Kirk stared into what looked like a small flashlight. "Are they intelligent?" he asked.

Somewhere, Spock stared into what appeared to be a fancy toothbrush. "They do seem to have a highly organized, efficient system of government. They have roads, monuments, scientific institutions, peace, prosperity, compassion, justice."

"Yes, but are they intelligent?" Kirk asked. "Have they got motels and car washes? Do they have Pepsi and credit ratings?"

"You hate my playing the guitar," Gerald accused.

He was watching television. Two men with walkie-talkies gestured wildly in the direction of a smoking ruin. Over the top of the rubble an immense humanoid head appeared. The mouth opened and a stream of fire engulfed the men with the walkie-talkies. The ground made a kind of sucking sound.

"You hate it when I have fun," Gerald said, not looking at me.

I walked over to his straw mat then. Gently, I pried the guitar from his lap. I walked into the hallway and swung the guitar at the doorjamb like a baseball bat. I beat the wood against the wall until the strings popped out and the guitar was simply a collection of wooden splinters.

Gerald began to cry. That's when I got the knife. I stabbed the brown Naugahyde sofa. Then I tore the white guts from the three oversized pillows Gerald always said we never needed.

"You're crazy," Gerald screamed. His pale gray eyes widened.

Suddenly, as if released from a terrible burden, he sprang awake. He was packing. We didn't have any suitcases. I was lying down in bed again, with the knife on the sheet next to my thigh. Gerald was running through the house, throwing his clothing and books into pillowcases. There were bits of feathers everywhere, on his shirt, on the floor, on my hands.

"I'll never trust you after this," he screamed from the hallway. He had four pillowcases in his hands. "I wouldn't trust you to sleep in the same house. Ever."

September came suddenly. In one day the interminable thick summer disappeared. It was cold. It rained. Even the trees in the yard below me, even the cars slowly casting their white headlights into the darkness, looked cold. Night had icy fingers. A black wind blew off the bay. I would run my fingertips across my breasts. Nothing lived inside. Inside was gray space, gray tiled corridors, narrow and dark, all straight and all leading absolutely nowhere.

Gerald returned for his mail. I didn't know where he was living. He refused to tell me. He still had a key to the apartment. Sometimes I would return from work and find another sign that Gerald had been there—a new patch of emptiness in the bookcase, a new slot in a closet where camping gear had once been folded.

When Gerald entered the apartment he was stiff and silent. His eyes darted back to the edges of the room, as if looking for threatening omens. He refused to share a pot of tea with me. I could feel him staring at me, searching for the correct nomenclature. Why, of course. A new category. Barefoot I was a small dark thing, a subspecies not reaching his chin. I was a kind of spider woman, dark and less than human, spinning threads through his torso, his pale chest.

He had come for his letters, and only his letters. He crossed the room carefully, as if the floor was filled with land mines. He avoided the bookcase shadows, the dark accusing glance of old titles, the lying threads of some other life. He stood in the doorway detached and tense, tearing his envelopes open. They were secret documents now consumed on the far side of the room, then folded and shoved into his pockets. He was gathering momentum.

"I wish I'd never met you," he said. "You've ruined my life. You tried to kill me."

His eyes were very dark. His big square hands with the new black ridges cut in his fingers by the guitar strings seemed to flap angrily at his side.

"I wish you were dead. I wish somebody would kill you," Gerald said. He was standing near the door. I stood on the far side of the room. Not even our shadows collided.

Gerald turned back once. He looked as if he wanted his fingerprints back and the drops of water from the shower. Then he opened the door. He shut the door. I never saw him again.

That year I would be twenty-one. Winter engulfed me. I committed to memory the periphery, the red enamel walls, the piece of overgrown yard below, the orange globes of street-lamps on Shattuck Avenue and the tiny balcony where I had once fed blue jays and where I stood now, in the wind-driven rain, letting the night pick at my face.

There was the matter of hard evidence. I knew I would never order the pieces. In time, the foundations would rot and the facts would grow wings and float through me. Gerald was gone. I would never understand. Gerald had been the student. I had studied him.

7

I walked back into the hospital. I found Francine in the cafeteria. She was sitting alone, staring at a round wall clock. Her amber eyes, eyes like slabs of yellow agate, were blood red from crying.

"I thought you'd run away. That's what you're good at, kid. And always when I need you the most. Oh, what's the use? You're strictly six," Francine said.

She meant I could run only six furlongs. Stakes races are longer. A mile and an eighth. A mile and a quarter. It wasn't enough to sprint. A great horse had to go the longer distances.

We sat in silence. Later we paced the corridor in front of the operating room. Much later the doctor came out. His hands trembled.

"It was touch and go." The doctor pushed past us toward the elevator. "Touch and go. But I think we got it all." He meant the cancer.

"What about now?" Francine followed the surgeon. He walked faster but she caught up with him. She grabbed his arm. She brought her face very close to his. Tears spilled down her cheeks.

"He's resting. I suggest you do the same." The elevator doors swung shut.

Francine and I looked at one another. Then we walked out to the parking lot. The air was very cold.

"I know he's going to die tonight. Trust my intuition. He's dying right now. I can feel his life force leaking out. Oh, God, help me."

I held Francine for a moment. She looked startled, almost embarrassed. Then she turned her face away. As I drove home, I kept thinking of her face, pale and frightened, skin white as a sheet draped over a dead man.

I waited for the hospital to call, formal and polite, crisp white words saying the man you call father is dead. Clear white words polished and hard, glistening, horrible, a kind of marble. He hemorrhaged. There was a sudden uncontrollable infection. White words like white stones, gravestones.

I waited. Nothing. Silence.

It was night, definitely night. The shadow battle had ended. The sun climbed back into Santa Monica Bay. The sun was a useless thing lying on the cool sandy ocean floor, eyeless and poisoning fish.

I turned on lights, trying to obliterate the night. I walked through the rooms of my house, the Woman's House, where I have lived six years watching the special seasons of the canals, the silver and grease-yellow, the abundant and quick-tongued shadows, the gray fog and sullen thickening brown edging into ink. For six years I have witnessed the water in front of my house, now churning, now changing, completing some cycle meaningful only to itself.

Suddenly the rooms of my house looked different, as if they were soft, as if they lacked edges and spines. As I paced the rooms of my house, I felt a chill. The chill was within. Something was stirring, beating strong wings and creating a current, a soft cooling wind. It seemed to grow, continually more urgent, insistent, something opening within, like a flower. And I thought, I am twenty-seven years old and a pine tree my age knows more. And I thought maybe this enormous opening flower should be named Rose.

I walked through my house, through the odd familiar rooms, opening closets and drawers, picking up objects at random like an amnesiac. I found myself holding an album of photographs. I found myself staring at Gerald.

Gerald had been a wound, cauterized and sealed shut, all in a limited way. Now it was somehow breaking loose, leaking out like blood. (Like my father's blood?) The passage of time had done nothing to alleviate the pain. Time merely softened certain essential edges. Things blurred. There was a loss of resonance, a slow irretrievable spillage.

I turned the album pages slowly. Each frame was clear, so clear it must have been autumn in Berkeley, the sharp Northern California fall when the wind blows hard, sweeping away the residues, the layers and veils that seem to separate faces and fence slats from another, more fragile reality.

I am standing in front of a polar bear cage in the San Francisco zoo. Wind blows. The picture was taken during a time when Gerald had to go to the zoo each day for a class on primate social behavior. He took notes on various animal interactions. He had a special notebook in which he assigned the gorillas and orang-utans names like Alpha Male or Juvenile and marked down each time they had dominance interactions or engaged in aggressive displays.

"Don't stare at me," Gerald had screamed, suddenly whirling around and facing me.

He had been going to the zoo every day for weeks. He refused to allow me to accompany him. Finally, on a day so clear, so perfectly etched, that even Gerald sensed a promise in the pale sunlight, he relented. "Just don't say a single word, not one," he cautioned.

I had left him in front of the gorilla enclosure and wandered through the zoo by myself. In the photograph I look directly at the camera. I look happy. I hadn't rushed into the North Beach night yet. Who took the photograph?

It is our apartment in Berkeley. Books, chess pieces and record albums lie in heaps on the floor around me. A chair has been pushed over. A lamp lies on the floor. The shade is three feet away.

"I want to document this," I told Gerald at the end of the argument. "I want to remember this." And he had taken the photograph.

I had been trying to convince Gerald to go to the student hospital. He said he'd rather see a shaman. We were discussing his impotence. Gerald said he was working on it. In fact, it was one of the fundamental aspects of his studies. Presumably from physics and mathematical psychology, from cave wall drawings and diagrams on how to set rabbit traps in the tundra, Gerald was going to find an answer to why his penis just curled in his lap like a fat sleepy worm.

"It's me, isn't it?" I screamed, terrified, sick.

"You have no concept of patience, of the right time and place, the natural cosmic rhythms. All you do is nag."

"Is that so?" I screamed. I walked over to the bookcase. With both hands, I emptied an entire shelf onto the floor. The books bounced and ricocheted off each other. They lay at pointed angles like a stack of plucked feathers.

It is our marriage picture. At the Las Vegas Palace of Marriage a photograph was included in the price. We stand near one another, posed in front of a fireplace where synthetic logs burn. We stand close but do not touch. We are not smiling. I am wearing orchids. I remember Gerald bought me two. It was very hot and they died almost immediately. It was odd having two orchids. I wore them pinned to my dress. They looked like grotesque twin breasts.

The longer I studied the photographs, the more interested I became in the periphery. Gerald Campbell no longer mattered. Always his shoulders slump into shadow. His face drifts off to the palest corner of the remembered room. It is not necessary to edit him. His presence is tentative and easily ignored. Gerald erases himself.

I find myself drawn to the objects. Whose fireplace did we stand in front of? Who snapped us, arms almost touching, in front of what mantel? What round wooden table is it? Whose green china teapot? Where is that black iron railing? On what terrace, in what city?

It is important to be precise. One must carefully assemble the details. I pour tea from a green china teapot. I draw the curtains apart and admit sunlight into my house. I bend down in noon sunlight to water a patch of new blood-red canna pushing up near my front-yard fence. The self has already been defined.

Suddenly I felt a terrible stinging uselessness. I assembled the few gifts Gerald had given me. There was a string of too big, too bright imitation coral beads I could never bring myself to wear, not even once. They looked like the sort of thing one sees wrapped around a mannequin's neck in airport gift shops, next to plastic leis and ashtrays saying HAWAII in gaudy goldish letters.

I found the blouse Gerald had bought me, one birthday or Christmas. It was a big billowing affair in yellow and magenta and red stripes. It was much too large for me, as if in Gerald's eyes I was enormous. I held the blouse against me. I looked like a soiled cloud.

There were more bits and pieces of Gerald. Pots and pans we

had bought when we first moved to Berkeley. They were old, stained by a dozen different sinks. I had scrubbed them a thousand times and they still stank of him.

The telephone rang. My hands were shaking. This is it, I thought. My father is dead.

"I'm cleaning it up," Jason breathed at me. He meant he was cleaning the globs of pink and peach and yellow from his square glass palette. He meant the model had gone home.

"You coming over?" His voice was water falling through dark green ferns. His voice was a slow wind brushing the crepe petals of poppies. "Give me half an hour?"

Half an hour? What did he have to do? Erase the traces of the evening he had, the two wineglasses, the rumpled sheets, the hard evidence of his life which he knows, after all this time, locks me in a terrible silence.

Jason is careful. He folds their blouses and jackets neatly in his bedroom closet. Still, I see the gifts they bring him, the handmade ceramic vases with pressed flowers pushed through narrow channels in the clay, the batik wall hangings with sea shells and stones glassy from waves and age tangled in the threads.

It is odd, but I have always felt myself superior to these women with their portable pasts, their interchangeable presents, their lives of endless transition. Of course, it is just a feeling, something locked within me for which I have no hard evidence.

I held the receiver very tight in my hand. All I said was yes.

I remembered the pile of clothing and knickknacks, household goods and photographs on my living room floor. I scooped them up into bags and threw the bags into the trash cans in the alley behind my house.

After what seemed a suitable passage of time, I wound my way across bridges and eroded pavement to Jason's house. In places, the sidewalk dipped down to mud or narrowed to a dirt trail. I pushed palm fronds back with my hands. I crossed an alley littered with parts of bicycles, pieces of stained rugs and piles of rusty nails glistening like red worms in the moonlight. The sky and water were an identical shade of deep purple, perfect mirrors. A thin haze was low in the sky and drifted across the cool water, a soft gauze.

I opened Jason's gate. I walked carefully past the rows of planted vegetables in his front yard, the artichokes, tomatoes, broccoli and strawberries all nodding their slow green heads.

Jason's door was opened. I walked in. I knew precisely where to go.

8

Everything requires an explanation.

Name. Age. Sex.

Today I named myself Rose.

I am twenty-seven and a pine tree my age knows more. A pine has stood without complaints or vision, accepting the burden of sunlight and the torture of night rain. A pine tree squares its spiked green shoulders and becomes a model for saplings and a guardian of hillsides, content with the cycles, flush of spring, stripping winter, and all the predictable repetition.

The sex is obvious. I am female, as you can plainly see, under the dress, across the flesh. I can meet you in the parking lot. A country setting could be arranged.

Weight. Height. Current addictions. Who's dying? How many

did you say? Just arrests or convictions? You're joking.

Marital status.

Marital status.

Jason was sitting in the kitchen alcove at a table that had once been mine. My father found it in a junk store and spent an entire month digging through the layers of old paint and sanding it, bringing back the fine oak grain. Jason said he liked the table. And impulsively, I had given it to him. Now it is the only place in his studio where I feel comfortable.

Jason was grinding up cocaine. He looked at me and smiled. After all this time, when Jason smiles at me I feel caught, captured, held circling frantic like a moth at a light bulb in summer.

"You said you have a problem?"

I thought of my father battling for his life. Jason was staring at me. And I knew there could be no connection between my parallel worlds. All was ordered and mutually exclusive. The pathways were clearly etched, straight and smooth as asphalt highways, deliberate as a surgeon's incision. The roads would never intersect, no matter the gravity, no matter the pull to the dark center, the cruel underbelly where I lived and watched worlds churn while stars clawed my face, floors dissolved and nothing was solid.

"It's O.K. now," I said, pulling my blouse over my head.

Jason nodded. "You always panic. See, nothing's that bad, right?"

"Right," I said.

Of course, it wasn't me speaking. The me I had once been had disappeared. Someone else remained, some pale relative. Now all I wanted Jason to do was tie my arm up. All I wanted Jason to do was tap, tap, tap the sides of the syringe and find a vein to fuck. We were always close when we shot dope. We were kin then, sanctified by blood.

Picasso was sitting near Jason's leg, a fine white and orange tabby cat with long thick fur. I hadn't killed him yet, hadn't come and taken him warm and trusting across the boulevard and down to the shoreline and strangled him.

"You get any rents?" Jason asked.

He was grinding up cocaine. My problems has been dismissed, inconsequential. Jason spilled a small white heap from a glass vial onto a mirror. Then he ground the particles into a powder with a razor blade. Jason was concentrating, looking down at the table, absorbed.

Six years before, Jason had said, "There's an art to needles." We were in Jason's house then, too. He was studying a new batch of needles. His movements were slow and precise, almost tender. I already realized that he kept his world small and manageable. Within the walls of his studio, he was absolute master. Within his rooms Jason controlled chaos. This was his oasis. Los Angeles was shut out, totally erased. Here it was always a late afternoon in an indeterminate but warm season. Jason had built a water fountain in his front room. Goldfish and turtles swam. I could hear them through the water in the darkness, just before I fell asleep.

Over the years I learned that Jason's studio is a museum of his personal life. Here the eras of his existence are preserved for possible study and reflection. Jason has been using the painting props for more than a decade. For more than ten years one woman after another has posed with the green surfboard near her shoulder or thigh, sending shadows rubbing against her breast like a live thing, a vine perhaps. For a decade one woman after another has lain on the beach towels with her legs spread or softly curled while the surfboard casts shadows against her flesh, shadows now red, violet or something heavy, a rancid-looking dark green.

In the beginning, I wanted Jason to teach me about needles. I wanted him to teach me about the goldfish that swam in his living room and the flowers and vegetables he grew in his garden. I was empty then, washed clean and ready for Jason.

I would prove I wasn't easy to erase the way all his other

women had been, the interchangeable women who posed for him and whom he let stay briefly, until the painting was finished, until he found someone who excited him more, offered him more, if only a slightly different voice or flesh history.

Six years before, Jason had stripped the needles from their disposable plastic shells. "These, see"—he pointed—"they're too big." He picked up another needle. "Perfect." He held the needle near my face. "You'll know the size next time."

I didn't memorize the size. I wasn't planning on a next time.

Then everything came to a halt. There were two of me. One of me was sickened with fear. The other, the outside one, sat calmly, as if taking notes. I watched Jason move through the late afternoon shadows.

We were sitting at a different table then. This was before my father spent one month stripping the table he would find years later, stripping it back to the original oak, slowly, with infinite care, bringing back the dark wood grain, the grain that was etched and smoothly polished as a sea stone wearing the embrace of waves.

Jason pulled the kitchen curtains closed. He walked through the house and returned with a bottle of rubbing alcohol and a bag of cotton. He filled a glass of water and tested the plunger again. He sorted through the hall closet and came back with a pale blue bathrobe belt.

"You know the bad reputation needles have?" Jason asked me the first time. "Well, they deserve it. Are you sure you want to do this?"

I nodded again, certain. I had a sense of the enormity of what we were going to share. There would be a bond in this. There would be discovery and change. There would be blood. Something would be decided.

It was a new world. The old forms had failed. There could be no decisions made by judges in courts of law, no marriage or baby. We had to develop our own bonding rituals. Our laws were a return to something primitive, the law of shared blood.

"Needles are their own world," Jason said. "You get into paraphernalia. It's part of the trip. The grinding up. The spooning in. You'll appreciate it later."

I wasn't planning on later. I was only doing this once, as a rite of passage, a special sealing ceremony, nothing more.

Jason was satisfied with the grinding. He drew two sample lines of cocaine on the mirror. With a knife he guided the powder from the mirror into a spoon. He dropped a small piece of cotton into the spoon. Slowly, concentrating, he measured 2 cc of water into the spoon. He put the syringe into the spoon, drawing the liquid, the cocaine and water, up through the cotton.

I extended my arm. It lay on the table in front of me like an alien object, a piece of driftwood, perhaps, curved smooth and white by the pressure of water.

"Me first," Jason said.

I watched him pull the bathrobe belt around his arm. He used his teeth to tighten it. He flexed his hand open and closed, open and closed. "Watch me," he said. His veins stood out like the blue ridges denoting rivers on a map. He rested the needle against his vein. He pushed the needle in.

Blood jumped up in the needle. The blood was very thick and very dark. "Blood shows you've registered. Hit the vein." He was letting the belt fall loose and drop to the floor. "As soon as you register, drop the tie," Jason said, pushing the plunger.

Jason took the needle out. He took a deep breath. His eyes went wide. He took another deep breath.

"You O.K.?" I asked. We would ask that of one another often across the years.

Jason nodded. Slowly, as if the floor wasn't solid, he walked to the kitchen sink and ran water through the needle, then alcohol and water again. "Got to clean the needle. Remember. Always clean it."

He sat down at the table. He dragged some white powder

from the mirror to the spoon. He poured in water. He took the second needle. He tested the plunger.

"I'm only going to show you once," he said, filling the syringe with liquid. He tapped the sides of the needle, tap, tap, tap, tap. "That's the rule. I only shoot people once. From then on, they're on their own. Tie up your arm."

I picked up the terry-cloth belt from the floor. My fingers were not my own. They were useless slabs of flesh. They could be part of some other form of animal, something with flippers. Jason helped pull the belt tight around my arm.

"Pump," Jason commanded. And I pumped my fist, now open, now closed.

"You've got no veins," Jason observed. He held my arm and turned it toward the light, studying it from another angle. He looked disgusted. "These are the worst veins I've ever seen," he pronounced. "You're not in this game for long."

Jason poured alcohol onto cotton. He swabbed my skin, just like in a doctor's office. I watched his face. He was intent, concentrating. He might have been gluing the mast onto a toy model of a ship.

"O.K.," Jason said. He was the man at the loudspeaker at Cape Canaveral. He was going to push the button and hurl the rocket into space. He was announcing all systems go, green and counting.

"Let go of the tie when I tell you." Jason was holding the needle against my vein. I started to turn my head away.

"Watch," Jason commanded.

There was a stab of pain. Blood came into the needle. I stared at my arm. The arm did not belong to me. It wasn't really connected to my body. Jason was holding my arm, balancing it against his raised knee.

"Let go," Jason said. I released the belt. It slid onto my lap.

There was a hot wind. Slowly, I realized the wind was within me. It was every wind I had ever known. It was the wind of childhood, the wind that brushed my six-year-old face when I skated the sidewalks of Philadelphia in autumn. It was the wind that came in the middle of the night in the east, in November, a wind rippling with the cool promise of the first snow. It was a wind tangled with greasy pronged summer oak leaves. It was a wind pitted with the charred bits of the oak leaves and maple leaves later, stained by sun in autumn, falling broken to the earth and lying there like severed red fists.

"This is your fit." Jason put my needle on the table in front of me. He had put it back in its plastic shell. "Take care of it."

I nodded. I knew I wouldn't have to take care of it. I was going to do this thing now and only now. It would be over at dawn.

Jason sat down again. He was grinding the cocaine with a razor blade. He was filling the needle. I watched his hands, then his face. His eyes were wide and clear, a light hazel. His eyes looked lit from the inside as if he had swallowed candles. His eyes widened. He sucked in his breath. "Yeah," he said, walking to the sink. "Oh, yeah," he said, walking slowly, carefully, as if the floor might open up and swallow him, as if there were secret crevices, sudden unexpected gaps.

Then he filled my needle. His finger was tap, tap, tapping the sides of the syringe. I tied up my arm, using my teeth to tighten the belt as Jason had. Blood came into the needle. I let the belt fall without being told.

"Don't forget," Jason said. "You're a junkie from the first time you stick a needle in. It's just a question of how long you stay clean."

Jason was talking somewhere in the distance. Perhaps he was talking underwater. Night had fallen. The curtains were pulled. The studio was sealed from the world. There was no world anymore, just wind rippling and surging through the hollow spaces that were no longer lungs and rib cage but fields now, low hills with grasses swaying lightly in a sea breeze.

Jason's words meant nothing to me then. They would mean

something later. Later I would come to Jason's studio at night. Later I would beg, "Do me, please."

It was always night. The sun burned my eyes. I kept my shades drawn. It was now a permanent shadowy twilight. It was not day or night but a glistening gray where soft things rustled and glowed and floated like birds and perched undulating to the walls.

I inhabited a silky underbelly. A pastel layer that enveloped me. I had been swallowed by fast-moving clouds. I was floating in a cloud's belly. Whenever I wanted skies to part, the clouds to gather momentum and rush blind over hills, over barely glimpsed cliffs burdened with lavender ice plant, I took another shot.

There was only the grinding, the tying, the filling, the cleaning, the feeling of tumbling exquisite. My mouth was wide and blue. When I yawned, clouds stirred and birds fluttered from my lips, a migration of orange and purple butterflies.

There was no reason to eat or sleep anymore. Cocaine was better than eating, better than sleeping. Cocaine was living curled in a cloud's diaphanous white side. Cocaine was wearing the sky for eyes.

I needed Jason. I had bruised my arm badly. I had used the same disposable needle at least two hundred times. The point was dull. I was clumsy, awkward and afraid. Later the glistening veil sailed down and draped itself around me like a tent. My hands trembled. I plunged the needle in and missed, no blood. I began again, tying off my arm, pulling it tight with my teeth and plunging in. No blood. It wouldn't register. Something was wrong. All night I stuck the needle in my arm and couldn't find a vein. It was only as the sun rose, as the sun spread itself fat and yellow through my rooms, that I realized I had been sitting in darkness, had forgotten to turn on the lights and had tried to find my tiny purple veins in the blue-black center of night.

"Do me, please," I begged Jason later.

He could find a vein through the four days of bruises on my arms. My veins were entirely hidden by green and purple and blue and black bruises flowering exotic across my skin. My arm seemed encased in a dark patterned snakeskin.

I looked at my arm dispassionately. It didn't really belong to me. It was oddly tattooed. It reminded me of the purple and yellow pansy Francine had pressed into my childhood book of fairy tales. It had been summer. Francine and I were sitting under an oak tree. She picked the flower and serious, concentrating, carefully pressed the purple and yellow pansy into the golden book. I still have it.

I was sitting on the floor of Jason's bathroom. He was shaving. His arms were a series of tiny red pinpricks. "You've got to slow down," he said to me through the mirror.

I felt disadvantaged and small. I wanted to feel like the inside of a cloud. I wanted my eyelids to be butterflies printed red, purple and yellow, and fluttering now warm and soft. I wanted to get off. I wanted Jason to shoot me up. I wanted to feel the world spin white, white of canvas, white of clouds, white of enamel and starched linen, white of lace doilies, roses, ice cliffs and sails.

"Let's see the arm," Jason said.

I held out my arm. Jason looked at it through the mirror. He shook his head. "You're butchering yourself," he observed. I felt his words hitting the glass mirror and bouncing back at me like a thin sliver of silver, a kind of beam.

I wanted the dream. I wanted to snuggle in shimmering drifting flecks of white, bone chips and shells and the spilled guts of storm-spent whirling white clouds. I was trying again. I didn't feel the pain as the needle went in. I was half drifting, startled when the needle finally registered, startled and dazed to see blood in the needle. I jerked back and the plunger moved too fast, bruising my arm. I forgot to let the tie drop. My arm swelled in an angry purple pocket. My arm ached. I thought I was dying. My arm was leaden, gray and cold. I felt that my arm was already dead.

"Help me, please." Was that what Jason wanted to hear? Would I have to beg formally? Would there be a ritual?

"You're done," Jason said. "That arm's shot. You'll have to use your right arm. Shoot with your left."

"I can't," I said. My hands were trembling. I have never been able to do anything with my left hand, not even write my name.

"You'll have to." Jason was patting his face dry. He looked at me. "You know, the wives of warriors were accomplished fighters in their own right. Are you a warrior, little girl?"

I leaned against the cool tiles of the bathroom wall. I knew why junkies died in bathrooms. It wasn't a secret inexplicable affinity for shit. No, it was much simpler. Bathrooms had doors that locked. Bathrooms had good light, a sink and floors easy to mop the blood from.

I began to cry.

In one motion, Jason whirled around. He slapped me across the face. "Don't start that bullshit, junkie. You want it bad enough, you'll do it." He walked out of the room.

I looked at my left hand. It was shaking. Slowly I brought my hand up to my mouth and bit it. After a while my hand stopped shaking. I held the syringe with my left hand. I found a vein in my right arm. I let the tie drop. I cleaned my needle and leaned back against the cool white bathroom tiles. My back grew into the tiles. My back was cool and white. I merged into the wall, glistening. I was marble. I was porcelain. I was lilies of the valley. I was the lily. And the valley.

Jason was near me. He was white, a granite hillside by moonlight. He was sharp rock, naked. He was the spine of the world, a stone mountain. He was the beginning, the bleached sand, the fundamental, before divisions, before chance and error, when it/I was whole. I was a white egg. Jason cracked me. He had cloud chips for teeth. His hands were white metal.

Jason was grinding cocaine. He was tying off his arm. He was cleaning his needle. He was running the shower. He reached for me, for the tattooed arm that wasn't mine, for the arm with the black flowers printed on like skintight bracelets. The arm moved toward him. The water was coursing down hot, a liquid silver exploding on my skin, oily balls rolling and spiraling. Jason's tongue was red like an apple.

The water was a mist, a fine white frost. The water was like smoke in winter, the smoke you smell on country roads, logs burning, country logs smelling of pines and clouds. The water was hot, steaming. The water was primeval, jeweled. It fell, a string of delicately carved ivory beads.

"Tell me you need me," Jason breathed behind me. He was pushing me against the blue tiled shower walls. "Tell me," he said, pressing into me. He was white, hard, stone, metal. He was the beginning, fundamental. I was still, dark, huddled and open. I was the earth. He drilled and tunneled.

"Tell me you missed me," Jason breathed behind me, husky, a kind of wind, a May wind, a spring wind, stinging with promises of gardenias and marigolds, fat red buds poised on emerald vines, dew in the new shoots, the air steaming with jasmine, the streets sinking bewitched by rushing bluebirds.

"I missed you, yes," my voice said. My voice was wind. My voice was a dark brown of just plowed earth. I was the smell of fresh brown bread steaming on a wooden shelf. My hair was wet. Jason pulled it like a rope, hard, jerking my head back. Why, I was a horse and he was riding me. I breathed through my mouth.

"Tell me how much you missed me," Jason coaxed.

He held my waist. My forehead was pressed into the tile. My mouth was opened. I tried to speak but my mouth simply drank the night. I was a river swollen and squeezed through a cliff's eye. The sky was empty. Jason parachuted down. I waited. The parachute opened magenta and red folds, billowing down like gigantic petals. He was lava. I was melting into thin strands of gold. He was breathing and pushing behind me. His breath was the wind in late May, a wind tinged with strawberries, cherries, all the pink tongues pushing up from hillsides. Jason was the storm, pressing and pumping electric.

We didn't have bodies in the conventional sense anymore. There had been some evolutionary adaptation, a sudden accelerated mutation. We were part porpoise. We could live beneath the great churning sheets of sea water. Our flesh was too thin, too pale and soft. It wasn't even the skin of fish. It lacked all substance. It cast no shadows. We had become dream creatures.

The dream was enormous. I had been someone else. And Jason had recreated me. I was his invention. He had painted me in the beginning. There had been an unexpected sharing and merging. I had been subtly altered. If painting began as a religious ritual, a part of the hunt, wasn't it possible that the magic still stirred? Hadn't Jason tapped into that other realm when he painted me onto canvas?

And the man with me was no longer the Jason he had once been. This man too was subtly altered. He was in part my creation.

The dream had a fragile domed shell. The dream was encased in a glistening hard enamel. But it could be punctured. It could be opened and closed like a fist, like my fist pumping open and closed, open and closed, waiting for the one small stab into blue vein, blue, blue as the sky, my mouth, the tides and Jason behind me, hard, invisible, the wind.

Now it was seven years later. It was the table my father had stripped and sanded down for me. Jason and I were sitting together. Jason was grinding cocaine with a razor blade. Picasso his cat sat near his leg.

"You know what I heard today?" Jason pressed the needle against his arm. "All over the country white toilet paper is the big seller. But not in L.A." Jason stuck the needle in. Blood jumped. He let the tie drop. "Here, the more ornate the paper, the bigger it sells." His eyes were wild. "Doesn't it figure?"

I said nothing. I let Jason shoot me.

"You look sick," Jason noted.

I walked to the bed, near the far wall. I could hear the goldfish swimming in the fountain. I could hear the sea breeze rustling the thin curtains, taking the curtains like a pale pair of wings. I curled into the shadows and waited for Jason and for the night to wrap its fine black claws around me.

9

"Don't go up there yet," Francine said. She was waiting for me in the hospital lobby. "It's bad."

"You've been there?"

"Of course I've been there. I was here at six A.M." In the hospital light she looked white and shaken. Her smooth face was somehow chipped, creased and broken.

"How bad?"

"Bad." Francine lit a cigarette. "He's hooked up to oxygen and IV tubes in his nose and throat. They're pouring liquids into him like a plant." Francine took a deep breath. "They had to cut more than they thought." She let it sit there.

"What did they cut?" I was terrified.

Francine looked down at the floor. "Everything," she whispered. "The whole throat. Vocal cords. Parts of his mouth and tongue."

"God," I began.

"There's no God, kid. You'll see that when you go up there."

We took the elevator to the third floor. The corridors were glistening and dim. The walls were the color of enamel mud. The ward was a damp shadowy green. The corridor opened to identical small green rooms where the Venetian blinds were drawn and the sun fell measured and tamed through their slats.

The sounds were muted. The nurses scraped by in soft shoes. There was the hushed bubbling of fluids moving through nose and throat tubes, the hiss of oxygen and the softer, more insistent humming of the life-support machines.

I glimpsed bodies absolutely white and emaciated. Flesh hung to the bones, pasty, already unnecessary.

Suddenly I thought of fish. The cancer ward was a kind of human aquarium. Here the almost dead lay in their own slow bubbles. So this is how it ends. It dries in silence. It dries in an afternoon the color of a childhood memory of an aquarium. The flesh dries. Finally the flesh is shed.

I kept walking. On each nightstand in each identical pale green room a philodendron sat with a red or pink ribbon wrapped around its green neck, its fat dull leaves blending into the greenish shadows. I thought of algae and sea plants.

My father's face was terribly swollen. His face looked dark and angry between the layers of white bandaging. The gauze formed a thick collar around his neck. The collar sprouted tubes. He was bleeding. He was draining. He was hooked up to oxygen. My father was curled small in his bed, so small that at first I thought they might also have amputated his legs.

The blinds were drawn shut. My father reached for a writing pad. IV dripped through a needle taped to a vein in his hand.

WHATS THIS. He gestured toward the oxygen hissing through a thick green plastic tube. The tube was attached to a hole they had punched through his throat. A round metal disk was embedded in the center of his throat and hooked up to the green plastic oxygen tube.

"It's oxygen. It's temporary. They're taking it out in a few days," Francine said.

My father's eyes filled with tears. He turned his bandaged face away from me and slowly, painfully tugged the edge of the blanket closer to his chest. He closed his eyes.

"He's dying," Francine said. She reached across the bed. She searched his wrist for a pulse. I stared at her. I felt an enormous scream building up somewhere inside of me. My lips trembled.

"I'll get a doctor," I said after what seemed like a long time. I rushed into the corridor. The green shadows were thick like sheets of greasy oak leaves across my face, a forest collapsing, a green storm, suffocating, blinding.

"Is he going to make it? Ultimately?" Francine asked, her words precise, her eyes amber lights, her breath grazing the doctor's flesh. The doctor couldn't inch away. His back was already against the corridor wall.

"There's no way to say yet. Hemorrhaging and infection are possible. And there's the matter of motivation."

"Don't give me that Marcus Welby shit. Who do you think I am? Some intimidated welfare case?" Francine grabbed his arm. "I'm asking you for the odds."

The doctor considered his response carefully. "It's completely undecided," he said finally. "Fifty-fifty." The doctor edged away.

We walked back into my father's room. There was the smell of something terrible, dark and rotten, rancid plant fibers. The smell was thick and black, overpowering. The smell was coming from my father's flesh. It was the smell of decay, of death.

WHAT TIME. My father inched himself into something like a sitting position. He pointed to his wrist. I could see the white line where he had worn his watch. He held up six fingers.

Did he think it was six o'clock? He must mean six at night. Time to turn on the news. Time for a shot of bourbon and a cigar. Time for day to shut down all around him while he watered the ivy, pruned the peach and apricot trees, the avocado tree, the lemon tree. Time to water the drained brownish backyard grass. Time to pick up a form sheet for the next day. Time for the Dodgers or Lakers on television while waiting for the next ambush, waiting, waiting for the cancer to return, a black swarm.

"It's noon." It was the first thing I had said to my father. He had been staring at Francine. Now he looked at me, squinting, trying to focus on me, recognize me.

WHATS THIS. He pointed to the oxygen tube.

"It's temporary. Oxygen," Francine told him. "It's only temporary."

How did she know that? I stared at her. She was biting her lip.

My father pulled on the transparent green tube running from the metal tank to his throat. With the blinds drawn, there was no time in the room, no seasons, no standard divisions. Everything was one long unbroken morphine afternoon, a dream without motion or direction.

"Sit down near him," Francine directed.

I sat down lightly on the edge of my father's bed. I reached for his hand and ran my fingertips gently across the skin, around the IV needle. The smell was like poisonous fumes. It filled my mouth and lungs. I could taste it on my tongue.

"Does it hurt?" I asked, softly. "Do you want a shot?"

"You can have morphine whenever you want it," Francine told my father. "I read your chart."

My father seemed to nod his head. Then he closed his eyes. His breath was soft, slow, a mere rustle. We watched him doze.

"It's worse than before," Francine assured me. We were walking toward the elevator. She was very pale. "You better prepare yourself. I don't think he's going to make it."

I stopped walking. I stared at her, hard. "We don't know that. It's still fifty-fifty."

Francine said nothing. We got into the elevator. We walked past the emergency room and into the hospital parking lot.

"Now you know," Francine said. "I was twenty-seven. Precisely the age you are now. Only I was all alone. With a husband dying and a child to support."

Slowly a haze parted. I glimpsed the world as it must have appeared to Francine. She had been stripped naked. The vultures had picked her clean.

"They sent him to California to die," my mother said. "They said he wouldn't last the winter in the East. Can you imagine what it was like for me? Holding him in my arms at night. Not knowing if he would just die at my side." Francine lit a cigarette. "You've always hated me, blamed me. I was in a strange city. Alone, no friends, no family, a child, broke, an invalid husband in bed."

I glimpsed Francine standing on the strange bleached Southern California plain with her back to the sea and the cruel sun going berserk, turning to blood above her head, above the flat white meaningless streets, above the stunted anemic palm fronds slatted and thick, the landscape itself strange and unreasonable. Now I was standing there with the sea opening its spiked gray mouth and the black vultures circling hungry just above me.

The wheel had spun. Twenty years passed. Now it was my turn. The first time I had been six years old. I remembered the world as black and white, before and after. One day it was precisely as it had always been. My mother had iron pots for hands. Soup was steaming. Snow fell but I was never cold. The old gray stone house was the perfect shell. There were no violations. My father left each morning in his special work clothes with the painting stains on the pant legs. My father carried his big brown toolbox. He was going to build another house. My mother was making things steam in the kitchen. She was humming. She met me at the curb where the school bus stopped. She was smiling.

When my mother baked, I baked, too. I had special tiny pie tins. My father would study the big pie and the little pie and eat mine. When my mother ironed, I ironed, too. I had a special miniature ironing board. My mother gave me the napkins to iron while she ironed my father's shirts. The seasons spilled around us gently. We were undamaged. We were waiting on the gray stone porch for Daddy to come home from work. My mother had taken a bath and put on lipstick. The pies were cooling. Soon we would see Daddy's car.

Overnight the world was torn apart, torn inside out, irrevocably stained. The stain spread out and became a dark spot I wore embedded in the center of my head.

"Do you understand?" Francine asked. Her face was very close. Her eyes seemed like beacons, iridescent and haunted, enormous yellow globes.

Did I have the power of absolution? Was I being asked for a blessing, a dispensation?

"You did well, Mother," I said.

We embraced awkwardly. Her body felt very warm, too warm, almost feverish. I walked quickly to my car.

It was late afternoon. I stood on the porch of the Woman's House. I could hear the slow drugged humming of insects sliding from one red plateau of geraniums to another, red patches scattered across the city like landing strips. There was a sense of frenzied insects leaping.

I sat down on the side of the canal. Yellow wildflowers rose in thick rows across the vacant field near my house. I sat very still, a part of the landscape, like a rock. In time, the edges of the canals would grind down and the vacant field reach out and push over me. Wild black grapes would grow in my arms. Vines would wrap around my ankles and dirt lick my thighs. In time, I would become a mound on a hill, a place for insects to rest their too thin veined wings.

And where were the fine crisp white words saying the man is dead. The man no longer breathes. The man lay in his small white bed. Life ebbed from him as he slept.

I picked up my mail. One letter, handwritten. I read the letter slowly. The paper was very white and thin in my hands. Near me, the ducks grew quiet, preparing to squawk their twilight pastel prayers of gratitude while the water beneath them browned. I read the letter again. It was from my cousin Rachel. She was in a Maine mental hospital. We had never met.

Suddenly it seemed to make perfect sense that she contact me. It was another proof that the wheel was indeed spinning. The evidence was piling up. It was my turn.

March 3

Dear Rachel,

You ask, did Medea take lithium?

The implications are legion. I know nothing about lithium.

You say you jumped off a bridge? You say the ground called to you, wanted you, arched its spine to you hungry? You ask if I think you are crazy.

I don't know what crazy is any more. I know our family harbors a manic-depressive streak. It runs like a stain through this family. There isn't even an undercurrent of stigma attached to it. After all, the kings of Europe were hemophiliacs. Is it so remarkable that their shopkeepers, moneychangers, outcast bankers and rag traders should also have a small dark anomaly? In our case, a certain inability to securely anchor a sense of proportion, a perspective lasting more than twenty minutes. Let me try to explain, although I must caution you, I no longer believe in explanations.

I do not think it "odd" that you would turn to me in your crisis, turn to me as the world you know tumbles and day itself collapses. You have heard stories about me? Your mother suggested this? Perhaps you both think because I am ten years older than you I have learned something of value. You'll have to judge that for yourself.

We share the same blood. There are blood truths. I am certain of that. There exist connections of awesome power and subtlety more ancient and virulent than you might at this point imagine.

Have you thought of me often? I ask simply because I feel the presence of things, a kind of chorus. I've felt it all winter.

I understand when you say your mother is difficult beyond normal expectation, beyond even the bounds of that antiquated concept some men once called decency. I have an appreciation for your situation. Aren't our mothers identical twins?

You ask why they scorn each other. I think it is simply that they cannot bear the undeniable stain. They must deny it. It is necessary for them that they despise each other. They have not even spoken in twenty-five years. They nest on opposite shores of this country as if the three thousand miles between them was a tangible demonstration of free will. I don't think anything is free.

Is your mother bleaching you clean of Poland? Of horse paths through the firs? Ritual baths and superstition? Of course she is difficult to communicate with. Her Ph.D. in sociology protects her from the root-truths. Doesn't she realize her doctorate is simply a modern piece of witchcraft?

My mother also denied me our exquisite and painful history. I believed I had a holy right to our shared past. I knew it wouldn't be given. I took it.

How will you take it, you wonder? There are no maps for this, no dress rehearsal. One empties the self of past latitudes. The arms can become sails. The self is the projectile. Do you follow me?

What do you know of our terrible shared history? The rot they do not speak about? Even now with their names clean and Anglo-Saxon, certain truths are sealed shut in their mouths, too dangerous, too dark and taloned to utter. In their way, they are still spitting the evil eye in claustrophobic dark Sabbath rooms.

You know by now (your mother has told you?) they were not orphans. Our grandmother still lives. That's where I saw your photograph. Our mothers pretend that she is dead. It is easier for them to believe this than to bear the simple truth of her alive, crippled (and have you heard it said demented?), in a Bronx tenement, living in her self-imposed hell, still punishing herself for the one terrible indiscretion. I am talking about the one virgin night she spent with the man, the infidel, the Christian who took her girlhood and left her pregnant with the twin curse that is our mothers.

Our grandmother named them Frieda and Fay. Later and separately, as they created new lives for themselves, they became Francine and the Felicity you know well.

Our grandfather was named Edward. I hired a private detective for this. Edward Geoffrey Richmond, though the name is meaningless and he is dead. He died a wealthy man in Houston, Texas, in 1964. I saw his grave.

He was married five times legally. There's no way to count the liaisons he had. His pattern was always the same. He was attracted to very young women of what was then called the lower classes. Our grandmother wasn't the first. She was simply one so deprived, so impoverished and terrified in this raw country of factories and sweatshops, of trolley cars and gray skyscrapers blotting out the clouds, that she had no recourse at all.

Edward Geoffrey Richmond probably never even knew his seed beat with life. (Two lives, in fact.) He has sets of bastards scattered across America. The detective said there could be as many as twelve children.

I met one, once. The private detective found her for me. She was tall, as we all are. She had the same giddy brilliance. She was vice-president of a bank in Boston. She was the bastard daughter of this man Edward. Her mother had been a fifteen-year-old Russian immigrant, much like our own grandmother Rose. She, too, was deserted in infancy.

She didn't seem surprised to see me, just as I am not really surprised by your letter. There are forces pushing toward order. I am certain of that now.

This woman, this half-aunt, took me to lunch in a glass citadel with chilled white wine and the city sparkling and fresh as a new-dug grave below us. She sipped her wine slowly, without bitterness.

Rachel, they are such Calvinists. Your mother Felicity with her professorship. My mother Francine. The bastard daughter bank president in Boston. America has ruined them. This half-aunt sipped her wine and spoke without longing or anger about her childhood of cots and poverty. She even offered the hypothesis that early suffering can lead to extraordinary achievements.

I could see that she could not bear the pain of me, my eyes, the something in me she recognized. There seemed little to say. I stood on the street with my half-aunt. The search had, for me, ended.

It was different with our grandmother Rose. I will tell you more about her later. I can give you her address. You can learn from her. She's a witch, in her way, red-haired as we all are. She would sense in you the dark amber eyes (almost coral, like the buds of certain orchids) and the erratic heartbeat, one of her own.

But you cannot journey in your condition. A serious journey requires preparation. Eat and sleep. You will need strength, no matter what. Perhaps by summer you will be ready. Remember, nothing is promised. Even the ground we walk upon is tentative, a mere approximation of something else.

I await word of your increasing health. We will share the blood-truth. I sense this.

I folded the letter carefully in an envelope. I had to mail it immediately or it would just sit there in my house amid the other remnants and relics of the lives I have led.

I mailed the letter and let myself wander slowly toward the ocean. The waves were gray. And I thought, don't die, white-haired father, you who have been beaten gray as rock. You are but momentarily becalmed. Winds will rise. The whitecaps will dance again, star haunted. You will mount the stern gray crest again. You will know the liquid mountains. Just keep breathing.

Then the gray sea was lost, engulfed by a gray haze, the first tentative claw of night. Somewhere on the sand a man began singing something like an Arabic prayer. I remembered the day I moved into the Woman's House.

"I love you," I whispered in my new darkness.

"Why?" Jason asked.

He was lying on his back, lying on the brand-new flower-print sheets I had bought, lying with his arms raised above his head, resting loosely on the new down pillow. The bedroom curtains were open. It was summer. Jason had strung rows of neon Christmas bulbs outside the window. The bedroom was washed by silver. It always looked like a full moon.

"You are my dark one. My solitary one. You are my longed for and absolute in black marble. You are onyx. We skate down the iris night, one body. We map the black warm flesh openings. Your tongue is moss. You are a flutter of wings and hemp smoke. Your breath is sweet lime. Your sighs are like a drum, a tree falling down. You are my charmer, my fire-eater, my wind-rider. You are the cloud dance."

"I know," Jason said. He turned and faced the wall. "I don't want that much love."

I willed myself to lie still in the darkness. It was summer. I had watered the backyard garden. I had fluffed the pillows, straightened the bedspread, swept the floor.

"Why does my love terrify?"

"You want so much in return," Jason said.

I sat up. It was our first night together officially. I wanted to open drawers and find flowers. I wanted to be carried over the threshold. I wanted some tangible demonstration that he wanted me there, some proof, some hard evidence.

"There's no room for all that junk," Jason repeated, over and over, while I dragged cardboard cartons up the three front steps, across the porch and into the living room. Jason watched the boxes collect, one on top of the other. He stared at them with a mounting horror, as if he had expected me to enter his life naked, empty of everything, a stretched canvas ready for the brush. I carried boxes and he looked angry. Jason looked betrayed.

"There's no room for that crap," Jason said from time to time.

Later I began to unpack the boxes. I hung my dresses in the bedroom closet. I put dishes away. Jason appeared from the bedroom, outraged, a clump of my clothing in his hand. He threw my dresses on the floor.

"Wrong," he said.

"Wrong?"

"You hung them in the wrong closet. Keep your clothes in the hall closet. Clothes are impersonal." He made it sound like an immutable law of nature.

"Jason," I began slowly. "Is this my house or not? Because after carrying in all those damn boxes all day, I—"

"Rents are due the first of the month. That means get off your ass and collect them the first." Jason walked out of the house.

I sat down startled, frightened, angry. I was filled with something burgundy red, thick and overwhelming. The air was liquid. What was happening? I was a holy shrine, ancient, perfected. Now suddenly I was besieged by vandals. There were vulgarities written on my elegant time-smoothed walls. They stole from the poorbox. They were monsters. Something horrible was happening, random, beyond imagination.

Jason came back at midnight. He got into bed and turned his body away from me, facing the wall.

"What's going on? Please tell me," I whispered. My head was collapsing into a black mass. I could feel individual atoms crumbling.

Jason said nothing.

"You act like you don't want me here. You seem to be imposing stipulations on my life here. I feel tentative and—"

Within the darkness I could feel Jason smile. The night between us thickened. Jason laughed. He was beginning to feel better, lighter. The cardboard boxes had frightened him. I had frightened him, standing at the edges of his rooms, violating his routine, his painting schedule, his very existence, with the meaningless clutter of my life.

I covered my face with my hands. I pressed my face, trying to shake my head, my skin, my cells clear. The darkness was strangling. Debris was spilling fast and unpatterned.

"Jason." I touched his shoulder. I felt him tense beneath my fingertips.

"Leave me alone. I'm tired."

"I need you," I whispered, words intoned, a kind of prayer. I was a shrine, old and holy. I was the silence of candlelight and bells. Why the hell was Jason tired? I carried all the boxes.

"You always need something," Jason said. "You're a goddamned bottomless pit. Go to sleep."

"What's wrong?" I could barely breathe.

"I said shut up. Stop interrogating me. All you do is make it worse for yourself."

Worse for myself? Was I on trial? Was my demeanor having an adverse effect on the case? And what precisely were the charges against me?

"What the hell are you talking about?" I yelled.

Jason jumped forward then. He pressed his hand over my mouth, hard. His face was contorted through the layers of darkness. The neon light glanced off his teeth. He began shaking my head. I felt his thumb pinching into my lip.

"You want to play another midnight round of Name That Problem?" He was still shaking my head, picking my head up off the mattress like a cantaloupe and throwing me back down. "You hum a few bars and I'm supposed to guess what's eating your guts and driving you crazy?"

I was frozen. Part of me wanted to run, wanted to run down the three porch steps, down to my car, to the sleeping city, anywhere. That was the real me. The rest of me was a shell, lying quietly, obediently, wide-eyed and amazed.

"Sleep it off, bitch," Jason said, angry.

Part of me was running down the stairs. Part of me had reached Venice Boulevard. Part of me ran flushed and hot under a full summer moon, silently repeating a chant, slowly, over and over, hypnotically. Oh, God, it's a mistake, a mistake, a mistake, I kept repeating. It's a mistake, a mistake, a terrible mistake. The chant in my head was hopeless, over and over it fell through me like big drops of dirty city rain banging down on trash cans in an alley.

I woke up with a sense of purpose and clarity. Jason was gone. The morning was white and quiet. I would have to go somewhere and think. I would have to find a new place to live.

I edged into the kitchen. Jason was reading the newspaper. I filled a pot with water.

"Always use the white pot for boiling water," Jason told me. He was working the crossword puzzle in the newspaper. He didn't look at me.

"Here's the way it is," Jason began. He lit a cigarette. "I wake up. I want complete silence. No good mornings. No breakfast discussion. Nothing. Do you understand?"

"Yes."

"Good. I eat. Then I go to work. I go back to my house and paint. I paint seven days a week. I begin as soon as I wake up. When I'm painting, which is every day, you forget I'm here. I don't exist. I disappear. Do you understand?"

"Yes."

"Because I'm fucking tired of the marriage trip," Jason said. "You take care of your shit. I'll take care of mine. Are you hearing me?"

"I hear you."

"Good," he said. "Just accept it. This is a timeless moment." Jason looked out the kitchen window at the plants near the side gate. A stalk of yellow canna, the petals thick and hard, waved gently in the early morning sea breeze. The canals were the color of a mirror.

Jason crossed the room. He paused in the doorway. He glanced back at the plants along the side gate.

"It's going to be a lovely day," Jason pronounced. Then he opened the front door and walked out.

I had lived with Jason for twenty-four hours. I realized I had a tremendous amount to learn. And I realized that I would never learn it fast enough.

❧ 10 ❧

"We hang tough. No matter what, we hang tough," Francine said.

We were walking down the corridor toward my father's room. The corridor was long and greenish gray, a kind of tunnel. The world narrowed to a thin channel the color of sheet metal. It might have been underwater. The ward was like a submarine, claustrophobic, gray, locked. There could be no escape.

I was assaulted by the sense of evil in the corridor and small cubicles. The white light was a cool luminous breath. The ward was antiseptic, the sky covered, the stars hidden.

A primitive man would never submit to a hospital. A primitive man would insist on being surrounded by his most magical objects. There would be communal chanting and prayer, the holding of a collective breath. Campfires would blaze into the darkness, spark of cedar logs, air bristling red into black, blood and smoke. There would be amulets, charms, totems. The masks would be repainted. The gourd rattles would be taken from the healer's hut. There would be dancing, sand paintings and sung re-creations of the tribe's victories over evil, the close calls and new beginnings, a special kind of ringing.

The healer would beseech the earth. The earth would answer. The sacred bones of the dead sage would gnaw at the red-black night and push off the dirt from the illusionary grave. The dream would bend, and the skeleton talk with real words from a mouth grown lips and tongue again.

The hospital was too blank and uniform. It was a space stripped empty, a waiting room for death. Here the shamans also wore special garb, white masks and white coats. They maintained antiseptic rituals. They communicated in a private ancient language. In their depleted fashion they attempted to preserve the mystery. They adhered to the old forms but lost the substance, the connections to the inexplicable power.

The doctors wore stethoscopes around their necks and communed with machines and it wasn't enough, not nearly. I wanted antelope horns on their heads, rattles and drums. I wanted some enormous rumbling benediction, magic salts, colored smoke, knees on dirt, stars beacons of prayer.

"He's stronger, you'll see," Francine said, desperate, betraying her lack of conviction. She was walking in front of me, a bright red straw hat balanced on top of her head. All I had to do was stay on my feet and follow the bouncing red straw ball.

Francine veered into a small cubicle near my father's room. It was a storage room. Francine opened her red canvas carrying bag and began filling it with bars of soap, thermometers, Band-Aids, plastic drinking cups, washcloths and hospital gowns. She moved quickly. No one noticed.

"Five hundred forty bucks a day," she observed softly. "They owe me something."

I followed Francine into my father's room. He was staring at the far wall. His face was a dark scowl between the white gauze. The feeding tube in his nose was red, a kind of tusk. I tried to think of something to say.

WHATS THIS. My father pointed to the oxygen tank.

"It's oxygen. It's temporary. They'll take it out of here tomorrow."

My father's eyes were very black. They looked liquid, a kind of ink. His hand rested on top of his writing pad. I noticed the IV bottle was gone.

"See? They've already taken away the IV," I said.

My father seemed to be dozing. He opened his black eyes. He reached for his writing pad.

WHATS THIS.

"Oxygen. It's temporary."

"Read him the paper," Francine suggested. She produced the morning newspaper from her red canvas bag. She had to tape a program in Burbank. She was pacing nervously. Her suit jacket was unbuttoned, revealing a low-cut white silk blouse. I walked Francine into the corridor.

"What are you staring at?" Francine demanded. "My dress? Listen, kid. It cheers him up, believe me."

Her high-heeled shoes make a hard click, click, click on the green tiled floor. When Francine rounded the corridor to the elevator, I walked back into my father's room.

"Do you want to hear the news?"

My father is fanatical about the news. He begins each morning with a thorough study of the newspaper, sports section first, then the front page and editorials. He knows what's going on in Cuba and Korea and Great Britain. He just doesn't care. Republicans or Democrats? My father would shrug the way he does at a Monday-night baseball game between the Padres and Braves.

"I'm an impartial observer," he would say, a cigar in his hand. "I just want to see a good fight."

Now he was lying motionless. His eyes were closed.

"I'll read you the sports first," I said.

I began with the race results. I hoped for large Exactas, two- and three-thousand-dollar payoffs that might excite him. When there were only favorites, first and second choices, I invented long shots for him.

WHATS THIS.

"Oxygen, Daddy. Do you hurt? Do you want another shot?" Francine and I always offered my father a shot.

"Five hundred forty bucks a day," my mother said once. "He deserves a buzz."

My father was lying very still. A tear fell from his eye. He batted it down awkwardly with his hand, as if it were a terrible insect perched on his cheek. A killer.

NO WORDS, my father wrote on his pad. Then he turned his bandaged face away from me, toward the green enamel wall.

I drove home quickly, west, rushing for the sea, as if I were being pursued. Trucks surged around me like ancient enraged beasts shaking the air, cutting a path through the day, leaving the morning bruised.

It was early, not yet noon. I did what I was supposed to do. I went out collecting Jason's rents.

I walked carefully. If I walk on any one stretch of street or beach too often, it becomes bleached and dulled. If I am not careful, the world can become composed of papier-mâché buildings dead under a pale blue painted backdrop of sky.

It is essential that each building, each storefront, café and apartment house, retain distinct qualities, now white stucco, now brick, now wood slats or asphalt slabs. I noted each terra-cotta pot of red geraniums on porches and balconies. The sun numbs and strips my senses. I forced myself to see differences, the shades of gray in shingles and the print in polished cotton curtains.

It was clear. A breeze had pushed the sullen air from rooftops and sidewalks. I understood that the entire world was precisely the same. It was composed of millions of streets with balconies, liquor stores and fruit stands. The earth was simply a matter of liquid blues, sandy places, brown gullies, the green of valleys, white rock, the indeterminate pales of dry brush and gray asphalt. Angles could be elongated. A horizontal plane could be pushed out, a vertical line stretched. But the basic elements remained the same, fixed, a series of almost infinite geometric patterns altering only in proportion and color.

I was surprised and saddened by this knowledge. I saw that the world was simply variation. One could add more. The blue-white of hillsides under snow, perhaps. But the basic elements differed only in arrangement. The combinations were preordained, defined and limited.

I realized my life was also defined. The boundaries of my world were the canals on one side and the ocean on the other. Jason sat squarely in the center.

I shrugged, a piece of the beach brushing against doors. I collected the rent from Mr. Gordon. He's eighty-four years old and lives alone in a brick building facing the boardwalk. I watched him, arthritic and deaf as he brewed tea for me on his hot plate. The sun beat itself raw against his streaked gray windows. I watched him pour the tea into porcelain cups and slide them expertly into the centers of matched saucers. He was telling me about summer in New York when he was young and played the mandolin on rooftops in a slow dull wet heat. He was speaking without sorrow, as if it had happened to someone else.

Then he remembered the mandolin. He went into his tiny bedroom. I heard him rummaging. I imagined the mandolin, the wood infinitely fine, almost reddish like a stretched heart. I was afraid of the exquisitely carved and polished wood, the row of tight strings, bunched out and still hopeful. If I touched it something terrible would be imparted to me, through my fingers and into my flesh. I stood up quickly, the room spinning, my forehead stinging hot, and left, forgetting the rent.

I often forget the rents. I found myself standing in one of Jason's wooden cottages. I stared at a woman with gray hair hidden under a red cotton kerchief. She could have stood pounding clothing clean on rocks in a stream in a Polish village with my grandmother and her mother before the whole world changed.

Her eyes were manic, bright blue, knowledgeable, measuring. I was afraid of her history and what she could teach me. All old women have buried husbands who were scholars, men who taught the children in small back rooms in the east side of some city once.

I watched the old woman write a check with trembling hands swollen from disease and age. I glanced at her captured plants in dirty pots and the shelves of books that I knew would leave a brownish clotted dust across my hands. I was afraid of this residue, the sense of an imprint on my flesh, alive like a leech burrowing in.

I could almost hear the old woman's thoughts. Who could have foreseen this place, this Venice, California? There was no hint of this in the Florida winters, no omen of this far west coast with the painted and ragged young, stumbling drunk or high on drugs at noon, throwing driftwood at stray dogs and meeting in alleys behind her cottage to conduct business of an illicit, perhaps even demonic nature. There was no sense of this isolation and chaos in all the years of ordered Friday-night suppers, Thanksgivings and graduations and all the good seasons without locusts, fires or plagues.

When the old woman talked, her bony hands fluttered at her sides. She could lift out the years as simply as one takes a lipstick from a purse, reach in and hold up '31 or '47 or '66. I was terrified that she would somehow do this. I didn't want to see the frail dissolving spines of a life. I didn't want to see the years crack and splinter in the sunlight, become dust before she could even begin to explain.

I knew she was a good old woman, a clean old woman without black whiskers on her chin or a noticeable deformity, a limp or cane, cataracts or plastic devices embedded in the flesh. She was a good old woman, a clean old woman who did not smell. Still, I turned away from her while she pulled sponge cake from her small dirty oven. Magic.

I must be careful.

I forgot the rents. I walked in the sea breeze, the sole inhabitant of an underwater city. The pressure was enormous, each breath a struggle, a battle with individual molecules of air, those invisible clawed cells.

I stood on the bridge near my house. The day turned gray. The air was gray. The boulevard was gray, like an old sick dog.

Soon night would fall. Stripped of the myth of purpose and order, the streets and buildings would return to their true forms, a collection of mud and brick, things dug from the earth and left to rot under drained banks of low rust-red clouds.

Soon it would be the hour of the amulet and magic chant. The moment when man remembers his ancient fear of being alone, separated from the tribe as darkness fell and the predators began to stalk, the leopards crawling out of shadows with their slow torch eyes and claws.

The whole earth seemed to hang at the edge, suspended, not day and not night. A long moment of indecision. Then the battered sun spilled one fine plum-and-coral line into the thinning sky. Gulls ceased shrieking.

I just stood on the bridge, shaking my head as I stared at the blackening water, shaking my head back and forth, back and forth as if trying to pry the dream splinters from their perch in the dead center of my scalp. Then I telephoned Jason.

"I've been going over my life," I began. "One miserable frame at a time. Thinking about how sordid it's been, how degrading and filled with mutual contempt. I really feel sick."

"You're so solipsistic. It's insufferable," Jason said. And, softer, "Why don't you come over?"

"Come over? I don't think I'll ever come over again."

"Oh," Jason said finally. "If I had known that two hours ago, I could have made plans for tonight."

"You still can." I hung up.

For seven years I have lived continually threatened, feeling that a good half of Venice, California, was constantly being auditioned for my position. And a good half of the time I did nothing at all. I lived in my special silence, my world within a world of cold white tiles and ice sheets, and thought, good God, won't somebody please come and take this walking, breathing, stinking nightmare off my hands?

And someone did.

And I did not speak to Jason for thirteen months. I lived here in the Woman's House four canals away from Jason and constructed my life in such a fashion that I did not run into him, not once.

❦ 11 ❦

We reconciled. It was that simple.

I met Jason for a drink. After all, it had been thirteen months without him. I had spent two months traveling through Mexico and Northern California with another man. Later I decorated a second man's Christmas tree. I attached neon bulbs and strips of silver tinsel to fir branches with fingers that were not my own, dead fingers, inanimate and oddly frozen, another layer of decoration.

Nothing touched me. Jason clung to everything. I went with another man to Mexico City. I tried to forget him under a gouged white tequila sun while bells rang. I felt stalked by the cathedrals festering like abscesses on wide cobbled plazas where women squatted by stacks of Chiclets piled into holy pyramids. Jason haunted me.

The men came and went. They were interchangeable, pushing meaningless pieces of themselves into me, a stab of quartz, glistening disks, a kind of dying alphabet drying without residue. I sent them away. I dismissed them as Jason did his women and felt nothing. I was a tree in winter, half asleep, whittled naked, enduring.

Jason called on his birthday. I knew he would. I had been waiting all day.

"It's my birthday." Jason breathed black warm into the telephone, black with night and expectation, black and warm through the wires, black over the black metal webbing of canals. Jason, a black hawk strutting. Jason with his whole black bag of tricks.

"I'm thirty today," Jason said, as if those were the magic words and everything would be forgiven.

"So?" It was the first thing I had said to him in four months.

"So I thought we could get together."

"Your girlfriend busy?"

"I've got no girlfriend."

"Too bad." I hung up.

My hands were shaking. I could still feel his voice brushing my face. Sealed parts of me breathed again, stretching awake, hungry.

It was dangerous to speak to him. His words echoed through my head and body like a kind of summer wind. The Santa Ana winds, perhaps, that blow fierce and uncontrollable. The sudden desert winds. The city captured, singed nightly. The crime rate rises. There is violence, confusion, a strange burning.

Jason telephoned on the Fourth of July. "I'm all alone," he said miserably. He made it sound almost like a crime.

"I'm not surprised." I was also alone.

"Let's just get one drink. Celebrate our illusion of freedom with the other enslaved jerks. Get some almost bicentennial maya. White maya," Jason offered.

I bit my lip. I remembered Jason tying up my arm with his bathrobe belt, my heart racing, my hand pumping. And hitting. The sigh and transformation into arctic white, enamel white, cloud chips, the white sea opening icy white lips.

I lit a cigarette. I was sweating. "Your timing is terrible. You should have hustled somebody last week. Everybody loves you for three or four days."

"Do you love me?"

"No." I hung up.

For the first time I considered the possibility that I might actually see him again. And if I did see Jason again things would be very different, very different indeed.

Jason telephoned at Christmas. He was drunk. Music played loud in the background. He shouted above it. "Sorry to bother you. Nostalgia. Just wanted to hear your voice."

"You always want what you don't have, Jason. That's your private hell."

"I hurt you. I was stupid," Jason said quickly. "Could we get together? As friends?"

"We're not friends. I don't even like you," I said. My heart was pushing black torpedoes through my veins. They exploded. It rained and the drops were gigantic yellow moths. Parachutes with red and magenta folds were opening, billowing down. A choir was singing.

"Could you just see me out of pity?"

I thought about it. Then I said no.

Jason telephoned on my birthday. I was surprised. I didn't know Jason knew when my birthday was. He had ignored the occasion for three consecutive years. I was caught off balance. I was alone. I agreed to meet him for a drink.

At first I didn't recognize him. He was standing near me wearing a black cowboy shirt and a big black cowboy hat. He looked thin and pale and miserable, vaguely unhealthy, as if he had spent the entire year subsisting on beer and potato chips.

When Jason sat down at the small round table he brushed his

leg against mine. I tried not to look at him, to look instead at the city below. The ocean was a solid blue haze. The streets were a simple collection of horizontal and vertical lines now elongated, now fattening into a wide blank gully of freeway.

Jason stared at his beer. "I thought you might have forgiven me."

He reached for my arm. His hand circled my wrist. His hand was hot, was lava, metal, a kind of girdle, a goddamn wedding band. And I was breathing in the texture of his skin, the pressure of his hand, his closeness. In a rush I began to remember, began to tremble.

I was sipping white wine and looking out the plate-glass window at the city, the pale blue gauzy sky, the slow pale blue sea pocked with sailboats.

"I love you," Jason whispered. "Don't you still love me?"

A sadness spread inside me, warm and pasty. Below, houses were a horizontal stack of pastel boxes framed by green patches of front lawn and backyard. Jason tightened his grip on my wrist. And air sparked, sparkled, and suddenly I was laughing.

It was Monday afternoon. We left our drinks on the table and made love in the back seat of the car, parked in the hotel's underground parking lot. And I was young again. It was before Jason. It was before Gerald. Before the blank cold silence and bricking up. When I was still half girl. When I had force and grace and a shapeless ambition, joyriding a streamlined concentric July and steaming awake in yellow mornings with blond boys, in back seats and bathtubs, in closets like moths, any door that locked.

Monday night we went to the ballet. Francine is held in some special awe by the management of the Forum, the Santa Monica Civic Auditorium and the Hollywood Bowl. At least twice a month envelopes stuffed with complimentary tickets arrive at my house.

"Don't leave me," I begged in the darkness. A ballerina swirled, a gauzy blue circle, a piece of sky around her waist.

"You give great head," Jason answered.

I glanced at him in the darkness. Fear was an avalanche, clotting my eyes, lodging cold splinters inside. Something rushed at my face with blinding speed. And something within me broke.

On Tuesday we drove into the Santa Monica mountains. We parked the car on a dirt road and pushed our way up an old narrow dirt trail. We made love under eucalyptus trees. Twigs and burs stuck to our clothes.

Then he was zipping up his pants, moving back toward the road, already somehow in a hurry. I watched the small patch of his white back. Thud. And something inside me broke.

On Wednesday night we were given a free pass to an X-rated movie in Hollywood. The actress had once been Jason's neighbor on the Grand Canal. He had painted her riding on the teeter-totter. She always sent him passes for her porno movies.

"I want to do it all. Just like the movie," Jason breathed, later. He was on his knees above me. He was watching his body in the mirror over the bed.

"We'll need a birch rod," I said.

"I'll get one." Jason was reaching for his pants. He stared at me, my wrists tied behind my back, my breasts pushed up toward him, twin offerings. "Wait here. Think about what it will be like."

I lay in the darkness. I thought. Jason came back with a strip of bamboo and a knife. He cut a rod. "Are you afraid?"

"Yes." I looked at Jason. He was looking in the mirror.

"Good. Turn over," Jason said.

I turned over. The bamboo slapped against my back. I gasped. I tried to sit up.

"Does it hurt?" Jason asked.

"Yes."

"Good." Jason slapped the rod against my back again. I jumped. I moaned. I heard the air whiz by, shattered. The rod slapped down again. My flesh was stinging, impossibly hot. The whole world felt red. And Jason was breathing warm against me, "There, there," and licking the red lines in my skin, sliding his tongue, a red moth, across the flesh grooves and cooing, "There, there," and I was tumbling, falling through soft pockets of luminous air, floating down, down.

On Thursday morning we drove into the mountains. It was the tail end of winter.

"You know the women don't matter. The ones I pay," Jason said out of nowhere. "They're still lifes. I try not to touch. It's my work, my job. It's business."

Outside the window the high desert coughed in my face. I couldn't think of anything to say.

Jason pointed to a yucca in the snowbank. He said the yucca needed one special beetle to complete its sexual cycle, that short season when it pushes out a massive midsection, explodes the thighs and lays down a suggestion of shell. "I saw a special on it, on Twenty-eight," Jason said.

The sky was cold blue splinters. I realized I never understood Jason or why I needed him.

"I'm going to suspend a girl from ropes next. Hang the raft on wires. Make it look like she's really floating."

I stared out the window. I thought of a young girl's legs floating above a tapestry of blues and yellows and reds. Jason wound up a road marked closed into an icy late afternoon mist.

He stopped the car. I sledded down a hill into a creek of fresh melted snow. I lay in the white and cold, wet, afraid to breathe, afraid to move. Jason was standing on the hilltop above me, above the timberline, where trees twist bizarre and unkept like the savages at the end of a race.

Jason dropped me off near the bridge over Eastern Canal. He seemed agitated, restless, a claustrophobic with the walls inching in. I didn't see him for three days.

Silence. Silence like a live thing, feeding itself, breeding. My house filled with invisible things, blood trails of old wounds, shadows, shadows like snails glued to the walls, shadows and the ghost glows of the women Jason had painted, the oily half-formed flowers that glared at me from his walls and the walls of the Woman's House.

Three days of darkness swelling and pulling apart like petals. Three days of sun tearing at the soft bodies of nesting shadows. And mornings startled, punched open, entirely yellow and wide as a lethal wound, a bullet hole from a magnum.

"Hello, baby," Jason breathed. The night opened then, opened into black warm layered pathways, hot currents of moon rays, waves, the wind rustling burdened with salt.

"I'm busy." I dropped my voice. I imagined I was sitting in a diving bell on the floor of the ocean. I filled my voice with the accumulated pain of everything, the thorn-edged darkness, my solitude, the weight of his absence, the hole it tore in me, through me.

"I want you," Jason said.

"I have a date."

"Send him home at midnight."

"I can't do it that way." It was a lie. I could do it that way, had in fact done it precisely that way many times.

I couldn't remember whose move it was. Outside it was late afternoon. The canals were browning, shadow-burdened, the color of charred wood.

"I started a new painting," Jason told me, as if I cared.

"A new whore," I said, pointlessly. I knew to Jason they were all equal. You cannot multiply zero.

"Who are you kidding?" Jason snapped. "How many have there been? How do you think that makes me feel?"

"Feel?" I repeated. "You're incapable of feeling. You're defective, Jason, like someone born with thalidomide flippers for arms. You can't expect someone like that to play basketball or lift weights. You're not whole, Jason."

"Neither are you."

Impasse. A house of mirrors. Quartz tunnels and blind alleys. A maze. A graveyard, perilous abundant web of sharp curves.

Sculpture garden of crashed automobiles, scrap metal, hopeless. Box canyons. Hopeless. Sheer cliffs. And the walls and floors are glass. And I am multiplied, exaggerated. And no one is laughing.

I hung up. The night was a sheared-open place, a crater on the dark side of the moon. The air was a fibrous network. I burrowed in. I made a cocoon and slept.

I woke up to the sound of pounding. It was after midnight. Jason was beating his fist against my heavy wood front door, against the dead-bolt lock and chain. I let him knock for a long time before I opened it.

Jason stared at me. He looked surprised. He looked as if he was prepared for a crisis, prepared to find me stretched out on a floor, comatose fingers wrapped around an emptied bottle of neatly labeled Seconal.

I didn't say anything. I couldn't think of anything to say. It was the seventh night of our reconciliation. It was the end of our first week together, again.

12

I found myself assembling the evidence from my life with Jason, mementoes from my isolation, my worlds of silence. All at once I wanted to see it separately, deprived of that lie context and simply objects in a small pile at my feet, a kind of still life.

It was the middle of a cold night, and glistening, like the wet hide of a black shark. I felt wide awake, wired, my nerves on fire.

I removed one of Jason's canvases from my living room wall. I studied the painting. The impression was stark and strangely cold. The room seemed inordinately small, squeezed together and encased in a permanent chill. Without realizing it, Jason had included a suggestion of the broken back windows and wind rising, whipping across the dull slumbering harbor.

"I'm a mirror," Jason said, squeezing more red onto his square glass palette. "You see what you want to see. I simply am."

I was quiet and still. I was posing. I was a lemon, a basket of apples, a beer can, a patch of sand. Jason was painting me. I could feel the brush stroking my new canvas flesh.

"Don't you like what you see?" Jason asked. He was painting a red crevice into the thick orange shadow on the wall behind my shoulder.

"I can be any fantasy. Pleasure?"

He let the word hang in the air like a perfect plumed bird. Then he put his paintbrush down. Then he crossed the room and the floor was against my back and Jason pressing in, pressing in.

"We'll do a white painting," Jason told me. "You all in white. Everything feeling white."

White. Yes. White. Yes. I practically ran to Jason's studio. Cocaine was the collected white star shine of all the orbits of all the stars since the start of time, since the first bell, the first white explosion, the first white stirring in that first blank void.

Jason was sitting at his old kitchen table. The curtains were closed. He was cutting the white powder with a razor blade. His movements were slow and exact. We were still precise then. There were still edges and warning signals. Jason could still set up his easel, squeeze his paints onto his palette and make his brush sail across the white canvas. We still had hands.

Later there would be no fine distinguishing lines. Later we would use the same needle, use it even after the point was dulled almost useless. Later there would be no night or day. Later there would be only the needle and the shadows, the hot dark swirl, the walls with wings, my arms canvas sails, the floor itself churning, a kind of tide pool.

Later the world would collapse under the sheer white weight of white starlight. My laughter was white. My teeth and tongue were coated with enamel. I was a star. I was a sea shell perfected by the churning of waves and the turning in circles of that maniac, that cold-hearted, one-white-eyed bitch, the moon.

Jason worked on the painting all night. Someone walked to a sink. Water ran. Powder was ground up with a razor blade. The needle entered the vein effortlessly, like a knife into soft butter. And I felt white as an orchid, as a starched linen tablecloth, as a bride in an ankle-length white silk gown.

I closed my eyes. I was draped in white silk. I walked down a white aisle past pillars burdened by white bouquets, white lilies, white carnations and white roses. I stood somewhere with a white bundle in my arms, a baby wrapped in a soft white blanket. I lived in a white house behind a freshly painted white picket fence.

"Let's get married," I said, laughing, my tongue and teeth and lungs a sparkling glistening white.

"No way," Jason said.

He stood at his easel, smiling. I tried to imagine a time, any time, when I did not love him.

I was living in Francine's Westwood duplex. It was the slow gray of night and day passing imperceptibly without residue, drained. Jason came to paint me. He arrived precisely on time, just as the bells from the nearby church chimed six, six. Jason stood on the other side of the door. He was carrying his big brown wood paint box. The brushes looked stiff and sharp, a kind of finger. It was an important moment. The church bells rang, six, six. I looked at Jason. It was the last moment I was free.

I picked up the canvases and leaned them near the front door. Suddenly I didn't want them anymore.

It was almost dawn. I wanted anything but the silence in my house, anything but the vision of my father in the hospital hooked up to an oxygen machine. My father terrified, with tears falling through the thick white webbing of bandages. My father lying wide-eyed and horrified with his throat gone and his tongue cut and the curse of the centuries boiling in his useless mouth. My father, the wild river impossibly dammed, damned.

My father locked in a strangling silence, words exploding in the centers of his eyes and tears spilling down between the gauze.

I wandered through my house. The Woman's House. Had it ever been my house? Who hung the mirror above the bed? What predecessor pasted yellow tile in the kitchen? Blue tile above the bathtub? Who planted the bed of purple and yellow pansies, their smooth petals the pattern of a healing bruise?

The sun rose slowly and heavily, somehow uncertain, a convalescent taking the first strained steps. I kept moving. I ran cold water on my face. I still couldn't wake up. The real me was sleeping while someone else, a clever impostor, continued the show. The real me was still sleeping under a quilt and three wool blankets in the gray stone house in Philadelphia. The real me was sleeping in a room with bright yellow curtains. The real me was waiting for morning, for Mommy to call. I would come down the curving brown wood stairs to hot cereal while Daddy drank his coffee, while Daddy read his newspaper and pulled on his denim painting overalls, grabbed his big brown wool coat and pushed through all the thick-piled snow.

I began to drive toward the hospital. I gripped the wheel uncertainly, punched in the face by sun. The commercial buildings along Venice Boulevard and the patches of lawn in front of small stucco houses stuck and forgotten between factory buildings and warehouses whirled and spun red. Red cannas waved arms, red arms like a man on flame. A lemon tree pushed blooms, blooms like poisoned tongues. The sun stalled, a pus yellow and hot, hot enough to make a sane man hang himself.

What am I doing? What am I doing? And a voice answered with a soft chalky white laugh, Why, you're cutting new paths to the hospital. That's what you're doing. Cutting at the city like a surgeon cutting at someone's father's throat. North to Olympic Boulevard. East to Highland Avenue. You're discovering the subtlety of Arlington Avenue, how it curves around once and becomes Wilton Place. You're learning how to strip a city naked, to gouge its flesh as if holding a scalpel. Pico to Vermont.

And see how white it is? The pavement, your skin, the asphalt all white, white as the picked bones of dead prospectors. The end of the trail.

But what am I doing? Doing? You're breathing the gray glue between hospital visits. You're living suspended, exhausted, silent and dulled. These are the long numbing preparations for finality. See death lick the flesh? See what a horrible pointed tongue he has? See death reaching over, that foul-smelling pervert? See him licking Daddy's poor scarred skin?

And what if I can't face it? Not face it? the voice inside me repeated, a dull thud, an empty beer can kicked into the night canals, the water the color and texture of black metal, air rising damp as if from a deep well. The voice within me was a kind of mirror. Not face it? Not face it? Not drive the car? Not stop at red lights? Not walk down the quiet corridors with their shadows and bubbles, quiet corridors that are a minefield? Not crisscross the city to the hospital sitting hunched on Vermont near Sunset Boulevard in the gutted ruined heart of Hollywood?

The city stretched on all sides, ripe with my intangible past. Not simply street corners but distinct places, invisible doors into other eras. The spot where I met Gerald, met Jason. The apartments where I have lived, loved, vomited, stuck needles in my arms, passed out and howled. Always malformed buds strangled on wiry bushes, twisted by noise and dust. Always residential side streets pushed up rows of stucco bungalows like sun sores, the world blistered.

The morning had the quality of steam. Gulls screeched in the shallow empty clouds. I realized that if these blocks and cement gouges were the alphabet of the future, then we lived at the edge of history. Los Angeles sits white and half dead, already after the fact, already somehow gasping for breath, slowly strangling.

From Fountain Avenue and Vermont the city was revealed. White gouges like white scars leading to the hills. I realized that

Los Angeles is a rented city. It was born fully formed from the daydreams and wet dreams of greedy little men pushing celluloid fantasies. Los Angeles is a Monopoly board with orange trees. There is danger, too distant to be a factor. Earthquakes last only seconds. It is too much to hope for.

I turned onto Vermont Avenue. I was facing the blank brown backs of the hills. What am I doing? And the voice within me answered, You're waiting, kid. That's what you're doing. Waiting. Don't you understand yet? Los Angeles is the great waiting room of the world. Wait to get discovered. Wait for your social security check. Wait for the cancer to come back. Wait for the break, the earthquake. Wait for the crisp white words that say the man you call father is dead. Wait with your small life leaking out into a white haze of a hot white afternoon.

I parked my car. Everything seemed to be humming. The traffic on Vermont Avenue hummed. The sun seemed to hum. The slow drugged insects hummed. The air hummed in the cubicles and corridors of the intensive care unit. I suddenly realized that Los Angeles is the terminal ward of the world.

The parking lot attendant smiled at me. He seemed to know me, my dusty car, my face white, parking in the hot sun every day for a week. Nurses smiled at me, still hopeful. Everyone smiled, still hopeful.

I walked into the hospital lobby. Francine was leaning against a cigarette machine. I willed my legs to carry me forward. My steps were wooden, uneven. It seemed the air had finally turned liquid, been transmuted and flowed like a poison, flowed like a creek suddenly erupting its banks and reaching up for the low hills and reaching up farther, reaching up for the pale drained useless sky.

❧ 13 ❧

"It's not healing," Francine said. "The radiated tissue won't come together. It keeps opening, toward the artery."

"What?"

I stopped in the middle of the corridor. I thought of my father lying still in his white bed while his artery burst. It would be a sudden red dream, his last. Perhaps he would imagine himself a young boy again, running fast in a Yankee T-shirt, blinded by a red sun. His ears would fill again with the red wail of childhood, sirens and whistles, slap of bat against ball, the ice cream wagon, children screaming into sun, a special eruption.

"The surgery isn't healing," Francine repeated. "He wants to die. He can't stand the tubes. If it doesn't heal, they can't remove the tubes. He's got no way to eat."

"The tubes could be permanent?" I asked, gasped. I thought of my father with a red plastic tube positioned securely in his nose, a red tusk, an experiment, part elephant.

"Or worse."

Francine lit a cigarette. Two orderlies pushed a middle-aged man in a wheelchair. The man was screaming. Blood had collected in a perfect red puddle on his thigh. The emergency room door swung shut.

"He wants to commit suicide. Death with honor, he called it."

"What did you say?"

"I said, die? How can you die? You want me to bring you sleeping pills for an OD number? You'll have to get rid of the feeding tubes in your nose first. Maybe that will give you something to live for."

"What do you think?" someone asked. It couldn't have been me. I was gone. Something remained behind, white and numb, asking questions as if they mattered, as if explanations mattered, as if the horror could be labeled.

"He's in a bad depression," Francine said. "If the tubes don't come out, do you blame him?"

I couldn't think of anything to say.

"I saw the surgeon twice," Francine said. "He's going to try a skin graft. Take skin from his legs and shoulders. Hope the new skin will grow over and close the wound. He called it a patch."

"Quaint," I said. I thought of patchwork quilts. I thought of warrior tribes that skinned their enemies alive.

"Patch, my ass," Francine said. "I told him to get the old man out of bed."

I thought of something terrible. When my mind touched it, my mind emptied and went blank. It was like waking up and staring at an enormous white iceberg. I felt cold, disoriented and strangely small. I sucked in my breath.

"What if the skin graft doesn't work? If he doesn't get the tubes out he can't commit suicide."

"I've considered that," Francine said. "Worse comes to worse, we pick the old man up and throw him out the window."

There was no time in my father's room. The blinds were drawn. The air seemed a special glistening gray, seasonless, the color of waiting.

AM A LEMON, my father had scrawled on his pad. He picked the pad up and waved it in my mother's direction.

"Stop it," Francine told him.

AM A LOSER. ITS HOPELESS.

Francine walked to the window. "Look," she screamed, pointing at the windowpane. "A private room with a view. The most technologically advanced conditions. Five hundred forty dollars a day. A day."

My father closed his eyes. He turned his face away from the window.

"Hold your ticket," Francine said to my father, her voice softer. "It's a photo finish. Anything can happen."

CANT STAND TUBES.

"The tubes are temporary," Francine said quickly. She began to pace.

WHAT IF????

"If the tubes stay?" Francine stared down at my father. "If the skin graft doesn't work? If they can't make a new throat for you? Then we'll pick you up and throw you out the window."

Something was struggling near my father's lips. I think he was trying to smile.

"Are you in pain?" It was the first thing I had said. "I'll get you morphine."

NO FRIGGIN DRUGS, my father wrote. He looked at me, his eyes black pits, the gateways of deep tunnels. He seemed to think of something and forget it, all at once. He sank back small and coiled, a white bundle in a white crib.

Francine pulled the blinds open. Overnight the lawn below had erupted with small star-shaped white buds and yellow daisies. There was a sense of dew in the new shoots.

"Can't you take some joy in spring?" Francine asked.

FUCK SPRING.

"Not in your condition," Francine assured him.

WANT 2 DIE.

Francine glanced at her watch. "I've got a budget conference in Century City. A whole day of wall-to-wall assholes. I'll come back later."

She bent down and kissed my father on a small corner of unbandaged skin, just to the side of his red plastic feeding tube. She pointed to me. "Read him the newspaper. Find something grotesque. Mass murders, a 747 collision. Something to give him a sense of perspective."

My father had closed his eyes. He didn't open them until Francine left the room.

I searched the front page for something exciting. An earthquake in South America killing twenty or thirty thousand and leaving a million starving and homeless. A train plowing into a stalled school bus. A hurricane, a drought. I found a story about a twenty-one-year-old college football star losing his fight against cancer.

AGAIN.

I read the story again. I glanced at my father. He was staring at the ceiling.

AGAIN WITH DRAMATIC EMPHASIS.

I read the story a third time, taking appropriate pauses, making certain sentences leap out of my mouth, small plumed birds with a life of their own. And I thought, go fly off, find treetops, build strong nests, drift intoxicated eating berries and blue air.

KID PULLED A BAD HAND, my father wrote. He paused, the pen gripped between his fingers. LIKE ME. He dropped his felt-tipped pen to the floor. A tear slid out of his eye and careened down his cheek. It disappeared in the cotton wrapped around his neck.

My father was lying very still. Outside the window the lawn

nodded rows of small white heads, sun-dazed buds, petals intricate, looking knitted.

"You know, you're betraying your own philosophy," I began, searching for and somehow finding Francine's tone. I felt myself almost assuming her stance, legs planted wide apart, one tapered arm on her hip. "All those years after the first cancer. The twenty years I was growing up. You always said life was a grab bag, a sweepstakes. Live every minute because there are no guarantees."

My father seemed to be watching the sunlight reluctantly dragging itself through the Venetian blinds. I thought he was listening.

"You taught me that, Daddy. I remember. We still lived together. We had just come out here, the same time as the Dodgers. It was before Chavez Ravine. Remember? We watched them play at the Coliseum. I remember the whole team, Daddy. Snyder, Hodges, Wally Moon, Gilliam, Charlie Neal, Roseboro. We had Koufax and Drysdale then."

NOTHING TEAM.

"I know. I'm just remembering when we lived together. You sat in the backyard at night, watering the peach tree and listening to the blue jays. You were always out there watching something. The yard. The sky. You were just glad to be alive. You took a joy in everything."

THOUGHT I HAD IT LICKED FOREVER, my father wrote. I held his hand. After a while he closed his eyes.

I walked into the corridor. I needed a cigarette. I usually smoked in an alcove directly across the corridor from where the morphine was kept. Whenever I lit a cigarette, a nurse or doctor would suddenly appear at my shoulder and tell me no one on the third floor smoked, from the head doctor through the floor sweepers. They saw what cancer was, saw it every day.

What was cancer, anyway? It was ancient as the hills, the stones, original sin. It spawned in the morning of factory whistles, iron and coal and steel and gray stone blocks, streetcars, black scars of train tracks like black rows of stitches.

Perhaps the wild cancer cells had taken for their pattern the spoiled horizon, the low thick banks of poisonous clouds, the slow rivers absolutely dead beneath soap bubbles, rusting tin cans and old bottles. Perhaps it was the final legacy of generations born with chips of bronze in their lungs, the soot from chimneys and city curbs. Was it surprising that the body erupted, spewing contagion?

I lit a cigarette. I imagined the disease blowing like a red volcano in the center of my father's throat. It grew like the sagebrush and yucca, the natural vegetation of the Los Angeles basin. Perhaps it gained entry through pores and pushed roots in, tentative at first and then taking hold, gripping the soft flesh linings and opening buds. The doctor said it was growing inside him for two years. Two years he walked with it, slept with it, ate and fed it. For two years he lived with a seedling death crop pushing up stalks inside him. Two years of it spewing cells in a mad fuck of death.

Suddenly I realized that he must have sensed it, some faint taste of webbing, some shadowy perception of inhabitation. He hid it. He wore it like a special jewel inside, a small sun, a tight little secret that warmed him. He must have felt the thorns in his cheeks and tongue and the splinters as the seedling pod exploded. Perhaps he sensed the invasion and bent into its special warmth and radiance after a decade of loneliness.

Once the gray-haired man was sage. But my father spent his gray-haired years alone. I went to Berkeley with Gerald. I crouched half dead in Venice with Jason. And my father turned gray as the storm that spends itself above a gray sea, two hundred miles from landfall spilling its promise into indifferent gray waves. He aged. His tribe disintegrated, savaged by the place called Los Angeles and the events that just happened, the things called fate and chance.

"I'm hip to Francine," I remembered my father explaining.

It was the night before he went to the hospital. It was the night I found him collapsed on his kitchen floor. "We were both hipsters, your mother and I. She was some kind of sixteen-year-old street bum. I was thirty-five. I knew it couldn't go on forever. The cancer blew it. Upset the balance.

"And she was crazy. I always knew that. Like uncentered, out of kilter. She picked me up on a street corner, hustling dinners. I told her you're one tired kid. You're six months out of a whorehouse. She believed me. She saw I had savvy. I said, I'll marry you, kid. What the hell? Any port in a storm, right?

"She had a father thing, a complex from being deserted. When I got sick the first time, she had to quit being a kid. That's what she was, too. A kid. Playing house with you all day.

"She took it personally when I got sick. I can see her point. We were gamblers. She took a flier and won big. Still, for such a big winner she's really pathetic," my father said that night before he entered the hospital, the night he was drinking bourbon from the bottle, the night the world began crashing down.

"I'll never forget the first time," Francine told me once. "They were wheeling him into surgery. He looked up and said, sorry, kid. Don't look back. Keep your shoulders squared and keep going. As they pushed him into the operating room, he reached out and grabbed my ass. They wheeled him in laughing."

I began walking down the corridor. Everywhere a muted insistent humming clung to the layers of slow-moving fluids drip, drip, dripping through bottles and tubes. Patients were hidden behind greenish shadows, their blinds pulled closed. The slow fluids oozed. The televisions stuck high in the walls leaked their soft radioactive blue glow, a kind of death lash.

I could almost understand their dreams. They lie plugged in, rooms dim, and imagine their poor ruined flesh has finally fallen off and they are at last dry of all the human rot. They wish to dry even thinner, thin as the skin of fish, but something catches

125

them. They fight back then, fight the taut string and the sensation of hanging. They taste salt and a terrible yearning for the cracking spines of waves poised like sentries guarding the sea gates and chimes, the soft channel down into spinning purple. Finality. The sea floor.

I peeked into my father's doorway. He was sleeping. I crossed the corridor quickly, trying not to look into the room where the morphine trays sat. I told myself I could pass the room and feel nothing, feel nothing.

In the hospital cafeteria the light was sharp and white and the whole world was a kind of bas-relief. A large round clock was fastened to the wall above my shoulder, a device implanted surgically in plaster. I heard it ticking/breathing. Hours passed.

Francine walked in. She had changed clothing. She was wearing a white tennis skirt. Her legs were long, tanned. A doctor watched her walk. A busboy froze as she passed.

"You look at my tennis racket like a personal offense," Francine observed. She sat down. She brought her face very close to mine. Her eyes were agate, flecked and somehow windy.

"You don't know anything, kid. One thing I've learned from all this is to live while you can. Fred knows that. He's a very vital man. He should be. He's only forty."

I was thinking about the clock embedded in the wall, permanently wide-eyed and somehow accountable.

"You look terrible," Francine observed.

I almost smiled. Our interaction had become stylized. We spoke by analogy, by nuances so coded and odd we reinforced our alienation with each breath. We spun in the same old cruel circles.

Once I left Gerald during a particularly virulent period of our life. The National Guard was stationed on the street corners of Berkeley. They slept in tents three blocks from our apartment. The men wore uniforms. They carried rifles with bayonets. They rode in special army trucks. The city resembled newsreels of World War II in Europe. A banner saying WELCOME TO

OCCUPIED PRAGUE was strung across the front of our apartment house.

Gerald and I had been fighting all week. I think we still slept in the same bed then. I seem to remember his back, white by the streetlamp glow.

"Is it me?" I kept asking him. I was sitting up and rocking myself in the darkness. "Why don't you go to a doctor? Why don't you just try?" And rocking in the darkness thinking he should do it, why isn't he doing it, trial and error, the scientific method, what the hell was the matter? Gerald wasn't even playing by his own rules anymore.

"You don't fully appreciate cosmic rhythms. Be patient," Gerald said to the wall. He sounded disappointed and tired.

Patient, I thought. Patient? And I walked into the living room. Slowly, deliberately, as if dusting, I picked up our lamp and let it fall to the floor. The pottery base shattered.

Gerald stormed into the room. He was wearing white jockey shorts. He always wore white jockey shorts like a white bandage. He looked somehow antiseptic, protected from thighs to waist. His hidden parts were safe, coiled tight, a small white secret. A secret that no longer seemed to matter.

"Are you crazy?" he demanded. He was staring at the fragments of what had once been our lamp. He touched the splinters with his foot. His lips twisted, as if tasting something terribly sour. Gerald hated waste.

Gerald was studying anthropology then. He was sitting on the brown sofa reading Claude Lévi-Strauss. I was interrupting him, placing obstacles in his path, the sacred quest for knowledge.

He ignored me. His white fingers moved slowly along the edges of the white pages. He was telling me silently with his shoulders and hands to leave him alone, just leave him alone. I watched his shoulders slump further into shadow. His left hand curled into a fist. Trembling and breathless, I persisted.

"There's something wrong with you," I screamed finally, feeling hollow.

Gerald let his book shut. Flap. A small white bird. It wasn't that he couldn't make love with me, his Las Vegas Palace of Marriage certified lawful bride, he explained. It was that he didn't want to. There was a vital distinction there. It wasn't a case of physical or emotional illness or weakness. There was no mind-body dichotomy.

It was a philosophical issue, a matter of his right to exercise free will. I was wrong. I had no sense of the ebb and flow of things. And who ordained that sex be a primary part of a relationship, anyway? I insisted only because of my middle-class American orientation, the Madison Avenue constructs that littered my brain like rat droppings.

I thought of my brain as an empty gray corridor strewn with land mines and hand grenades, fragmentation bombs, napalm. Gerald was still talking. It was late at night. He was facing the wall, his back to me, a white slab, a cliff, icy, untouchable. Americans made a mania of a simple inconsequential biological function. The Trobriand Islanders and Samoans weren't like that. The natives of Saturn weren't like that. Where was my anthropological sense?

"I thought you had potential once," Gerald pronounced sadly into the darkness. "But you're just like the others, waving their fat ugly breasts like leeches. You have to know the sand in order to exhaust it. Deaf men don't retreat."

I tried to get to the airport in the morning. I tried to get to the airport again in the afternoon. Each attempt left me exhausted. Classes had been suspended. I didn't know where Gerald was. There were curfews. Six people had been shot. Helicopters were dropping clouds of CS gas. I was carrying my suitcase through streets blocked by the National Guard, through troop trucks and demonstrators, police, paddy wagons and dazed housewives. Parts of the city were sealed off by soldiers marching shoulder to shoulder, like a gigantic gray sausage slowly undulating forward, bayonets jutting from their rifles. I could see the sunlight glancing off their bayonets.

"You look terrible," Francine told me at the airport. "And those shoes are a bad joke."

I stared at my feet. I had never seriously considered the topic of shoe styles. I thought about primate social behavior, kinship designations and creation myths. I started crying.

Now I was sitting in the hospital cafeteria. The Formica tables were a pale yellow. We were drinking coffee from styrofoam cups.

"You hate my tennis racket, I can see that," Francine said. "Do you want me collapsed? A hag in black? You got black in your eyes, kid. I got news for you. I keep going. I do more in a day than you do in a year."

"What are the odds on the skin graft?"

"Good," Francine said. "If the graft works the tubes go out. Then he gets to go home at some point."

Home was the pastel house in West Los Angeles, the rooms sturdy, purposeful. Home was the black grapes growing wild at sunset in the shadows along the bamboo gate. Home was 6 P.M. Time for a shot of bourbon with the news.

I looked at Francine. She was balancing a hand mirror in her palm. She was putting on a reddish lipstick. I realized my head was nodding slowly, back and forth, making a kind of circle. I touched my forehead. I felt I needed a big white bandage wrapped across my head. A bandage to keep the jagged pieces from pushing out.

This is real, I thought, jolted by it. This is actually happening. It begins without warning. One lives as one has always lived, waking to an empty yellow morning, the sun a hammer. One pokes a dull head through a gray haze. A call is made. Someone says, Go to your father. He's sick. He needs you. And suddenly there are two of you. One is small and terrified, a child who cries, don't leave me, Daddy, I'm only six, Daddy, still sweeping leaves off the fall pavement in front of the gray stone house waiting for your car, waiting with Mommy. And you are waving, back again from building houses, paint spots on your pant legs, your toolbox full.

And there are two of you. Two of you sitting under a strange gouged metal eye planted in the wall. Tick. Tick. Tick. Tick. One is small, coiled up inside, hiding, screaming, Don't die, Daddy. Don't die. They'll call me a woman if you die, not a little girl.

And the other body moves. The other finds the father slumped in his kitchen crying, angry and bitter, already half broken. It's cancer, he says. It's cancer again. And the whole world stalls.

"Fred and I really connect. I mean this guy is something else." Francine leaned toward me. "He's got a faster recovery rate in bed than a twenty-year-old. Meanwhile I'm letting him put me into energy."

"Energy?"

"Alternative fuel sources. You know, Colette got very rich at the end. Stock tips. She knew certain men in government," Francine mused.

"The skin graft," I began. "Maybe if he sees the skin graft is working. Maybe he's just preparing himself to die. Maybe he doesn't believe he's going to live."

"Maybe," Francine said cautiously.

Things lay unanswered between us. Debris collected in the small corridor of white air where our shoulders almost brushed. Something hung suspended. Three floors above, my father lay suspended, undecided about living or dying.

"Let's look at the babies," Francine suggested.

We rode the elevator to the fourth floor. We stood in front of the viewing window where the daily crop of newborn infants were displayed, wrapped in white and perfect, their tiny fingers curled like the petals of certain utterly white orchids.

"Your father and I wanted this for you," Francine said. She looked sad. "Was it such a terrible dream to have? That you'd marry someone? Form bonds with meaning? Let a child grow from your love?" Francine studied me. "I loved being a mother, remember?"

And it was Philadelphia in winter. Snow fell soft, crystalline, a fine layer of white gauze sealing us together. Logs burned in the fireplace. Francine was reading poetry out loud. She was baking an apple pie. I was given my own slab of dough, my own small pie tin. We made a big pie and a little one. Sometimes Daddy ate mine. Mother was ironing. I ironed handkerchiefs and napkins while she ironed Daddy's shirts. We were waiting for Daddy to come home, to make the house warm, make Mommy laugh, make us safe for the night. And Daddy was pulling off his dark wool winter coat. He was standing at the kitchen sink scrubbing his hands, the room smelling of turpentine and soap, a dash of hand lotion, a sense of meat in the smoke.

"Your father would have liked a grandchild. He would have been good with a kid. He loved children, remember?"

When I remember my childhood it is always winter. My father is shoveling snow. My father is a big dark bundle in the center of the blizzard-sheeted street. We are dragging my sled through the snow. The sky is a net of whittled branches. My father is pulling me to the top of hills. In a vacant lot we find a stream. I dream rafts, barges, harbors. And I'm sliding through snow and laughing.

Beyond the viewing window the babies were slowly swaying in their identical white cribs, responding to an inner tide. First one, and then another, like a row of white dominoes. Francine was tapping her hand on the glass.

"You probably can't even have one now, after all the drugs," she said. She let herself shudder.

❧ 14 ❧

The hospital doors snapped open for me, a kind of glass mouth. An older man sat hunched and weeping on the grass near the emergency ambulance driveway. No one looked at him. He was still there as I drove out of the parking lot, a small mound lost beneath the shadows the building cast.

I walked the three steps up to my porch. My cousin Rachel had written. I sat on the porch and read her letter twice. Then I telephoned Jason.

"I miss you." I paused. Did I miss him? "I missed you last night."

"I'm here now. Do you want me now?"

Now, now.

I said yes.

Despite everything, when Jason offers me a piece of a day or a night, I feel six years old again. I am driving with Daddy in the old gray Hudson. He's going to buy me an ice cream cone. Daddy is taking me to the circus, the aquarium, the zoo. When Jason offers me anything I feel whole. I feel loved.

I studied my house. The last vestiges of Gerald Campbell had been thrown away. Jason's canvases were stacked neatly near the front door. The house was thinning. I could strip it down further.

There were the gifts from Francine that I no longer needed, had never needed. All the hard hooks and little anchors she gave me. They were attempts to weigh me down to the thing she called the real world. When Francine talked about the real world she made it sound as if she held the patent.

I assembled hand-painted vases Francine had bought on business trips to Rome and Jerusalem, Buenos Aires, Paris. If I could just cut back the unnecessary shape and mass, the sense of past inhabitation, perhaps I would be able to understand. Perhaps with the walls and floors free from the weight of furniture and tourist artifacts, the truth would snap loose, dusted off, perfectly clear.

"You can't do this to me," Jason said. He was stunned. It was a year ago or two years ago, after our reconciliation.

"Do what?" I asked softly.

I knew precisely what. I had been gone that night. I had been gone the better part of a week with another man.

The other man meant nothing. He was irrelevant, a kind of driftwood. He didn't stop the pain that was Jason. Beneath the surface weren't men the same, encased in their separate sets of idiosyncrasies? I no longer had the ability to memorize a new set of boundaries. Jason had burned me out.

"Where have you been?" Jason demanded.

"You don't want to know," I said softly, evenly, enjoying the tension in his voice.

Jason hung up. He opened the front door of my house without

knocking. He grabbed me by my shoulders and pushed me against the wall.

"Bitch," he hissed. "I want to know."

"I was with someone."

"I know that, bitch. I can smell it."

Once I had smelled it on him, too. It was like an invisible stain, the small tendrils of someone else, a faint impression left on the skin, a kind of resin.

"Does he fuck you like this?" Jason demanded. He was tearing off my jeans. He was pushing me farther against the wall. "Does he, bitch? Fuck you like this? Fuck you like I do?"

"Nobody fucks me like you do," I whispered, my forehead pressed against the cool plaster walls.

"Why spoil it?" Jason asked. He was finished.

I was sitting on the floor. I lit a cigarette and looked at him. "I don't trust you, obviously."

Jason's face was tight with a slow white spreading anger. There would be retribution. It didn't matter. His new weapons could only be variations and refinements on the old. And I had already been singed past bone. I was almost pure, beyond ash.

Later there would be escalations. Later I would come to Jason's studio when night was already thinning and going gray.

"Get laid?" he asked, opening his front door for me. I brushed his naked body as I walked in.

"Yes," I said into the darkness. I felt Jason walking behind me, a special dark heat at my back.

I lay down on his bed. I was a prop being taken down from a shelf. I would be dusted and polished, briefly admired. Then Jason would put me away again.

"Did he make you feel this much alive?" Jason asked. He was breathing in uneven short angry puffs like smoke.

"Actually, it was soft and gentle."

"Gentle? Since when is that your bag?" Jason sounded mildly surprised.

I didn't say anything. I had gone to a party. I found myself talking to a young woman. She was nineteen. She played a harpsichord in a small orchestra. The woman needed a ride home. I had driven her.

I watched the woman move through her rooms. She was graceful and deft, strangely confident. I had never been nineteen in that way. I had doubts. I leaned over toilets and vomited. I stood in the steamy shadows of Giovanni's Italian Restaurant with the pasta in big fat black pots and dragged myself half asleep, half dead, through the rooms, the streets.

All at once the girl turned her face toward me. She looked younger than nineteen. She played a harpsichord. She didn't want to marry, ever. She looked younger than I had ever been. She leaned over and kissed me. Her mouth startled.

I surprised myself. Something sparked electric, risky, raw. I stayed with her. I took off my clothing. I felt determined. She left a light on in the hallway. I sat down on the edge of her bed. I watched her light a candle and hoped it would be simple, painless, something I could wash down the drain, change clothing, stand in supermarket lines and no one would know. And I offered my face to the other. My lips were kissed, my chest pressed. I was a good grape, breaking and scattering juice.

"Come from your gentle lover?" Jason asked.

It was the next night. It was late. Still, he had kept his lights on. Still, he had waited for me.

I nodded. Jason glanced at the kitchen clock. "Only midnight," he observed. "What happened? The guy's wife show up?"

"As a matter of fact, it was a she," I said. "And her husband came back."

I liked the way my words sounded. They filled the air between us with something white and sharp. I felt surrounded by spikes, little marble columns where I could hide. A safe place in the ruins, almost definable. I wanted to smile.

Jason grabbed my wrist. "You were with a chick? Is that what you're telling me?" The veins in his forehead leaped out. His eyes went black. "A woman?" Jason paused. He looked at the kitchen wall as if searching for something, a common household object that might explain everything. Finally he said, "That really disgusts me." He dropped his fingers from my wrist. He glanced at his fingers as if expecting to find a glossy dark stain. My wrist fell to my side, a white fist hitting my hip, a kind of gong.

Was I imagining it? Was his face slowly collapsing in slabs of grayish clay? But yes. His eyes were dark. They darted. They raced. I could feel them spark. They seemed to be tearing at themselves, growing claws. Inside Jason's eyes there was turbulence, as if suddenly he had a vision of a thousand possible futures and in each one he was dying, falling hacked, trapped, boiled.

I felt light, airy. I could drift like smoke. I smiled sweetly, my lips perfect, my mouth half opened, silky in darkness, a flower, flawless. I stretched myself on his bed. I had stumbled on gold, nuggets and chips, gold by the pound, the ton. I waited in the darkness for Jason. I didn't have to wait long.

Later there would be escalations.

"Who was it?" he asked, talking into my body. "A man?" Jason bit my breast. I could feel his tongue, eyelids, fingernails, warm breath, lime breath. "A woman?" His voice seemed to flutter and tremble.

I was a kind of mirror. Dark formless things snaked and jerked in the smoky rippling glass. His fear brushed against me, a pulse running through the darkness, a current, electric.

"Was it a man?" Jason seemed to plead. He held my face hard with his hands and looked down through the shadows, looked down for something. I knew he would find nothing.

"No," I lied easily, looking straight at him. My face was solid. Nothing leaked or shook. "It was a woman."

"Jesus," he said. He slid away from me. He coiled himself into the darkness, stung and withdrawn. His face was a sail suddenly deprived of wind. The canvas flapped in useless white sheets.

Jason pressed his face into the pillow. He began to cry.

"There, there," I said, stroking his back lightly. "There, there," I said softly, gently, running my fingernails across his flesh, skating my fingers across his small back. I was smiling in the darkness, smiling where he couldn't see me. The smile felt odd and heavy on my mouth.

All at once I didn't care any more if he was painting naked blond teen-agers crouching over a pile of oranges in a sandbox like strange young hens. It didn't matter if he was painting women humping beer cans on a tapestry of floral print beach towel, their pink and yellow and orange legs disappearing into the gold and red and blue threads. I didn't care what young woman with what flat girl's stomach knelt on a yellow plastic beach raft with her hips jutting forward in the universal and cross-culturally validated position of absolute invitation. It had taken years not to care anymore.

"Where are you going?" Jason sat up in bed.

"Out," I said. It was another night, another battle.

Jason pushed the covers back, angry. He followed me into his bathroom. I combed my hair slowly, carefully arranging the long red strands around my neck. In the half-light they were a kind of coral. Why, I could be a mermaid draped in sea shells.

"It's one A.M."

His words were a kind of gong. One A.M. How dare you? I am the man. I am hard. I am metal. I am time, boundary, longitude. You can't defy me.

I put on gold hoop earrings. I was conscious of Jason watching me, his eyes, his face splintering. I was putting on pink lipstick. My hair was the color of sea bells. I was a mermaid. I didn't care what time it was.

"Don't go," Jason said.

My eyes were lined with luminescent blue. They looked like the insides of abalone shells. I rubbed rouge into my skin until my whole face glowed.

"You're doing this to piss me off," Jason said. He was following me through the front room. His voice seemed small and shocked.

I closed his front door. I could feel him behind me as I walked across the bridge over the Grand Canal. The air felt agitated behind me, a series of small black eruptions. Something inside me smiled.

There were truces, brief states of calm beneath stripped blue skies. I sat on my front porch. I was a shell surrendering to the currents and tides. It was late afternoon, another day in an indeterminate but warm season. I had collected my rents. I watched sunflowers nod, their faces a string of fat yellow beads repeated in the water. The canal seemed to be breathing.

Suddenly Jason appeared on the horizon. He was paddling his yellow rowboat under the Howland Canal bridge. He edged closer, yellower. He tied the boat to the stake he had driven into the side of the canal in front of my house. The Woman's House.

"I've come to take you away from all this." Jason mock-bowed. He smiled. He offered me his hand. I took it.

Jason rowed. The sun was raw in the sky, a slow thick red. A dozen black-and-white ducks pushed out of the way of the boat.

"It's just like the old days," Jason said.

His voice had a certain sparkle. I boiled potatoes in the kitchen alcove of his studio. Jason was in the front room, painting. The old days? I plopped the potatoes into the pot. They floated like the brown bloated bodies of drowned men.

Jason stood at his easel. He was watching a news special on the labor movement in Argentina. He looked from the television screen, then back to the canvas. He stared at the announcer. He dipped his brush. He faced the canvas, taking a geometric patterned towel and darkening it, adding crevices of shadow within shadow, another, more subtle design.

"You know I need you," Jason said, staring at the canvas. A cigarette was burning in the ashtray near his palette. He sipped a beer. The announcer was talking about agriculture, the birth rate and religion.

"You always need what you don't have," I said sadly.

"We could try," Jason said with conviction. He put his paint-brush down.

I turned away. I walked back into the ktichen. At that moment I realized that I didn't need him anymore. Jason had been a mirror. I had seen in him a reflection of who I once was. I had been empty and frightened. The image was frozen. It was all Jason saw.

In time I became a mirror. I learned to show Jason his fear and sorrow, the outlines of his failure. I showed him pieces that were a sketchy gray, the color of his pervasive unhappiness.

The mirrors were inaccurate. They only reflected back what was already past. The mirrors had half-lives like radioactive elements. The mirrors had time gaps like messages sent from distant stars that even at the speed of light take centuries to arrive.

There had been a strange filtering process, a sealing out of certain vital elements. The mirrors were limited. They were ice sheets. They contained a passed vision more inconsequential than a dream. In short, they were useless.

Now it was late afternoon. The canals were turning muddy. I was waiting for the hospital to call. There was something. Infection. Internal bleeding. An artery erupting, a red glow in the glistening dim cubicle, an ember. Something happened. Unexpected. A gasping. A sinking in.

I was waiting for the doctor in his nice white coat. I was waiting for the bad news about Daddy's throat. This is the last white scene. He is bleeding. His neck is falling apart, collapsing under the white gauze. He is coughing in his sleep. It is his last dream. He hears an ambulance scream into the hospital parking lot. In his dream it is the wail of boys playing softball in a vacant field, Bronx farmland then.

Suddenly I wished the house were completely empty, stripped of the false unnecessary residues. Why, the walls were a kind of membrane. Didn't they breathe and lean? Didn't they long to feel the sea breeze sting them naked, unadorned? Didn't they yearn to be freed?

I gathered the undeniable hard evidence of my life with Francine. I made a neat pile of Greek peasant blouses, Mexican wedding dresses and French silk scarves. I wrapped hand-painted vases carefully in newspaper. I filled up cardboard cartons and carried them to the trunk of my car.

The phone was ringing. I ran back into my house. The air rattled and broke off in sharp spinning narrow white spokes, like arrows. The sound scratched my face. My heart started racing. I could feel myself getting ready to run. The phone seemed to snap and growl. Afraid, I reached out for it, reached out to quiet it.

"I'm worried sick," Francine said. "I couldn't hit a ball to save my life today. I think he's dying."

"Don't think that. Thoughts have a certain power."

"You sound like you're taking LSD again."

"I'm not. Don't dissipate your energy."

"What energy? I feel like I'm dying. I'll be all alone. I'm getting old. It doesn't show, but I feel it. In my bones." Francine began to cry. In the background there was talking and the sound of plates clattering, the special rattle of china and glass. "I don't know what to do," Francine admitted.

"You're doing it. We're on defense. We're on the one-yard line. We hang tough." Who was talking? Outside my window the canals were slowly browning. Autumn on the canals.

"What if the skin graft flops?" Francine blew her nose.

"It won't. We won't let it."

"I wish you didn't hate me," Francine began. "Fred says it's temporary, a phase. He's been in analysis twenty-two years. He says I'm threatening to your identity. You feel competitive. Is that why you're so ungiving, so hostile? Fred says—"

"Fuck Fred." Outside my window two young boys climbed the bridge over Eastern Canal. They dropped small rocks into the water. I noticed they had a bag filled with rocks. They began throwing them at the ducks.

"Fred is something special," Francine whispered. "I'm in the Polo Lounge waiting for him. He had a meeting at Warner's this afternoon." Francine sucked in her breath. "I think this guy is it."

She thought each man was it. They were intelligent, vital and alive. They had whole histories packed solid with immutable hard evidence like Harvard and town houses and Panamanian bank accounts. Then they failed her. The well ran unexpectedly dry. Winds began howling again. And suddenly she was sitting alone on the stoops in front of a row of identical dark brick buildings where it was always winter and she never had a key.

"I'm worried," Francine said. About my father? About the deal at Warner's?

"It'll be O.K." I hung up.

It was beginning to get dark. The newly stripped walls sucked at the shadows. New dark nests formed.

"Spring cleaning?" Jason asked. He walked into the half-empty living room. He noted the blank walls. He looked at me.

I shrugged. I knew the cardboard boxes had to be packed. I was cutting grooves through the glue inside me. It was as if I had somehow stumbled on a new dimension. There was change, after all. Days did not simply rise and fall, open and blink shut one after another, unbroken, inexhaustible and meaningless. There were certain extraordinary events that altered the course of things. One had simply to wait for these events and in time they would shake apart the old order. Change was a river, snaking and dancing, fat with fresh melted snow, now cutting a channel through a mountain, now bending, now flooding, now rearranging the shape of the soft valley floor.

My father was going to die if the skin graft didn't work. My father's face was a swollen black smear in a white frame, a gauzy white casing. He was wearing a collar around his neck. The bandages sprouted feeding tubes. He was being watered like a plant.

"Can you feed a hungry man? A man with his own spoon?" Jason smiled. I watched him take the glass vial from his pocket.

I would be a collection of starsides soon. I would be a bleached moon soon. I would be swirling white hot beyond naked, beyond bone. In the beginning, white sun, white foam, a sudden unexpected churning.

"Is this premeditated? The way you don't talk to me?" His voice was soft. It rubbed against the shadows.

"Hardly." I was measuring water into the spoon. "One thing I've learned from you is never plan anything."

Jason glanced at my arm. "You're not cut out for this," he said, his voice still soft. "You've got to slow down."

"I'm going to quit soon."

"Quit now."

"Why? You never liked me as a hausfrau," I said matter-of-factly.

"I don't like you as a junkie, either."

"We have no range, you and I. That's the problem." I was tapping the sides of the syringe. "We can bite or be bitten. There's nothing else. In between, we yap and howl like kicked dogs. Yap and lie in the dust."

I stood up. I pulled the kitchen curtains closed. I offered my arm to Jason. I shut my eyes. Outside, the canals were sealed and locked into the night. Then he pushed the needle in.

❧ 15 ❧

I woke before dawn. I had slept a drugged sleep, dozing and tossing. It was like drifting on a too calm silvery sea. I kept glimpsing slivers of stars.

I sat on my front porch. The gray haze covered me, a kind of wave.

Dear Rachel,

You sound so well and so quickly. And so many questions like a flock of singing seabirds. I think of a certain bloated white bird circling the harbor at Ensenada, swooping down for the tossed heads of cut bonita, screeching at the rusty burned-out boats. Birds fatter than longed-for children. You see, I have a certain distrust for the sudden. It's not easy to erase what was.

And the genuinely new emerges slowly, one pale part of an inch at a time.

You want to know more about the family? Our family grief is flat and wide as those dark barren lands that strained us through cursed generations. Our history unwinds in slow pieces like a bolt of wine-red velvet then in fashion at the Czar's court.

They were peasants, Rachel. They were the poorest kind of farmers. They were rootless and ignorant, arrogant and despised. They knew better than bowing down to the North Star to ensure the fertility of their goats and cows—but barely. Their religion had become portable and abstract. They were confused by and simultaneously proud of their sheer alienness, their undecipherable manuscripts and haircuts. They burrowed, isolated and dark as the poor shubbery, the monstrous skies pouring always too much or not enough.

The original landscape did something to our eyes. I believe people grow the organs they need. Our eyes are enormous, eyes stained by Polish skies, eyes of the ghetto and suspicion. We have the mutant eyes able to see the periphery, to detect disasters waiting in shadows—Cossacks, droughts, pogroms, floods, and the idiosyncrasies of kings.

Has your mother told you nothing?

They came in slow pieces. First Rose's father, Joseph. He called himself a tailor, had tuberculosis and went blind hemming and saving pennies to bring the others across the Atlantic in steerage, almost like pieces of freight. In the end there were sixteen blood relatives in a three-room East Side tenement.

Rose's mother, Katrina, died almost immediately. She was an exceptional woman. They said she read books in Hebrew and Polish, an amazing feat for a woman of that stifling and rigid culture. She died the first winter.

At thirteen Rose was the oldest child. She went to work in the sweatshops. She had never ridden on trolley cars or even been to a real city.

The private detective located her brothers and sisters for me. Our great-aunts and uncles. The people who do not recognize our mothers as kin. I walked into their houses and it was like being in a time warp, a new dimension. One hasn't simply crossed a room but opened a portal and bounded centuries. A kind of black hole in the fabric.

I asked these great-aunts and uncles about Rose. And across

the decades her younger brothers and sisters spit the evil eye in protection. I stood in front of them already tried and infinitely guilty and I felt the dark strangling strangeness of ten thousand claustrophobic Sabbaths.

A horse kicked her head back on the farm, they warned me. She isn't stable mentally, they said. The head wound. They turned silent. I was amused by their image of a mythical horse. The sheer simplicity of the explanation, its inadequacy and child-like quality of assigning a tangible physical cause to the unique and inexplicable, filled me with something that might have been a combination of laughter and rage. It was neither.

Later I asked our grandmother if a horse kicked her head. She smiled. They're full of shit, she said.

Rachel, I tell you this about the horse as a bare beginning, an arbitrary symbol. Our line was poisoned with this misshapen intensity some called mental illness before our grandmother. What of her mutant mother, Katrina, who read poetry, read in an age when women were mere extensions of the kitchen, important as a metal soup pot, a necessity, not requiring serious thought? Why, women grew arms only for sweeping and stirring and rocking children. God must have glued them on last, an afterthought.

Why do I tell you this? It's part of our family history. You'll see in time.

The telephone rang. This is it, I thought, running back into my house. He's dead. The final white apology.

I grabbed the telephone and glanced at Jason. He looked white and small in my bed. A pale beached sea mammal, some kind of seal.

"They just wheeled him in for the graft," Francine said. "I have a real bad feeling about it."

"Tell me."

"He's been in pain since last night. Bad pain."

"What did the doctor say?"

"Mumbo jumbo." Francine paused. "I'm scared."

"Don't be scared," I said, my heart racing, blood pumping, everything cooking, grinding, shooting off sparks, going berserk, a body filled with sudden raging storm clouds.

"I feel that I'm being punished," Francine said.

"That's a common reaction." I was trying to be precise with my mother. I was trying to be quiet and calm and take deep soothing breaths like the ones the Red Cross recommends for snakebite victims. I had to be very slow and careful or I would start screaming. And I was afraid that once I started screaming that way I would never stop.

"Listen, kid. We are, all of us, many ages at once," Francine began. "My ordinary boundaries were malformed. I have arrested development. I am both your mother and your daughter. You are the only thing I've ever really loved."

I didn't say anything. I couldn't think of anything simple to say.

"Do you love me?" Francine began crying.

"Yes."

"But you hate me, too?"

"Yes."

"You are cruel. You are one callous daughter, may it haunt you. Not that I want to curse you, but—"

"Don't curse me, Francine," I said, hard.

"You're mean to me. You know how lonely I am. Unspeakably lonely. You never visit me. And you know it's never going to work with Fred. He took the midnight plane back to Miami. He—"

I took a deep breath. "I have to hang up now."

"Why? What's the matter?" Francine demanded, all at once wounded and offended, terrified and hurt.

"I feel like I'm dying," I said.

Outside, the front yard seemed strangely wrong. The gladioli were too bright and sharp. Their fist-sized petals opened like screaming mouths. Their stiff pinkish undersides looked like the organza party dresses I never wanted, the ones Francine pushed me into in the long girlhood I never wanted, never understood.

The mums along the side gate were better. The yellow of

bleached linoleum kitchen floors, the sort Francine always wanted for me. The mums were the yellow of a child's playroom. A room I would never have. The yellow mums were sturdy and undemanding. A practical flower perfect for bedside or table setting. Could I take them to the hospital? The cemetery? Would they stop the slide into day, that yawning crevice, that gaping hot yellow bull's-eye?

"What are you doing?" Jason asked.

He drank orange juice from the bottle. He left the refrigerator door open.

"I'm writing a letter."

Obviously, you bastard. Are you blind? And I'm waiting for Francine to call. They're doing the skin graft today. He's in surgery. The half-ass sadists in their starched white suits are taking neat little squares of skin off his back and thighs and sewing them to his throat. He's been in pain all night. Even the butchers are worried.

"Come back to bed when you're done," Jason said.

He walked back to the bedroom. I heard the television go on. The announcer seemed to be discussing the Harbor Commission.

I looked into my front room. A row of cardboard cartons lined the far wall, so many small caskets with my past buried in them. A preparation for another burial, something enormous? And I remembered that I was waiting for Francine to call me from the hospital. I remembered I was writing a letter to my cousin Rachel.

Somewhere my cousin wondered if she should take the thing they called lithium. Somewhere they were cutting up my father. Somewhere a man was talking about taxation of pleasure yachts. It had become clear to me that I was no longer playing with a full deck. Did anyone notice?

History. Yes. It was during the Great Depression. Our grandmother Rose got off a bus at a wrong stop. A simple mistake.

Imagine the immensity of New York City for her. The sheer urban web, the unmeasurable dull winding rot of boulevards for a girl who had lived on a farm, pulled water from a well, fed chickens. New York opened its deranged mouth. Our grandmother had never even been to Warsaw.

She was fourteen years old, with our red hair and dark amber eyes. She literally walked right into him. An accident on a wrong street corner. How dashing and American he must have seemed to her with his stiff black suit and private car. Remember our grandmother had a sense of other things. Didn't they say she brooded through too dark eyes? Didn't she sit at her sewing machine and dream pink taffeta?

The sin occurred in his car. He took her driving to the country on a secret Sunday picnic. He dropped her off back at the street corner near her tenement and never saw her again. Our grandmother's mother, Katrina, was dead by then. Imagine Rose with her belly swollen at her sewing machine hardly knowing what had happened until the monstrous thing became visible. Even then she needed an explanation.

It was the Depression. Times were changing, all right. The patriarchy felt besieged. Her father, Joseph, abandoned her. He scorned her during her pregnancy and literally threw her out into those savage poor streets alone. She could barely speak English. And when she bore twins, particularly twin girls, they took it as an evil omen, proof absolute of the horrible contamination in those alien gentile genes. Besides, who needed more daughters? As if the world wasn't hard enough.

Our mothers were born that January night in a charity hospital. Rose took the subway there herself. The city was sheeted by blizzard. Her father, Joseph, got as far as the head nurse. When he heard of the dual birth he spit the evil eye on the hospital corridor floor. Perhaps he shuddered with visions of unspeakable sin.

It's not uncommon for primitive people to react to the birth of twins with fear or revulsion. Perhaps our great-grandfather saw in the identical red-haired girls the twin horns of some satanic force, some new world demon, stone gray, hard and towering. He refused to see his daughter or the twins again. I think that was the definitive moment, the incident that pushed her into the strange exile she has lived this half century. But then, they say she was never well, not even on the farm in Poland.

Of course, she couldn't work and take care of the infants by herself. But she tried. She was fifteen years old. She went to the factory each morning and left the infants swaddled old-world style. She kept them nearly two years that way. A welfare worker stumbled on them. They brought Rose documents to sign. She was illiterate. Your mother had temporary blindness from untreated measles. My mother had whooping cough. They were removed by ambulance to the state orphanage.

Our grandmother didn't realize she had signed away her right of custody. She thought she could get her daughters back. But she never made enough money.

Rose began working as a waitress in the Catskill Mountains. Perhaps she was calmed by some green vision there she never gave a name, not even in Yiddish. Perhaps she was able to walk barefoot on the grass in the late afternoons on her one day off, days she wasn't carrying the trays of rich soups, steaming meats and potatoes, the trays of chocolate and fat cream pastries.

Rose returned to New York in the off seasons. Our mothers would come from the orphanages on subways on Saturdays. They would sit in her tiny kitchen in the apartment where Rose lived, where Rose still lives.

She had a fascination for geography. Our mothers stole books for her, atlases from libraries. They would sit together in the late afternoons with the maps spread open while Rose traced with her fingertip the exact route she had taken from Krakow to New York, and cursed half the world.

They call themselves orphans. Lies. Our mothers simply choose not to remember those Saturday afternoons when they were six and seven. Years when they stood in the tile courtyard below her brick apartment building and Rose called to them from her sixth-story window and dropped pennies wrapped in pieces of old newspaper down to their outstretched hands.

The chain is long like a string of black pearls. Expensive. Magnificent. But one mustn't wear it too tight around the throat. One mustn't choke. We must take it bead by bead, one at a time, and savor the black depths, the gouged black eyes and the shine the color of dried blood.

Rose never took a lover. There was a chef four or five summers in a row who wanted her. But he could not accept her twins and in return she refused him. She was still a teen-ager then, thin and dreamlike. Men must have wanted her. But she felt stained,

149

guilty beyond redemption. There must have been certain temptations during the years of her twenties and thirties as she carried the heavy trays, the meats, the creamy pastries in a sea of starched white linen. Prosperous city merchants with fat bellies must have propositioned her in the carpeted hotel hallways and on the grass near the bungalow where the help slept. But Rose resisted them.

And perhaps her madness was a factor even for men on a holiday. They must have sensed her blackness burning like an open wound and shining in the center of her dark ambery eyes. A certain intensity men find impossible to deal with.

At eight our mothers were sent to foster homes. They did not see Rose again. Our mothers both married during the war. Shortly after that our grandmother woke one day with her legs almost paralyzed. Since that day she has needed a cane to walk and she rarely leaves her apartment and then only under duress.

Is it odd that she should stop walking the year our mothers married? The year our mothers sent her terse announcements of the fact, after the fact? Perhaps on some level she realized fully for the first time that she would never get her daughters back. Perhaps there was no longer a reason to keep walking.

That was years ago. Ever since, she has lived self-contained and crippled, a small bent woman in a miniature invented world in a corner of the city called Washington Heights, with its brick and darkness, the streets and buildings and people. There is a certain smell to rooms inhabited for so many years. You may discover that.

Our mothers have erased her apartment from their memory as simply as an advancing army removes a village, severs it from history by mortar and fire. So in their own way did they bury hers.

Rose lives on a narrow street, one jagged fork from a poor gray boulevard that seems to lead nowhere, seems to be a piece of something immense but now forgotten. One can't even reconstruct the meaning it might have once contained.

I came by cab. I clutched the address the detective had given me. The little piece of paper was sweat-stained. My hands trembled. Young Puerto Rican and black men leaned against double-parked cars shouting and laughing, tossing coins against brick walls laughing. The air was alive. It was early in the fall. Children played in the apartment courtyard, a square expanse of chipped orangy tiles. As I crossed the courtyard my feet seemed to dig into the tile. They echoed. Voices echoed sharply, flying pointed arrows.

I walked past a sagging wrought-iron gate. I felt as if I was walking into something breathing, not an apartment building but a body still warm. Everything had the quality of echoing. The sunlight fell in bouncing splinters. Radio music filled the gray tile corridors. Bass drums echoed and rumbled and curled on the tiled stairs.

It was six flights up to her apartment. Sixty-seven steps, I counted. Imagine her stumbling up one steep cement plateau to another with her cane and pieces of kosher chicken wings, with her disability checks and crippled legs and her hair dyed red. Yes, she still dyes her hair. She is so crippled she can barely bend her neck forward over her old chipped sink. Still she keeps that one small vestige of vanity, of her girlhood, of some intrinsic and overwhelming necessity. And it occurs to me that when I saw her, she was still only in her early fifties!

The walls lining the corridors leading to her apartment were covered with spray-painted red obscenities in Spanish and English. Even through the thick walls smells drifted, sounds drifted. Dogs barked. Infants squalled. A smell of onions and old meat was draped like a sheet across the building. It was chilly in the corridors, a chill that seemed to cut. I found it hard to breathe.

I knocked on her door breathless, a knapsack on my back. I had taken the Greyhound from Berkeley. I moved randomly, a wind creature not in a hurry. This was seven years ago. The world was different then. Doors had opened then that are closed now, probably forever.

Still I had certain expectations. I wanted a grandmother with a pale blue gingham apron. I wanted still warm from the oven butter cookies in round embossed tins. I wanted my history neat and complete, down to dates and localities, velocities and body counts. I was not prepared for the old woman behind the heavy metal door chain, red-haired and stooped.

The phone rang. My arm leaped out for it, made contact and felt shocked.

"He's out of the recovery room," Francine said.

"And?"

"And he's sleeping. They cut him and he's sleeping." Francine paused. "They're going to take him for tests when he wakes up. If he wakes up."

"What kind of tests?"

"Liver. Kidney. I think this is it. Wait by the phone."

"What about you?"

Francine laughed a harsh wisp. "Me? I was at the hospital at five this morning. I'm working like every other day. Why don't you go back to doing what you do best? Nothing." Francine hung up.

Rose studied me as the light faded, as day shredded and fell down beyond the brick. I've been waiting for you, my grandmother said. She laughed and the sound was like wind tearing through something dark and wiry, wind ripping scrub brush.

I will tell you more about Rose later. You say you are walking along the ocean. I also live near the sea but this sea is different, shuttered and untouchable. The sea is important, of course, the patterns and salt.

Is lithium a kind of salt? A white powder? Does it open new channels in the sea's face? Does it help you ride above whitecaps on a gull's wing? Does it let you sing?

I folded the letter into an envelope. I crossed the bridge over Eastern Canal and mailed it. Somewhere my mother's twin sister's daughter was considering the myriad possibilities in a thing called lithium. Somewhere a young girl was learning her personal history. Somewhere my father was sleeping after being skinned and patched.

It was noon. Jason was lying in my bed waiting. I let him wait.

❧ 16 ❧

He looked like a racing dog, lean and sleek and infinitely prepared. He was lying on his side, balanced on one elbow, the afternoon draped across him like a sheet. The shadows where curtains pinched sunlight glanced across his skin, small exploding stars. He was wearing a pair of my white lace panties. They were very tight.

The television was loud. Dust danced in the crevice where sunlight bounced against the paler light radiating from the screen.

I sat down on the edge of my bed. The windows were open. I could see the canals below, a pale buttery patch beyond sunflower stalks.

"Tell me you like me in white lace," Jason demanded. "Tell me."

He meant tell him a story about sex. He wanted me to spin a fantasy that might excite him. It was something that had evolved after our reconciliation. We discovered a place where we could forget our life was a continual state of war by curling into the soft silvery underbelly of invention.

I might wear a silk dressing robe. I would light candles in my bedroom. Or wash him slowly in a bathtub fat with bubbles and dry his body with warm towels. I massaged his neck and rubbed oil into his back. We found a cherry-flavored cream that turned hot on the skin and still hotter when the cream was rubbed. I poured it on him straight from the bottle.

Jason flipped through a magazine of color photographs showing women making love together while I did this. I licked his ankle and the inside of his thigh. I buried myself in his lap. I was sweating. I was working hard.

"You should buy black garters," Jason said, looking at the magazine.

"Do something to me," he said. He closed his eyes. "Tell me a story."

It was another night. It was raining. Jason lay on his back with his mouth half open. His face was swollen with expectation. In the half-light his legs looked like porcelain.

"A gallery is having an exhibition. The room is empty. I bring you out"—I was watching his face, watching his back dance across the sheet—"on a chain. I lay you down on a platform. You're the exhibit. A crowd has been invited. Everyone gets to use you." Jason's mouth was wide open. I thought he had started shaking.

"Who uses me?"

"Whoever wants to." I studied his face. "Men use you," I said softly and watched Jason's hips rise from the bed. He was pushing himself into the darkness. "Men sit on your face, Jason. You're tied up. You can't move. One after another, they sit on you. They push their cocks down your throat. They sit on your face and you push your tongue into their asses. You lick them."

"Men use me?" Jason whispered. He was moving from side to side on the bed, doing a kind of dance with the darkness.

"They fuck you."

"No," Jason cried.

He meant yes.

"Don't you feel better now? Working out your anger like that?" Jason asked softly.

I thought about it. It was later that night. We were in bed. After a while I said, "No."

"Tell me about women," Jason might say, leaning his small body deeper into the mattress and slowly rotating his hips.

And I might tell Jason a story about meeting a young woman at a party, a girl who was younger than I had ever been. I might tell him that I drove her home by accident, expecting nothing. I hadn't wanted a lover that night. I hadn't even bothered to bathe. My panties were still damp from his sperm. I would tell him about her young hands slowly sliding my blue jeans down from my hips and her tongue flickering, a moth wing licking me and licking him, his wall of white glue still curled up inside me. And Jason's hips would be moving from side to side silky and silvery on the white sheets while the neon bulbs in the backyard bathed the whole room in a light like a full moon's.

"Let's play," Jason breathed on the bed beside me. "Tell me you love me in lace."

On the television a reporter was pointing to a group of starved-looking children lying in a rut at the edge of a thin muddy road. They could have been a stack of old broken boards. The camera came in for a close-up of their wide dazed horrified eyes.

"Do I look like a woman?" Jason asked. He was running his fingertips across the tight white lace panties, across the place where the elastic waistband cut a tiny red groove into his swollen penis.

Yes? You look lovely. I'll lick you, seduce you. No? You look awful. Do penance, I'll beat you. Why, I could be sixteen. I could be a man. The captor or victim. We were beyond distinctions. Things danced and snaked sharp and sparkling. Things floated on crisp wings, nameless. It had all become simply a matter of shadow and light, shape and patches of color.

And white. Marble white. Gravestone white. My father in his white crib. My father newly bandaged again, new wounds, more stitches. And white, the tight white lace panties. Jason's skin a kind of perfect porcelain.

"You're lovely," I breathed. "You are my jade and flame breath bitch."

"Take them off," he whispered. "Take them off with your mouth."

I lit a cigarette. "Do they hurt you? Do they cut into you?" Outside it was still noon, unmoving.

Jason moaned. We had done this before. "Oh, yes, yes." He sounded like a little boy. A little girl?

"They burn," Jason whispered.

"Good. Think about how much they hurt and burn. I might make you wear them for days." How could I make Jason do anything? "You know what they would become like?"

"Yes," Jason whispered.

"Tell me."

"A diaper."

"Let's get high," I said.

The alcohol and cotton were already on the nightstand. I sat on the floor. Jason held my arm balanced against his knee. Blood jumped into the needle.

Suddenly wild moths were beating my eyes wide. I was the candle and the arc of light. Jason had found my fragile blue pulse. The room was inordinately yellow. I smelled alcohol. The room was filled with ripening lemons. Even the light bulb was a glistening yellow metal, as a captured moon might be. And I was sailing the warm water of a tropical harbor and swimming above darting black sharks to a cove with a waterfall choked by ferns spilling down moss-smooth rock.

I sighed. I was arctic white. The sea opened her icy lip. My path edged avalanches and albino seals. I was white under a white skull of sky in my own white season. It was a kind of permanent childhood Christmas. I stood in a room with tables covered by white linen. There were big white boxes tied up with white silk ribbons. I unwrapped knee-length white lace-up leather skates. I skated down pavement white with snow. There was ice. I didn't skid.

The afternoon was leaking out, white blood into white air. And I was white beyond reason. The poisonous shoreline disappeared, singed pure as old shells, their white wormy grooves scorched crepelike, thin as wings. Fat white gulls shrieked in a thick white lull.

I closed my eyes. In the beginning a white sun. In the beginning white amino acids strung together with white ribbon. And I am white marble. No. I am white gravestones. No. I am wearing white bandages around my face. I am tongueless. My mouth is sewed shut. Small white hairs push out in the empty places between gauze and feeding tubes. No.

I sat up. It was better. Yes. I was freshly painted white fence spokes and ivory piano keys. I was giving a piano recital. I had white smooth flesh and a perfect smile. I wore the most expensive white rose. I tossed on whitecaps. I knew the true depths of sea water. I drifted past the last reefs naked in pale silk stockings. My lungs unfurled white canvas on whitecaps while I sailed, sailed.

The telephone rang. I watched my white arm float from my pure white side. "Hello?" I said. And when my mouth opened I drank in clouds.

"He's in bad pain," Francine said.

"What?" I was a whitecap, a slice taken from a star. I was untarnished, afraid of nothing.

"He can't tolerate anything in the tubes. Not even water. Wait. I see the doctor. I'll call you back."

I looked out the bedroom window. The canals were an ink. And I was an empty gray corridor. A dull wind blew.

"You want to play now?" Jason asked, resting his hand lightly on my bare back. He had taken the tight white lace panties off.

Silence. Silence of ice sheets. White sheets. Hospital sheets. Marble. Gravestones. A white eulogy. Everyone polite. We did the best we could. Life's a grab bag. There are no guarantees. I felt like screaming.

"Let's pretend that you love me," I began. "I'm your wife. You've been gone a long time. But now you're back."

"Shit." Jason yawned. "But we do one of mine later."

I closed my eyes. Jason was licking the hollows my bones form in my neck. "I'll never leave you again," Jason managed with real feeling. He breathed into me, a May wind, strawberries sticking up new pink tongues along hillsides. A pink fluttering. "Let me show you how much I missed you," Jason breathed into me.

My back was pressing cooling sheets and Jason was whispering into my neck and my eyes were closed and I was digging my long fingernails into the small of his back. I was tumbling, floating, falling down moss-green channels. Night was a kind of silky tunnel. Night rustled and glowed and opened arms of black feathers. The heat was incredible, searing and intense. And I was willing to believe anything, everything, all over again.

❧ 17 ❧

"You better get here fast." Francine's voice was tight and absolutely sober. I was seized by a sense of horror. The horror was a pile of enormous bricks. The bricks were falling on my head.

"Tell me." I was already looking on the floor for my jeans. I willed my legs to keep moving, just keep moving while I paced the small hallway in front of my bedroom. Morning was a blank haze. I had gray pebbles for eyes. I didn't think I was going to make it. The cliff ended, a sheer drop.

"He's in terrible pain. Terrible. They can't even pour water into him. He's crazy from the pain." Francine paused. Then she said, "They put him in a strait jacket."

I felt something like an electrical shock. It began at my toes and surged through my entire body. A cold rush. A mainlining of ice. A sensation of small things crawling and hopping in my bloodstream. Goose bumps appeared in a sudden flush across my arms. I felt my hair rising from my scalp. Then I screamed. The scream began somewhere in the blank hazy distance. It took a long time to weave from my toes and finally tumble out black from my mouth. After a while I realized I had dropped the telephone. I picked it up. All I said was, "What?"

"They don't know what the pain is from. But he pulled out the tubes. Yanked them out. They found him in the middle of the night. He was shadowboxing in the corridor." Francine lowered her voice. She took a deep breath. "It took four nurses to put him back in bed. In restraints."

Dogs were barking on Howland Canal. I heard a man shouting, "Did you hear it? Some lady screaming?"

Francine began to cry. "It's horrible. He's slipping. He's dying. Help me, please."

"I'm coming."

Jason was sitting up in my bed. "I demand an explanation," he said, angry and still half asleep.

I was looking for my car keys. I moved towels and skirts from one corner of the floor to another with my foot. I was pulling on a blouse. I realized that somewhere along the line I must have lost my incentive for keeping a house neat and sparkling clean. I found my car keys on the floor under my shoes. My shoes were under a beach towel and an overturned ashtray. I paused in the bedroom doorway.

"I need you tonight. I haven't asked you for anything in a long time. Wait for me at your place. Promise me."

Jason stared at the sheet over his feet. "Give me an explanation first."

"I can't now. Just be there." I looked directly at him.

Then I was walking into the blank early morning haze. The grass in the front yards along Eastern Canal seemed damp. The air was pale and thin. Not the air of earth at all but some other, smaller world with an ancient decaying sun. A world where it was always a stripped dawn. A woman stood on a porch near the alley. "You hear that screaming?" she asked me.

I shook my head no and walked to my car. The rush hour traffic engulfed me like a cold gray wave.

The hospital loomed enormous, five stories of neo-Spanish grayish walls poked into the blank morning. The building itself looked cold. The morning seemed fragile, somehow slippery.

Francine met me in the parking lot. She was sheet white. Her hands trembled. I suddenly realized that the woman who was my mother smelled somehow old, vaguely dusty, musky. Beyond the flush of youth a sense of something else, a kind of ripening. Or more. A sense of decay?

"He was shadowboxing in the corridor," Francine began. She stopped. "This is the worst thing that's happened to me since the mice fell on my head. I lived in a foster home where they locked the refrigerator. I was only allowed in the kitchen to clean. I slept in a room where I knew there were mice. I could hear them in the sewing machine. Then one night the ceiling fell down on me. Pieces of plaster and mice. Mice running all over my head, the bed. I wasn't really surprised." Francine smiled. "I knew all along there were mice in that room."

We were riding in the elevator. We were walking down the gray expanse of narrow corridor on the third floor past the portals where the dying lay in fine greenish layers of shadow while the fluids slowly bubbled and oozed and the sunlight fell slow and measured through Venetian blinds and the philodendrons dreamed dark green dreams on the nightstands, dreams of impossible stalks, vines winding into cloud, the sky green, green.

"He says he can't go on. The tubes. The pain. He told me, wrote me on his pad, he was going to jump off the balcony."

I noticed a certain chill in the corridor, something cool clinging to the tiles and enamel walls. I shivered.

It was important to be precise. "What did the doctor say?"

"He's staying pat. Says the skin graft is going to work."

"What about now?"

"We give him the will to go on," Francine answered immediately.

She stopped near my father's room. The door was closed. A sign had been taped to the wood: NO VISITORS. I had seen that sign on the doors of the half-dead, the pasty skeletons curled in greenish shadows while their life ebbed. I saw the NO VISITORS sign tacked to doors just before the chaplain came. Just before the whole family suddenly appeared out of nowhere with the last bouquets, enormous arrangements featuring carnations and roses. Just before families appeared laden with grotesque baskets of fruit and boxes of chocolates. My mother's hands were shaking.

"I asked him what kind of funeral he wanted. He said just bury him with his spikes on. He also wants to wear a 1927 Yankee baseball cap. He's got one somewhere. You go in," Francine said. Her eyes were very dark, very wide. She seemed to be gasping for air. "Maybe he'll be better with you."

I opened the door. My father was hooked up to oxygen again. The IV was back, taped and embedded in his hand. The skin on his arms was an unusual mottled yellow, his twenty-year California suntan collapsing in uneven streaks. The blinds were drawn. He was back on morphine. He watched me approach his bed through pitch-black too wide eyes.

DONT WANT THIS. He wrote the note with his left hand. His right hand had the IV. The note was an ugly black scrawl.

"You don't want the hospital?" I was terrified. "Are you in pain? Do you want a shot?"

DONT WANT THIS STINKING LIFE. My father shoved the note at me.

I was standing near his bed unmoving, oddly frozen. I was a slab of ice bobbing in a cold empty stretch of too blue too deep sea. I felt my mother enter the room. Somewhere through a cold haze I saw my mother square her thin shoulders. She glanced down at my father's notes. Then she walked across the room and pulled the blinds open. My father averted his face from the sudden rush of sunlight as if the sunlight hurt, a kind of yellow slap.

"You don't want life?" Francine demanded. "Some example you set for your daughter." My mother was pacing the small room. She crossed it, touched the window with her fingertips like a swimmer making contact with the poolside, and crossed the room again, another completed lap.

"You should have thought of that sooner. You wanted life plenty before the operation. What is this? A suicide threat?" She leaned over. She picked up my father's note and studied it as if it were written in code. "Suicide? After the mice jumped on my head? After the things that happened to me? And her?" My mother pointed to me. "You would set that kind of example for your daughter? You know this kid is sick already."

CANT STAND THIS. My father handed me the note. For a moment I considered the possibility that he might be talking about Francine.

"You weren't expecting a picnic, were you? Remember the first time?" Francine asked. "It was worse. The cobalt. Remember? You don't remember. The mind forgets. You'll get better. Trust me."

My father pointed at Francine. Then he pointed at the door. My mother stared at him.

"I think he wants you to leave," I suggested. "Get some coffee downstairs."

I sat down lightly on my father's bed. I could see the outline of his body beneath the sheet. His legs were thickly bandaged where skin had been removed from his thighs. The red plastic feeding tube was still attached to his nose. Three times a day a nurse held the feeding tube in her hand and poured in a thick brownish liquid from a jar. They didn't even call it eating. "Time for your feeding," they would say. Feeding, as if he were a dog or a plant.

My father was looking down at the gray tiled floor. Maybe he was tracing the pattern the sun made spilling lazy, slowly swaying and uncurling. My father closed his eyes.

"Daddy, what happened? They said you were shadowboxing in the corridor last night. They put you in a strait jacket?" I handed my father his pad. I handed my father his felt-tipped pen.

DONT REM. FRIGGING DRUGS? SAW DEATH GOT UP?

"You saw death? You got out of bed?"

FIGHT BASTARD BIG.

"Death's big?"

My father nodded his head. His eyes seemed a kind of black liquid.

"But you saw death before. The first time around. You lived through it, remember?"

He had lived twenty years waiting for it to recur, waiting for the black ambush.

But he had found a way of coping. He played horses in the sunlight. He sat near a water fountain in front of the outside odds board, mountains in the background, Santa Anita. He watched the odds board lights flicker and the water falling, butterflies brushing their wings against the spray, the odds changing, a bed of orange and purple pansies like a circle of bruises around the round fountain with the names of the champions engraved on the sides. Native Diver. Round Table. Swaps. Omaha. Man o' War.

The sun would be setting above the bamboo garden gate. My father would read the form sheet for the next day. He sat on a chaise longue at dusk with the form sheet across his lap and the wild black grapes rustling, slowly growing near the side of the house. The house would be a pale yellow pastel lost in the pastel twilight. He would bring out the radio. The Dodgers would play while he hosed the apricot tree and the lemon tree and the orange tree. And they would breed for him.

And his daughter? In the distance, through pastel layers, his daughter grew into a strained and crippled womanhood. A senseless womanhood. My life was a stain. Did he see it as a retribution and blame himself?

I picked up his hand. I wanted to say forgive me for failing you. Forgive me for giving you no grandchildren, no son-in-law. My father had longed for a son-in-law, a regular guy, he called it, a regular guy who would call him up to go for a pastrami sandwich and watch a fight. Instead I gave him Gerald. Instead I gave him Jason.

I gave my father nothing, not even the sense that he could leave me safely flowing in time, once a daughter and then a mother. I had spent my girlhood wearing a secret sneer inside. No one came with corsages. No crisp introductions to fine upright young men who knew how to bring a fifth of Scotch with them and planned on becoming dentists or building contractors and marrying me.

I brought him the blue denim brigade. I brought him foot soldiers from the revolution, the crusaders of the new order. They were scarred by visions of irredeemable hells. Or the other, some green-wooded Mendocino paradise of redwood branches and leaves falling across the insides of their eyes and remaining embedded there forever.

I had ignored his firm history. I had labeled his experience irrelevant. It meant no more to me than the rubber plants growing along the back gate or the shower of bougainvillaea above the barbecue. And he watched in the pastel distance as I slipped away into my darkness and wild manias. My teen-age years were a blood clot of savage unnecessary rage. He must have sensed this.

My father's hand was thin, sculpted to the bone. What was he thinking?

"You got up to fight death off?" My father nodded. "I'm proud of you, Daddy. You fought death off man to man. You did the right thing. Primitive people, people in tribes, get up to shout and jab out the evil spirits. You did a natural thing. Don't be ashamed."

AM DYING.

I had never seen him so pale. His hands, suntanned from years of sitting at Southern California race tracks, where it is always hot and sunny and the track is always fast and even cripples run six in 1:10 and change, were ashen now. His chin was a frosted gray. White hairs pushed out from the bandages between the feeding tube and the green tube attached to the metal thing embedded in his throat.

I remembered that my father had boxed as a young man. It was before he married my mother. It belonged to the time when he rode trains around the country, working a few months in Chicago, St. Louis, New Orleans, and pushing on again, searching for something. Did he ever find it?

"I don't think you're dying," I said softly. "I believe that you had your confrontation with death last night. You got up on your feet and fought death off. I think you beat it."

WAS STUPID. STATISTICALLY HAD LIVED ALMOST FULL LIFE. WAS STUPID 2 SUBMIT 2 THIS. SHOULD HAVE ENDED IT ALL MYSELF.

Slowly, he closed his eyes and sank back against the pillow. He seemed to drift and doze.

There was a smell in the corridor. It was chilly but stale. There was a sense of something sweet slowly rotting. The chill. I thought of the rusty hull of a burned and abandoned ship. I thought of furnished rooms with threadbare brown rugs stained and stinking of old cigarette butts and whiskey. Rooms with the windows shut and bolted for weeks. I thought of drought air, a hot swirl across brittle dirt.

I walked quickly. I did not let myself look through the doors into the green cubicles, the human aquariums where vines twisted in the shadows and built slow webs with clawed fingers and called to them, Come down, come down. Surrender. It's cool and green here. It's better. Be one with the green vine and green shadow. Be one with the gouged hole in the earth. It's better. Your skin is illusion. You can shed it like an old coat.

Come to me. Be one and cool and green with me. It is your bone I want.

I did not turn around. I knew death was standing in that corridor directly behind my left shoulder.

"He's dying," Francine said.

I sat down at her side in the cafeteria. My mother's yellow-brown eyes were filled with tiny black flecks. Now the black lines in her eyes seemed to be blowing. She was wearing the debris of a terrible storm inside her.

"He's dying," Francine repeated. "The room smells of death," she said dully.

"He's not dying. That's why he got up. He fought death off. The crisis is passing." Francine did not answer me. She looked unconvinced. I went on. "There are forces that can be tapped. He plugged into one when he fought death off."

Francine studied me. "Your timing is way off," she noted. "Settle down. You're in this one. You've been dealt in. You got in when I decided to make you born. Are you following me? He didn't want you." Francine lit a cigarette. I stared at her. "He wanted to live that crummy life style forever. Riding trains. Wake up in Baltimore. Get on a train. Ride to Belmont. Go to a fight at the Garden. Get on a train. Wake up in Philadelphia. Go to a baseball game. Eat lunch in Washington." Francine shook her head from side to side.

"He thought I'd go on like that forever. Like my childhood wasn't bad enough. Like I needed more dislocations. I never had a home." My mother studied me in the sharp white hospital light. "I'd already had two abortions. He thought kids would slow him down, cramp his style. He thought I wasn't ready to be a mother. That's what he kept saying. I wasn't ready. Wasn't grown up enough, he used to say. He said I didn't know how to be a mother. So I finally said it's this kid or I'm walking. He knew I meant it by then. You taking this in?"

I nodded my head. I was thinking about my father shadow-boxing death in the corridor. He must have felt death leaning over. He must have felt the cool green breath. And he stood up. He squared up against it, man to man. Death was big. But my father was still breathing.

"You're in this one no matter what," Francine was saying. "I mean you'll bring his food to him, if he ever eats again. If they build him a new throat. If he lives through this. If he gets the tubes out. If the skin graft works. Are you following me?"

"Yes."

"I mean you'll sit by his bed. You'll talk to him. You'll do whatever it takes. We will give him the will to go on. So I'm telling you straight. Pick up your cards and play."

I was six years old. I took piano lessons after school. I collected clay models of dinosaurs. I collected butterflies. I was fascinated by transformations. But something terrible was happening. My father spent entire days in bed. She brought him lunch on a tray. I had a sense that my father, that big man, was turning back into a little boy. He wasn't talking right. He was whispering. He was thinning. He didn't drive his car anymore. He sat in mother's seat while mother drove the car. He went away every day for the cobalt treatment. And what was cobalt? Why, cobalt was blue, a kind of blue machine, a sort of gun they aimed at my father's throat. It made him throw his food on the floor, rasping, It tastes like garbage, garbage.

And Mommy was leaning against the front door crying. She was watching the strangers walk across the street, the strangers who came and carted away her brass lamps and the new china plates. The sofa was gone. The big glass and wood cabinet in the dining room where she kept the plates was gone. In school I was learning colors. Nobody had time to look at my red apples, my yellow bananas and green trees. Daddy wore an old gray wool bathrobe. He was cold all the time. Mommy was crying.

"Something has happened to Daddy," Mommy said. We were in her bed together. Daddy was gone. Mommy's eyes were stained red from crying. "Daddy's gone to the hospital." Did I know what a hospital was? "When he comes back he won't be the same," my mother told me. "He'll have to rest for a long time. He will talk funny."

"Funny?" I asked. I was lying in bed with my mother, in the big bed Mommy and Daddy slept in together. Funny? Daddy was always funny. He watched me play with my clay models. He came into my bedroom and pretended to be a dinosaur. He hunched his shoulders and swooped me up. He watched me study my butterflies. He spread his arms wide and pretended he had wings. We both spread our arms and pretended we had wings and ran down the street breaking fallen red leaves with our feet. We were laughing.

"Funny," Mommy said again. "Like Billy."

Billy was twelve. He lived across the street. He had been born deaf. When he talked the words sounded painful and deformed. Everyone said he talked like that because he ate worms. I thought about my father talking like Billy. Would everybody say my father ate worms? I stood up. I stared at my mother. She was watching me from the bed. She was reaching out her arms for me. I thought about my father talking like Billy. Then I fainted.

"We'll get the tests back today. It might be his gall bladder," Francine said. "He can't take another surgery now. We may have to make a decision."

"About pulling the plugs?"

Francine stared down at the table. She nodded her head. She was biting her lip.

Slowly I managed to stand up. The world had broken down into still frames.

My father is taking me to my first baseball game. The Philadelphia Athletics are playing. I feel I've been sitting on my strange hard seat for a long time. I stand up. It is the National Anthem. "I want to go home now," I tell my father. He is looking down at the big green field. "But the game hasn't started yet," he says. Then he shrugs. He laughs and his laughter is big like the wind. "O.K., kid. O.K." And he takes me by the hand and leads me out of the stadium.

I sit under a tree. Horses pass in front of me. It is Delaware Park. My father is whispering to me. "Pick one," he whispers. I watch the horses pass, enormous near my face. I point to a gigantic grayish beast. My father tells me to sit by the tree. "Just a small flier," he tells Francine. She is angry. In the car on the way home she doesn't speak to my father. She leans against the car window, crying. From time to time she says, "Jesus Christ. A hundred bucks. Jesus Christ. You went for the whole goddamn hundred."

My father goes away on the train. It's a holiday. He doesn't have to go to work. He waves to me from the train. He's going to the race track in New York. He comes back late at night. He is laughing. He walks into the old kitchen. He takes out a pocketful of green bills. He throws them on the table like cards. My mother and father are laughing. "Buy a hat," my father tells my mother. "Buy that coat you saw downtown." My father puts his arms around both of us. He hugs us so tight I think we'll break.

He hunches up his shoulders and swoops me up. I ride on his shoulders. He makes his arms go out wide at his sides like wings. He carries me that way all through the house.

"Where are you going?" Francine asked. Her face seemed broken, pale, unsolid.

"To take my best shot," I said. I kept walking.

It was morning, still before noon. The sky was a sheer blue. The haze had lifted. The day was becoming strangely hot. It seemed a wind was somewhere beginning. I had a sense of being watched.

When I came home, Jason was gone. I could still smell my father, the chill, the sense of rotting fibers in the cobalt-scarred flesh refusing to heal on my father's butchered neck. I could still breathe in a sense of blood, contamination and evil, evil.

The telephone rang. "The doctor just left his room," Francine whispered. "He brought in a heart machine." My mother took a deep breath. "The doctor said he may be slipping."

"He's going to live," I told her. "The crisis is passing."

I still felt chilled inside, felt my bones branching out in cold spokes sharp and blank as twigs in winter. Philadelphia in winter. The whittled branches. The mounds of soft snow pressing against the front door. Daddy finds his shovel and digs us out. A new channel. We are saved again. We are grateful. We watch Daddy drive away.

I sat down on my front porch. It was time to consider death. Death was clever. Death was a taker who left nothing, who even hid the bone. Death had great shadowy arms and shale breath. Death was big. It had teeth and wings. It left claw marks in the skin, torn-out flesh pockets and rows of black stitches, black stitches like train tracks in snow. It could make a big man into a boy. It could make a big man talk funny, talk wormy. And death would have to be considered now, in the slow noon before the world began to spin again into the black, sky filled with ink-squid blood stinking, seething and hungry to bury someone.

My father had pulled out his tubes. He had shadowboxed death in the middle-of-the-night hospital corridor. He had done battle alone. A force had been tapped into, a passageway perhaps inadvertently etched out. It still stirred. It stretched out enormous scale-encrusted arms. It had talons and fangs. It took bites out of the sick and helpless. It stank. Its breath was a dull wind on cobblestone alleys cut between ruins of buildings, narrow ruts of stone streets smelling from the piss of a thousand generations of beggars and cripples and lepers.

A door had been opened. It would have to be closed.

❧ 18 ❧

The early afternoon was a glassy blue, pale as imitation amethyst. The afternoon was unusually clear.

The full horror was slowly leaking down, the way rain fights to enter blank dry dirt. My father might not live through the night. I thought of my father with his fresh scars burning. My father webbed in white and counting his missing parts. The hollowed out neck and tongue, part of the cheek gone, vocal cords gone, gone. My father sat on the horizon, an undecided exploding red sun.

I sat in the kitchen alcove of Jason's studio, at the table my father found for me in a used furniture store. A kitchen table, symbolic, a woman's anchor, a gift for a daughter. The cat

Picasso sat on the chair next to me. Jason's car was gone. I had asked him to wait for me. I told him it was the first thing I had asked of him in a long time, years perhaps. And Jason was gone.

Picasso licked his right front paw. It was simple. If my father could just live through the night the storm would pass, spent and forgotten. Winter would pass. There would be a chorus of erupting blossoms and drugged insects, spring and the possibilities strung fat red and yellow on the vines.

The day turned strangely hot. I heard sirens. I thought, you must not die, Father. Be slowly warmed. The worst is behind you. The singed canyons are spitting new cactus. You have lived through the cruel turn from the sun. Believe me, Father. Winter is over. You have survived it.

The afternoon seemed suspended. The heat increased and turned harsh. Sirens shattered the late afternoon shadows. I heard ambulances and howls. The Santa Ana winds were blasting through the streets, bristling and smelling of desert, of white sunlight, sharp wiry plants and white rock.

The winds had a taste. I thought of scrub brush and the thorns desert plants wear. A hot madness was enclosing the city. It found me. It could inch east to my father's hospital bed. It could pry him from the oxygen again and the saline stuck in his hand. A small crucifixion. And what if the winds burned their way across the city to him?

Night was sharp and clear and hot. Jason didn't come back at dusk. I sat in his empty studio. Picasso and I regarded one another. Night was a black trench. The moon hung in the dead center of the window, absolutely round, a mirrory disk embedded in the night's throat.

Picasso felt the winds ripping at the house. He could sense the full moon's special heat and how she seemed to call to him with longing, a strange circular lust. He was agitated. He wanted to go outside, wanted to taste moon sheen, that white light substantive as snow. He wanted to brush his claws against the night bodies of conspiring plants. He longed to hunt and make his throat ripple with small growls like small harbor waves. He wanted to draw blood.

I watched him for a while. Then I closed the door leading to the front room. I picked Picasso up. He settled into my lap.

I stroked the cat. I rubbed his back. I noticed his long fur was badly matted. Jason rarely brushed him. Pieces of things were caught in his coat, twigs and leaves and small round oil stains from sitting under cars. His long bushy tail was tangled up around a green vine. I realized that he looked as if he were already growing out of the earth.

I rubbed Picasso under his chin and thought, what retrograde centuries to beach you thus small and inconsequential. Remember when you were predator? When you dreamed bigger than lizard and mouse and blue jay? You knew the way to the jugular, the way through the jungle, the millenniums of yellow wind in yellow grasses.

I pushed at an oil stain on his head with my thumb. The cat purred. The moon seemed oddly and whitely hot. I had the sense of being watched.

I have things to tell you, little one. There is another man. He is my father. He is being held in a white web by a black spider. An enormous spider with a command of technology and history. A black spider who practices the cruel art of knives. He is being slowly eaten. He is being skinned alive. I know you have a certain appreciation for a slow and painful death. I have watched you torture birds, watched your claws dart across a feathery neck. I have seen you intoxicated by blood.

There is another matter. It is a thing called cancer. Hard claws were jammed through my father's mouth. It took his tongue and throat. They cut the first grooves. Later roots took hold, blood-fed and blood-warmed. They sprouted buds. He was colonized.

Now his face is dark and swollen. Bandages form a thick collar around his gutted neck. They sprout tubes for feeding and bleeding, branches. Why, he's part tree now. And he always thinks it's six o'clock, time for the news and a shot of bourbon. Time for a cigar and the next day's racing form.

I watch his mouth twist and curl. He tries to make sounds that no longer come. I can barely read his scrawled notes. Over and over again I explain the oxygen machine to him. Perhaps he hears it hiss. He points to it and scowls.

Do you see what I'm getting at, cat? There are certain channels, small crevices in life as we pretend to know it. There are places where the hand-painted mural that is the world separates into individual tiles/time/cells. These cracks in the fabric can be lethal.

Hot wind assaulted the house. It was furious, enraged. I rocked Picasso in my arms. He arched his oil-stained head to me and closed his yellow eyes. I stroked the soft white fur on his neck. He purred, a deep humming. And I thought of the humming in the hospital, the fluids slowly oozing, the hiss of oxygen. The humming.

A boundary is crossed. The hand-painted mural that is the world shatters into separate fragments. The sky swirls. Ink rushes like a lava flow between the torn seams. It's enough to make a strong man drown. And my father is weak, helpless. And the sky caves in. Black chunks fall.

Outside I could feel the wind driving toward the sea, a wide hot spoke. In Philadelphia it was kite season. I was six years old. Daddy was supposed to take me to the park and make my kite windborne. But Daddy couldn't come that day. Daddy couldn't come any day. Daddy stayed in bed. When he spoke it was whispery, windy, harsh. He had to lean close to your ear. Had everything become a secret?

I went to the park alone. I had a kite in a bird's shape. It upended in a tree stump. The sky was a child-eyed blue hung between low hills, grafted onto the day like a patch of blue flesh. Cobalt-blue flesh? The sky was a severed bull's-eye. "Stop crying," Mother said, making soup steam. "It's only paper. I'll buy you another." But something happened to Father. Kite season ripped him to pieces. Maybe Daddy was only paper. What happened to the sky? Blue sky with white chipped mouth of clouds was rolled down like a used sail. Big hands packed it away.

Then big hands packed the brass lamps and the new china plates. I sat in strange rooms assigned to me by smiling strangers. Mommy drove the car. And Daddy didn't talk at all. And we were taking a cab to the train station. Why were we going to the train station? We were going to California. And what was California? It was where the oranges grew and there was no snow. No snow? Then what? Well, just sun and palm trees. And just sit nice and quiet in your seat. Let Daddy try to sleep.

And I am squeezed small and airborne in a hawk's belly. I nest in a raped oak shell. I break my dolls. I tear their arms off. I burn their almost porcelain faces. I practice invisibility. I lean into shadows and walls, making cold metallic connections. And I scream, I don't like it here. There's no sky, no sky. No sky in city apartment inches from a boulevard where Daddy curls small in bed all day. No sky in city apartment glued to a wide gray boulevard where trucks heave and shove. And where is Mommy? Will she stop working soon? No. And Daddy's lying in bed all the day and the sun is strange, defective. It falls plop into the ocean. It bleeds. And father bleeds. Father has a drawer of special bandages. And Mommy's gone. Will she come back soon?

Life's hard all around, Mother says to the mirror. Mommy is making her mouth red. Mommy is making her eyes big. Her teeth are polished sails. If it's that bad, divorce him. He's a small soft mound. You don't need his broken strings, his useless arms. You don't even have to bury him. Mommy is talking about Gerald. She is saying just go. Maggots will do the rest.

Outside it was very dark and hot. The wind made a sound like a long harsh cough. The air seemed gravelly. The sky looked like a sealed grave. I rubbed the cat's soft white chest. Sirens cut at the night, black knives. There was a sense of smoke.

Maybe it would have been different if Jason had been there, if he had waited for me, or come back. Maybe it would have been different if the moon weren't so bright, so clearly gorged on blood.

Maybe if the Santa Ana winds weren't blowing, tearing at the air, turning the night into a kind of scrub brush. Maybe if the night hadn't been pitted with sirens, howling dogs, screaming and wails.

I waited for Jason, and night was an avalanche, air molecules insane. I held Picasso on my lap. His purring was a soft hum. And night pressed down a savage fist. The air was pointed and sharp and clearly alive. Picasso was warm and soft on my lap. He was listening to me, hearing my thoughts as if I were reciting a lullaby. Then it occurred to me that the cat might want to sleep.

Picasso nestled against my chest while I crossed Pacific Avenue. He seemed untroubled by the occasional car, the moon full and shrieking, the wind a torture. He trusted me.

My feet touched cold sand. Suddenly I turned around. I stared at the deserted strip of boardwalk behind me. I was afraid someone would see me. My heart was racing. My head was a seething black storm. That's when I realized for the first time what I was going to do.

I sat down just above the wet sand, Picasso on my lap. I stroked him and he purred, a soft humming. I held him warm against my chest. Our hearts beat together. The waves broke on shore and withdrew, broke on shore and withdrew, a kind of humming.

It was simple. A door opened. A crevice was torn in the fabric. Something entered. It stalked. It was a hunter. It was hungry but mindless as a shark. It would take anything. It was enormous.

And it wouldn't go back empty-handed, humiliated with no new scalps, no dried hides or skulls. It was rude not to acknowledge its presence, its chill and teeth. Something was required.

Picasso never really struggled. He stared at me, disbelieving, his eyes startled yellow marbles, oddly frozen. And I thought of the certain marbles children call cat's eyes. I heard sirens behind me. I felt the wind whipping my shoulders, hot breath, desert breath rubbing my flesh. The moon was breathing platinum above me. There was a slow cracking sound.

Picasso took a long time to die. I was surprised. My fingers were stiff and itching at the end, after the bones in his neck broke and he finally went limp. A thin trail of blood slid from the corner of his mouth and drip, drip, dripped down his neck onto my hands.

I let him fall to the wet sand. I let the waves wash the blood from my hand. I dipped my hand into foam and swish, the blood was gone.

Then the waves circled the cat's dead body. The waves reached out black hands and embraced him. Salt leaked into his wound. He was wrapped in black coiling swirls.

I turned my back to the sea. I felt the power of the waves at my back hurtling and gnawing the shoreline, crashing and withdrawing, a kind of humming. I felt the rhythm, the wind, salt spray, the land groaning while cold black water lapped around my ankles.

I looked up at the sky. Would that blood satisfy? Would it be enough to glue the torn place shut? And something inside me turned incredibly hard.

That night the moon was impossibly full and the yellow of a child's gold locket. It seemed to follow behind me as I walked back to my house.

I locked my door. I could still sense the moon, feel its special yellow heat. It sat suspended in the center of the sky as if precisely placed there by an engineer. It hung directly above my head, fat and glowing like a terrible promise.

I thought, what is it, anyway, this moon? It's simply a pinprick, a sliver, a coin glued to a useless black metal sky. The moon is an empty beacon. The moon is a cyst, dead to my curses or, worse, cursed itself, stuck there, abandoned, useless and blind.

The moon was the yellow of a marble. The moon was yellow as Picasso's eyes after I dug my fingers into his neck until bones broke and blood drip, drip, dripped down on my hands.

I lay very still in my bed. Now things will change, I thought. And from now on, death, you bastard, you deal with me.

꒰ 19 ꒱

Everything requires an explanation.

Name. Age. Sexual persuasion. Occupation. Tribal rituals completed. (Check where appropriate.)

1. Search for visionary experience/hallucinatory connection with forces called magical, spiritual or even philosophical.

2. Marriage.

3. Birth.

4. Death.

5. Contact with evil force, place or person. Also contact with evil spells sometimes called concepts, art, science and history.

6. Contact with holy forces sometimes called miracles or luck.

7. Rebirth.

8. Physical torture.

9. Blood sacrifice, exorcism, etc.
10. Other. (Specify.)

Francine telephoned at precisely nine. Nine, I thought, looking at the clock. Nine, a kind of chime.

"His heart stopped last night," she said. "Then it started again. I wasn't here when it happened. I just found out. Actually, he looks considerably better today." She sounded surprised. It was the first energy I had heard in her voice in weeks. Was it weeks? Her voice had a new dimension, some rumbling of a white mania to come, one suspicious perfect white cloud.

My body was weaving, secretly drunk. Your father's heart stopped she said and my heart stopped and I felt the blood empty from my face, felt the chill, the cells within collapsing. But it started again. His heart started again she said. And I realized that he wasn't dead. No, of course not. She was talking. I was twenty-seven when he got it the first time. Now you're twenty-seven. The wheel spins she was saying. Or was she?

"He looks terrible. Gray. Like hell. But somehow better. For the first time I feel he has a chance," Francine said.

The Santa Ana winds had disappeared. The day was warm and clear. I found Francine in the hospital cafeteria. She was wearing a white tennis skirt. She seemed rejuvenated. An intern passed our table carrying a tray of fried chicken. Francine watched him walk. "You look lousy," she said to me.

I shrugged. I was holding a white styrofoam cup. It might have been a small warm white rock.

"Listen, kid. You think I'm ridiculous, obscene? Forty-six with a tennis racket? If I drop dead tomorrow, and I might, just tell them I was here, alive, trying. Are you following me? I haven't given up. I'm still in there punching. Just like your father."

But no, Francine wasn't saying that at all. She was smiling. She was sipping coffee from a white cup. She was saying, "He looks so much better today. They're going to make him walk tomorrow. The skin graft looks good. The pain has stopped. I'm taking the whole day off. Let's go shopping in Beverly Hills."

"I don't think so," I said carefully.

"Come on," Francine said, almost gay. "We'll start on Rodeo. I'll buy you a milk shake."

I shook my head no.

"No. No," she screamed, banging her fist on the table. "That's all you know how to say. No. No. And you're getting older. You're almost thirty. And you're missing it all."

I didn't say anything. Francine was wearing a white blouse over her tennis dress. She looked as if she were wearing a pale pair of wings.

"You'll never give me a break, will you?" Francine demanded.

Yes/no/maybe. All of the above. None of the above. Are there gradations? Can you use an attached sheet? No?

"There's so much you don't know," Francine was saying. "Your father taught me. All we have is the moment. It can be snatched away at any time. I learned late. But I learned. Don't you see?" My mother brought her face very close to mine. "Each second is important. See him struggle just for a chance to keep living? Where is your sense of life?"

Gone, I thought, like everything else. The impulse was finite, meager from the beginning. It was chipped into. Francine had taken pieces of it. My father. Somewhere Gerald sneered at me and in that special darkness took a piece. Jason came with a shovel. He dug out pieces of me by the cartful, the truckful. I had a paper kite in a bird's shape. It broke. Everything broke.

Francine was staring at the girl in the chair. She was examining her/me. "Don't let your father down," she said after a while. "I mean it," she added. Her words were sharp white splinters.

My father's bed had been raised to a sitting position. He was reading *Esquire* magazine. His eyeglasses were stuck through the gauze near his ears. He heard my footsteps. He let the magazine fall to the floor.

AM DOOMED.

I sat down carefully near his legs. I could see the bandages on his thighs through the sheet. I was staring at his eyeglasses stuck into the head bandage. In the beginning my father had refused to even touch his glasses. He said he would never need them again. He would never read again.

AM DOOMED.

"What do you mean, doomed?" Was that me talking?

CANCER 2X NOW.

"You beat the rap twice. You're way ahead," somebody said.

LOOKED IN MIRROR. MUTILATION HORRIBLE.

"There are many different kinds of scars," I began. Scars of childhood. Francine's scars of sitting on the cold stoops of brick buildings in winter. Houses where the refrigerator was always locked. Houses where the ceiling collapsed and mice ran across her head and she wasn't really surprised, she knew they were there. And scars of the first footprints and tire tracks in the new snow. And scars in the neck, scars across the throat. And scars like an invisible web fallen across Gerald's lap, a kind of glue in his lap where nothing stirred. "There are physical scars, Daddy. And mental scars, emotional scars."

I HAVE THEM ALL. I HAVE A 3 HORSE PARLAY GOING.

I sat very still. The blinds were partially open. I could see the new white flowers poking star-shaped through thick-looking vines. The morning was still clear.

SAD SAD SAD. A tear slid down my father's cheek. SURGERY MISTAKE. SUCKER BET. My father threw his writing pad on the floor.

I reached for his hand. It felt almost lifeless, brittle, a severed leaf. "Daddy," I began softly, very softly. I had noticed that loud noises made him nervous and angry. "What are you afraid of? The skin graft is working. They're going to take out the feeding tube soon. You'll go home. You're beating this one."

My father nodded his head. He seemed to be listening.

"Are you afraid the cancer will come back?" Sprout new branches? Grow more tumbleweed in another place, your lungs perhaps? I handed my father his writing pad.

INSIDIOUS DISEASE. ALWAYS COMES BACK.

"Doesn't everything come back in a way?" I said. I wasn't thinking about the cancer. I was thinking about Venice Beach, the way the waves came up and embraced Picasso. I realized if one stood on Venice Beach long enough the sea would be revealed absolutely. If one stood there long enough sooner or later everything would wash up on shore. The sea's dead returned as rows of coughed-up white bone. Old beer cans, pieces of galley ships and a strangled long-haired orange and white cat.

WANT 2 DIE.

My father wrote that note in a heavy black scrawl. I pretended not to notice.

AM DYING.

"Nobody knows that," I said. "It's a photo finish. I wouldn't throw away my ticket."

YOUR TRACK ANALOGIES STINK.

I stared at my father. There was a tiny spark in the center of his too dark eyes. I thought he might be smiling.

The telephone was ringing as I walked into my house. It was Jason, warm and apologetic. Was I angry he didn't come back last night?

"No," I said. It occurred to me that a person needed hope to be angry. Anger implied expectations and violations. I wasn't angry.

"Picasso's gone. I came back this morning and he was gone," Jason told me. "You know he always waits for me in the morning."

Was I supposed to say something? Silence. The quiet space was a whirlpool, some kind of vacuum sucking all the air in, swooshing, eating it all up. In the silence black waves wrapped black ropes around a throat of cracked bones.

"Yeah, old Picasso's gone. I guess he packed his bags and hit the road." Jason laughed.

Easy come, easy go, I thought.

"I'm going to check out the rents," Jason said. "Want to come?"

"No." My, how easy it was becoming to talk to Jason. A shrug. A grunt. Why, it didn't require anything at all.

"I'll see you after I paint." Jason hung up.

I crossed the bridge over Eastern Canal. I crossed Howland and Linnie canals and waited for him to drive away. Then I began carrying his possessions back to his house.

I put his things in a neat pile near the water fountain in his front room. It took six trips to carry everything back. Things were changing, all right, I told myself. I had a pile of hard evidence on the floor near his water fountain. I was becoming certain. When I walked back into my house, the telephone was ringing.

"The old man's dead," Jason said.

"The old man?" The room turned black. Why had they called Jason? Jason didn't even know my father was in the hospital. I was reeling. I was chunks of black ice. And the room was slanting now. There were no edges.

"You know, Gordon? The decrepit old—"

"I know," I said quickly, said as quickly as I could. The room was slowly returning to a normal color. Mr. Gordon was the old man with a mandolin, wood fine and polished and reddish like a stretched heart. He used to play the mandolin on the roofs in New York in August. He was going to show it to me the last time I saw him. He was looking for it in a back closet but I left. I was afraid to see it.

"He was coming back from his doctor on the bus, on Pacific when—"

"Don't tell me," I said, and hung up.

They said it went in threes, didn't they? If I counted Picasso as the first and Mr. Gordon as the second, there was only one question left. Who was going to be third?

My living room was almost empty. Sunlight spilled across the walls freely, exuberantly. I wondered how I had ever stood the unnecessary clutter. It was much better now. It was airier. It was much easier to breathe, to think clearly and remember.

I stood on my porch. A fat duck floated by, a dark stain on the water. The air was warm. It could have been summer. A dog barked. I felt the sea breeze slowly uncurling and thought if he just lives a few more days, he'll beat it. Spring would unravel, bewitch and enchant, sun silky across the new wounds. If he could just live a few more days he would eat and walk again. If he could live a few more days he would be victorious. He would be tougher than leather, yes. He would be terribly aged, yes. Crazed, yes. But he would be on his feet, punching. And I was gaining a deep appreciation for being ambulatory. A moving target was considerably harder to hit.

I sat in my bedroom. I became conscious of the clock ticking, ticking, ticking. Ticking like a special secret code. Ticking like small teeth nibbling the dark air. Ticking, the quality of something entering and breaking. The ticking was harsh and whispery. And Daddy had to edge up close to me to speak. He had to put his lips right next to my ear. And Mommy said, when Daddy comes back, he may talk funny. He may talk like Billy. But Billy ate worms. My father wouldn't eat worms, I knew that.

And the clock was ticking, ticking, ticking. And Francine said, "Listen, kid. Your clock's ticking. You're almost thirty. You don't have forever. A week becomes a month, becomes a year, becomes a life. Define yourself," my mother said once. Or did she?

I picked up the clock. I threw it on the floor. Then I picked it up and threw it down harder. The fourth time I punched it against the floor, it broke. I realized it didn't matter anymore what time it was. Time was frozen. It was always now. Terminal now.

The telephone rang. I picked it up with a stiff arm. My hands were shaking. Get it done with, I thought. Butcher the third one and be gone, back to the depths, you bastard, you shark-hearted monster.

"What's all that crap doing in my painting room?" Jason demanded. He made it sound so exotic, like they weren't simply boxes but a series of strange tan ornaments.

"I'm just cleaning house," I said.

"Then you're not mad." Jason sounded relieved.

"Of course not," I said carefully. What in the world do I have to be mad about, mad about, mad about? I howled inside.

"What are you doing?"

I am just thinking about the mind, Jason. Thinking about my father and how night drills and tunnels. How night has harsh sagebrush breath. And my father was pinned in his white hospital bed. A hot wind was blowing. The sirens were screaming. And it was the first moments of April. And I would not let my father die. I would not let him be thrown away like a page from a calendar, cast off with the perfect still squares of February and March.

"I'm thinking," I said out loud. Yes, Jason. Thinking about the radiated tissue that won't heal and is opening toward the artery. I was wondering about the skin they took in nice neat squares like white calendar pages from his back and shoulder and thigh.

And they have to build him a new throat or he'll be stuck with a red plastic feeding tube in his nose forever. And that wouldn't be a long time. And I'm thinking that I should just tear the phone out of the wall, just sever its stupid thin neck and be done with it, done with it.

"And yourself?" I inquired. My, how nice and formal. Was this the great lull? The calm before the storm. The calm my mother and father settled into right before their divorce. When they stopped shouting and breaking things. When they looked up at the same patch of thin blue sky and realized they saw different dimensions.

"We'll get dinner. Pick me up in ten minutes," Jason said.

I felt light and airy. I could let go of the edge of the chair, just unwrap my fingers from their blood-draining tight grip and float to a far wall. Float like light, like smoke, like a big transparent bubble.

I didn't have a clock anymore. I just left my house and parked my car in the alley behind Jason's house. I was early. I was always early for him, always waiting. He got into my car.

"Were you painting?" I asked.

"Yep."

I was driving. "Did you get a lot of work done?" Did you get a beer can perched on a cunt exactly right? Did you find some way to send a rancid shadow through a woman's thigh? Did you notice I've begun hating you? I glanced across the car seat. Jason was staring out the window.

"They repainted the liquor store," he said, pointing. "See? It's red and white stripes now."

My father's red and white, I thought. Bandages and blood. I felt hot. I wanted a shot. It was a lull.

I parked the car. The market was closing. The lot was practically empty.

"You're in crooked," Jason observed.

"I know." Did he have his sword out? Was it off with my head? And imagine, it wasn't even dawn yet. "They're closing the store. There's only four cars here." I pointed to the almost deserted parking lot.

"I still don't like it." Jason slammed the door shut.

We walked into the market. Two steps forward. Four steps back. I am moth wing. You are fire. You are snow. I'm a steam shovel. Why, it could go on that way indefinitely.

Jason stopped dead in his tracks. "You're barefoot," he said. He sounded shocked. He was staring at my bare feet. He looked miserable.

I ignored him. What was he talking about, anyway? I didn't even have feet. They were white, of course, and somehow attached, but why call them feet? Weren't they the color and texture of mushrooms? They were a kind of web. They were a form of a pod, clearly a device for locomotion. But then, everything was if you considered time and the wind as part of the equation.

I picked out a shopping cart and began pushing down an aisle. My arms felt very strong and zingalong, zingalong. It wasn't any trouble at all.

"I don't like your attitude," Jason pronounced.

"Incredible, isn't it?" I kept pushing the cart. "Bare feet one day and who knows what next? The crossing of any boundary. The end of life as we know it." Did that mean the burial of a father?

"You're such a bitch," he said.

"A bitch?" I stopped pushing the cart.

"Shut up," Jason said.

I shut up. I started pushing the cart again. I was the path to heaven. He was a toll gate. I was a girl wrapped in the skinned white sides of stars. He was a blind troll. I tossed a loaf of bread into the cart.

"Wrong," Jason said. He was staring at the bread as if I had picked out a big brown turd. He removed the bread from the cart. He replaced it with another, one with a better fiber count, I was certain. One with fewer carcinogenics and preservatives. He had probably heard about it on a consumer affairs program on Channel 28. I almost laughed.

"Everything you do is wrong," Jason said. "You're incorrigible."

I stopped pushing the cart. I stared at him. "Your whole terminology sickens me. What are you? A probation officer?"

We were face to face. It occurred to me that if Jason got angry enough, he wouldn't spend the night with me.

"You want it one hundred percent your way," Jason said.

"You are talking about yourself," I said. And it was echo, echo, echo, echo chamber time again, time again, time again.

"You have no sense of order," Jason yelled.

"Oh, leave me alone," I yelled back. I was getting tired. I gave the shopping cart a jab. All at once I didn't care if he fucked me tonight, or ever.

"I'll leave you alone, cunt," Jason screamed. He walked out of the market. I watched him leave. Go, bastard. I hate you. And he was gone. And I was staring at the market door. Everything seemed darkly gouged out and too cold and I wasn't at all certain.

I had the sensation of sinking into black circles, liquid whirlpools, dark air hissing, the chill, and I thought, now easy, take big breaths. Calm down. It was all a dream. I was wrong. I was dark, too sharp. I was bleeding, seething, mistaken, misshapen. And I'll go insane without him. The roof will break off and winter strike without warning and the ground dissolve with a small sucking sound. And the earth will be barren, skies clotted with fat yellow clouds of dust and hopping locusts and I'll die.

I ran into the parking lot. I searched the sidewalk, the street, the gray shadow-driven pavement where haunted fat dark shapes floated. I got into my car, aching and resigned, part of me breaking, breaking.

Jason was lying on the back seat. He was eating a Mars bar. "I really don't know what to do anymore," he said.

❧ 20 ❧

I crossed the bridge over Eastern Canal and wound down an alley to the beach. It was early. The sky and sea were a lively blue. I thought of Jason curled small in my bed, his breath slowly rising and making the sheet softly sway. The morning waves sashayed onto shore, pastel blue, petticoat blue, and I wondered how it had all gone so bad. I walked along the wet sand to the place where I had strangled the cat, the place where the waves curved around his body in a black embrace. The sand was deserted, pale yellow, popsicle yellow. Waves curled slowly and lapped at the shore. And I thought, how did it happen, the ruin? Like everything else, one sad blind step at a time.

I drove to the hospital. The day was clear, finely etched, the edges distinct, the centers solid. Lawns and slices of sidewalk pushed up spring flowers. Pink and white lilies, mouths starched and wide open. Dark stalks of purple iris. Yellow and red and lava-colored cannas. Gladioli, roses, and the bougainvillaea that never slept, never went into remission, but just kept spreading across garden gates and roofs, luxuriant. And plateaus of red and pink geraniums, azaleas, blue clusters of agapanthus. The city almost looked real.

Francine was sitting in the hospital cafeteria. She was wearing white slacks and a white straw beach hat. A vision in white. She was reading *The New Yorker* magazine. "Borges is a great writer," she announced. "Márquez. Neruda. All those greasers are great writers." She closed the magazine.

We considered the great greaser writers in silence. I drank another cup of coffee. I was conscious of the round black and white clock embedded in the wall just above my head. Why, it was a kind of eye. It saw something, measured something. It breathed and blinked.

"He looks so much better," Francine said, sparkling. "I'm taking the day off. I'm going sailing."

"You deserve it," I said.

Francine leaned across the small table. She brought her face very close to mine. "Phillip has fallen in love with me," she whispered. "Totally smitten. But he's afraid to get involved. He knows he could become serious. He's afraid to be vulnerable. What do you think?"

"I'm tired of what men are afraid of."

"I know what you mean. I thought about that reading the *Wall Street Journal* yesterday. News is merely the way men gossip." Francine stared at me, stared into me, through the skin, directly into my brain. "It's tedious pretending to be subservient, isn't it? But Phillip is a whole new ball game." Francine leaned her face so close to mine I could feel her breath against my face. "He's a Scorpio," she whispered. "You know what that means."

It was becoming clear to me that Francine was missing important cards from her personal deck. An ace and two kings at the least. Maybe it had something to do with the mice that fell out of the ceiling and bounced across her ten-year-old head.

"They want him to walk. He says he's waiting for you. By the way, I called his bluff."

"How?"

"He asked for the *TV Guide*," Francine said. She laughed. "He didn't ask for it. He pointed to the TV up on the wall. Then he put out both his hands like a book and pantomimed turning pages. I ask you, would a man planning to die want a *TV Guide?*" Francine stood up. "Make sure he walks," she said.

"Francine, have fun today," I said softly.

My mother looked stunned. "You've never wished me a good time in my entire miserable life," she said. "And you're going to be one guilt-ridden woman someday."

My father was sitting up. The oxygen and IV were gone. The other machines were gone. He was reading *Playboy*. When he saw me he shoved the magazine aside and removed his eyeglasses. His expression darkened. He had already written a note.

BUYING TIME AT THIS EXPENSE CRAZY. PUT U & F. THRU THIS. F. ACTING NUTS. MICE ON HER BRAIN AGAIN. AFRAID 2 DIE. U & F. CANT TAKE CARE OF SELVES.

I read my father's note. He looked alert. His eyes were a dark brown. The inky liquid was gone. They had removed more of the bandages from his face. He looked incredibly sad.

"Are you in pain?"

My father nodded his head.

"Do you want a shot?"

My father nodded yes. He reached for his pad. ASKED NURSE 4 SHOT. NO DICE.

"They won't give you a shot any more? They must think you're getting better."

BS. THEY R SADISTS.

My father stared at the floor. After a while a young nurse

padded into the room. "Time to go on your first walk," she said cheerfully. She gave my father a big smile.

My father stared at the nurse. He gripped his blanket with both hands and pressed it tightly against his chest. I could see a grayish scab on his hand where the IV needle had been embedded. My father shook his head violently from side to side.

The nurse smiled sweetly and left the room. She returned with another nurse and a doctor I had never seen before. "Time to walk now," the new doctor said. He sounded as if he meant it.

My father studied the new doctor. Then he gave him the finger.

Everyone sprang into action. One nurse pried the sheet from my father's hands. The other nurse and the doctor gripped my father under his armpit. They were pulling him by his good arm, the one they hadn't taken skin from. I tried to help my father put his bathrobe on. His shoulder was too thickly bandaged from the skin graft. He couldn't push his arm through the sleeve. I draped it over his shoulders.

My father was standing on his feet. His legs were trembling violently. He seemed startled and breathless, clearly in pain.

"One foot in front of the other," the doctor said firmly.

My father gave the doctor a brief black stare. With his eyes he said eat it motherfucker.

We edged into the corridor. My father leaned against me. He took tiny broken steps. I tried to match them. My father has always been a good walker. It was one of his hobbies. After the divorce, my father had tried to walk his rage out. He would walk from his house in West Los Angeles to City Hall downtown and back. Or he would walk west, to the ocean, and back again. Walking. Walking. Once he walked forty miles in a single day. He went back later to measure his route exactly by the car odometer. Forty-two miles, he told me proudly.

On his sixtieth birthday my father bought a set of weights. His arms were suntanned and strong. He showed me new muscles in his back. My father wasn't planning on growing old gracefully. He wasn't planning on growing old at all. He was deeply motivated. He wanted to outlive Francine, he said.

Now he was bent, thinned, a Lear in his gauzy white storm. He walked the distance of two hospital rooms and collapsed shaken against the corridor wall. They brought him a wheelchair. My father lay trembling in his bed. He seemed to be gasping for air. He could barely hold on to his pen.

AM DYING.

"I think it just feels that way. The doctor told me he saw new pink skin under the bandages. The graft is working."

DR. LYING. COVER-UP. OPER. WAS FLOP.

"Look at it this way. You're turning for home. It's the stretch drive. Anything can happen."

My father seemed to think of something. He picked up his pad.

CANT WALK FROM PARKING LOT 2 TRACK. COULD PHONE IN BETS. SUCKER PLAY. CANT SEE ODDS OR BANDAGED HORSES. BUT I CANT TALK!!!

"We'll work out something."

My father gave me a long hard black stare. THERES NO PT. 2 ALL THIS SUFFERING. WHY???

I thought about it for a while. When I looked back at my father he had closed his eyes. I reached over and felt for his pulse. One thing was certain. The old man was still breathing.

I walked into the corridor. I passed the chaplain. He smiled at me and tipped an imaginary hat. I was struck by his pallor. It occurred to me that the chaplain would know about that bastard death stalking the corridors, that foul-breathed monster. But no. The chaplain wasn't considering the evil serpent with its coiled stinger and claws. The chaplain seemed to be discussing the dispensation of an unclaimed philodendron with the head nurse. I kept walking.

The emaciated woman in the room next to the alcove where they kept the morphine had her first visitor. He was wearing a business suit. He was writing something down on a large yellow pad. I assumed it was her will.

I darted into the morphine alcove. The nurses were organizing the lunch trays, scurrying like white mice, phones ringing in the nurses' station, visitors crowding through the narrow gray enamel channel of corridor between carts stacked with half-eaten plates of food, mounds of too-green and too-yellow ground-up mush the dying were served. The morphine alcove was deserted. The key was stuck in the locked drawer. It dangled out like bait. I unlocked the drawer.

What's the point of all this? my father had asked. I held the morphine bottles in my hand. They were warm, charmed. I was holding plucked hot moons, clear white stars. I could have put them into my purse. I didn't.

A certain disease had been cut from my father. He had been mutilated, skinned, patched, gouged, stitched. I thought of my father's painful broken steps in the corridor. My father had always been a good walker. I could barely keep up with him at the track. My father. A short man with broad shoulders and a sturdy, purposeful stride. He had a firm grip. When I held my father's hand it felt warm like the earth, felt like sun-bloated grains just pulled from the ground.

I put the morphine bottles back into the drawer. I walked into the crowded corridor. There had been a man in the room closest to the elevator. Now the room was empty. I had known the man was dying. There had been a sudden flurry of visitors with too bright, too expensive bouquets. Now the bed was newly made, white and empty. The plants and baskets of fruit were gone. The IV pole and machines were gone. The blinds were open. Sun spilled lazy onto the crisp white sheets. The room was ready to kill somebody else.

I sat down on the strip of grass near the emergency room

entrance. I put my head down in my hands and cried. Perhaps someone would come and help me, a kindly churchy-looking older woman with hair sprayed a stiff white-blue under a pastel pillbox hat.

I prepared an explanation. My mother, Francine, had gone sailing. I was worried about her. She was both my mother and my child. In a sense we were sisters. Francine had been a foster child, repeatedly beaten and abused. She lived in homes where she never had a key and the refrigerator was kept locked. And mice fell on her head. She wasn't surprised when the mice scampered across her skin. She had known they were there in the sewing machine all along.

The man who had been her lover and husband, friend and protector, was lying mute and haunted in the cancer ward, poised between life and death. My father.

And he thinks he is going to die. It's the second time the black cells ambushed him. And he was up four grand on the Santa Anita meet. And he doesn't know how he will manage walking from the parking lot into the track. He could bet with a bookie. It isn't good that way. You can't see the changing odds. You can't see if the horse comes out with bandages. Not that bandages mean that much. Bandaged horses win, too. But he can't talk anymore. He doesn't know if he'll be able to drive a car again. You see, the skin graft is pinching his shoulder and neck together so that he can't really turn his head.

Just today I stood in the morphine alcove just now and put the bottles back. I'll never be a small white star again. I'll never dance draped in moon hide again. Or feel a Santa Ana wind slam through my lungs and know myself as young, naked, my navel filled with platinum. I'll never drift past the last reefs draped in white garlands, eating grapes, the sea a glazed blue eye unblinking.

I cried a long time. I waited for the kindly woman. I

would tell her about Jason and my seven years of paralysis and suffering. I sensed feet passing near me. I heard steps. I caught a glimpse of pant legs, a brush of white skirts. The hospital doors snapped open and shut, open and shut. A cold gray mouth.

I waited for something to happen. No one stopped. No one said a single word to me.

❧ 21 ❧

I slept and tossed, haunted, shivering, burning and dreaming of Gerald, of Jason. I was being chased under a white lid of moon through streets empty and white and filled with a sense of the sudden and inexplicable, fire and danger. Somewhere a woman I almost recognized was counting, was chanting, was saying over and over if Picasso was the first and the old man with the mandolin was the second, then who will be the third, the third, the third?

I drove to the hospital. It was early morning, already warm and sharp, without haze or fog. A boundary had been crossed. The hills beyond the city seemed hard, substantial, possible.

Francine had just come from my father's room. She saw me and bit her lower lip. A bad sign.

"The graft is working. I looked under the bandage. There is new pink skin." Francine leaned closer to me. "It's just the mental shit now. The depression."

The light in the room was sharp and white. The wheel spins, all right. It's got machete sides. It moves faster than light. And is it dangerous? You bet, kid.

Francine was wearing a long lavender sheath dress. I could remember when she bought it. Her first designer dress on her first business trip to Paris.

She telephoned me breathless, just back from Paris. "I kept wishing you were with me," she said.

It was night in Berkeley. Outside my kitchen window the Bay Bridge was amberish, a line of gouged-out eyes. Gerald was studying mathematics then. It was the era of the slide rule, equations and chalk board of symbols that were going to make Gerald well, going to make him whole.

Or was it later? Suddenly I remembered that Gerald had begun a process of physical transformation just before he left me. He decided that he needed a strong body.

"Strong," Gerald demanded of the mirror. He punched his fat belly with his fist. "How can the universe be an orchestra if the body is badly tuned?" Gerald asked the mirror. Perhaps the mirror answered.

He joined a yoga club. He did special breathing exercises. He was given a Xeroxed copy of a diet consisting of certain fruits, nuts and brown rice. He taped the diet to the refrigerator door. He informed me that I could no longer cook for him. My vibrations were wrong. My aura was wrong. My karma was a pile of shit.

"Are you telling me I contaminate your food?" I was getting ready for work at the restaurant. I had already pinned up my hair and squeezed into my short black waitress skirt.

"You don't see fat people in healthy societies," Gerald said. "Western culture kills for pleasure."

"Are you talking about chickens and cows and things?" I was going to be late for work, I was certain.

"The body is a holy temple. And they're not things," Gerald corrected. "They're life forms."

Whenever Gerald spoke about life forms, his voice became somehow dreamy. When he spoke about life forms, I felt I was standing on the bridge of the U.S.S. *Enterprise*. First Officer Spock was staring into a painted tin can. It might have been a tomato juice can with the label removed. Captain James T. Kirk was looking into what might have been a small flashlight.

"What is it, Spock?"

Spock shook his head with its gracefully pointed plastic ears. He tried to look green and grave. "Most curious readings, Captain," he told the tomato juice can. "An entirely new life form."

"A new life form?" Kirk whispered, stunned and breathless. He made it sound as if they had never encountered bizarre species before.

"A new life form," Kirk repeated. "But can we use them? Can we force them to join the Federation? Can we tax them? Farm them? Eat them? Most of all, can we fuck them?"

"I kept wishing you were with me," Francine repeated. "I wanted you to see Paris with me. Imagine a city where they even sculpt statues under bridges. Imagine a city with that sense of beauty." Francine seemed humbled and awed.

I tried to imagine. I was holding the phone in one hand and stirring a pot with the other. The steam rising was a soft white veil between me and Gerald. My mother was saying that she went by herself to the flea market at Clignancourt. She mastered the intricacies of the Métro. I held the telephone and felt like an insomniac poisoned by fatigue. I couldn't wake up. I was intimidated by her vision of the City of Light and her appetite, her appetite.

My mother told me she walked her shoes down to nails. She walked and wanted more, more. The river was not enough. She gobbled up bridges, monuments, both banks. I imagined she could have walked to Normandy in her fur coat and tennis shoes, her seven weeks of Berlitz.

When my mother described the river to me I saw it as somehow waterless, containing stale things, hopeless and gray. I thought if I had gone with her, my feet and hands would have turned into stone. I would not have returned. I would have become the spine of a sixteenth-century bridge, catatonic and without eyes. And Francine was telling me about the Tuileries, where she touched pink and red flowers to her lips. She wanted to name and breathe everything. She ate dinner on top of the Eiffel Tower with the city below glowing, an immense perfect circle cut by a river that even in the darkness seemed alive, seemed to sway and breathe.

Gerald glared at me from the living room. Even my hushed voice was an intrusion. Gerald did not care about my mother's trip to Europe. Paris was a symbol of Western culture, decadent, draped in the sins of imperialism, and spent. Gerald was concerned only with meaningful journeys. He wanted to go to Andromeda. He wanted to go through the black holes of space. He wanted to go back into the Pleistocene with a camera and snap photographs of *Homo erectus* discovering fire. And back even further to trilobites, lava flows, invertebrates. Would that be back far enough?

"What are you staring at?" Francine asked.

"I was remembering that dress."

"My first trip to Europe." Francine smiled. "You remember? I wanted to take you with me. But you refused. You were married to that sick jerk. You should have left him and come with me."

I nodded my head. She was right.

"I finally had dinner with Bernard," Francine began.

Was Bernard the one with the six-picture deal and the legal separation? The one who was going to take tennis lessons? Or was he the psychiatrist with debilitating inertia and a drinking problem? Was he the goddamned man in the moon?

I stopped listening. I could feel the white chips in the room when I moved my arm through the white air, when I moved my hand through the white air to my cup, my white cup. I could feel the hard sides of the cut-away spaces.

"How long has it been?" I asked.

"With Bernard?"

"With my father. Here."

"Almost a month straight up. Why?"

"I'm losing track of time."

Francine seemed to consider the possibility of losing track of time. "You don't look well," she observed. Suddenly she thought of something. Her eyes widened. "Remember when we were young? In Philadelphia? We got to stay home together all day and play. I made up fairy tales for you. I ironed the ribbons on your baby smocks. Can you imagine? Even the little ribbons on the collars? I'd never had a toy before and suddenly I had you. Remember?"

I said yes.

It was as if my mother and I had been children together. We baked and ironed together. We crayoned together. We waited for Daddy to come home together. Francine had a chance to be a child again. No, it was more. Francine had a chance to be a child for the first time.

Francine is leaning over my bed. It is my bedroom in the old gray stone house in Philadelphia. It is winter. Mommy makes me bundle up and put on my blue furry-looking slippers. I must whisper. I mustn't wake up Daddy. He's sleeping. He'd be angry if we woke him up. He would think Mommy was crazy. I pad down the cold wooden hallway behind her, down the wooden stairs to the kitchen. Why do I have to wake up in the middle of the night? "To see the first snow of the year," Mommy says. She is making hot chocolate. But couldn't I see it in the morning? Mommy is shaking her head no. "It won't be the same by morning," Mommy whispers. She explains that by morning the first snow would be scarred by footprints and tire tracks, impure, ruined. We stand at the kitchen window waiting for the birth.

It is raining. I am coloring. I am putting different dresses on my dolls. Daddy is gone. He is busy building houses. It is afternoon. Mommy is working in the kitchen. She calls to me, excited. "Look," she exclaims, pointing out the window. I look. I see only rain. I keep looking. And there it is, in the tree directly in front of our house. A red bird. "It's a robin," Mommy says. And what's the robin doing? "Building a nest," Mommy says. "Someday you'll build a nest," Mommy says. "Watch." I see the robin carrying twigs in his beak and things that look like pieces of string. I am bored. I want to go back to my coloring book. The robin flies back and forth, back and forth. Each time he returns with more twigs, more bits of brownish things. I want to color. My mother says, "Stay here. Watch the bird. See how many times he flies back and forth? Watch him struggle. See how hard it is, how long it takes?" Why do I have to watch this tiny patch of red glistening in the rain, mouth impossibly small for all the bits he somehow finds and somehow brings back again. "It's important," Mommy says. "It's rare." And Mommy and I watch the robin from the window all afternoon, watch until Daddy comes home.

And the wheel spins. And twenty years pass. And I realize that she was right. I have never seen a bird build a nest since. Just that once. Just one rainy afternoon. A robin in Philadelphia.

"Do you remember when we loved fairy tales?" Francine asked.

I looked at her. She was leaning her elbows against the Formica hospital cafeteria tabletop. Her eyes were a pale dreamy yellow.

Mommy gives me a book of fairy tales. The cover of the book is a glistening sunny gold. When I touch the golden cover I feel like a princess in one of the illustrations. Francine is reading a story to me. "Remember this moment," she suddenly says.

I look up, startled. We are sitting under a tree with big thick dark green leaves, leaves that seem heavy, larger than my father's hands.

"If you only remember one pure moment, remember this," Mommy says. She brings her face very close to mine. "I love you. I want you to remember we sat here together and I loved you. I'll help you remember. Watch me."

I watched my mother. A purple and yellow pansy was growing near the sidewalk. Francine picked it. She pressed it gently against my face. "See how it feels like velvet?" she asked. "Look at the sky. See how blue it is? See the leaves? How green they are?" I nodded my head. What was my mother doing?

Francine picked up the purple and yellow pansy. She opened the fairy tale book with its fine golden cover. She placed the flower carefully on the front page. Then she closed the book. When she opened the book again, the flower was pressed into the page, a purplish imprint.

"Whenever you open this book you'll see the flower. You'll remember when we sat under the tree and how much I love you. And this moment will last forever," Mommy said. That was before my father got the first cancer. That was before strangers came and took away her brass lamps and the new china plates. That was before they carted off the sofa and chairs and my mother watched from the porch and wept.

"Was I a good mother?" Francine suddenly asked.

"You were imaginative. Remember when we froze the moment absolutely and took the flower and—"

"It was a pansy. I pressed it inside the fairy tale book you had. It had a gold cover," Francine said. She lit a cigarette. "Do you still have it?"

"Yes."

"I was inventive in my neurotic way, wasn't I? Remember when you had measles? You were sick. You were always sick, right from the beginning. You were burning up with fever. I sat by your bed all day and sewed red spots onto your rag doll. It took eight hours to stitch all the red patches on. I wanted to amuse you." My mother looked at me. Her eyes were like a cat's, a tiger's, a fiery yellow. They looked lit from the inside.

"What went wrong?" Francine asked softly.

I was sitting up very straight in my scooped-out plastic chair. It was essential that I remain calm under all the layers of sharp white light, under the chips and spokes. Yes, of course I knew where I was. In the hospital cafeteria with my mother, drinking coffee, trying to wake up, waiting for something to start kicking, to explode in my bloodstream like a newborn yellow sun. And I want to be warmed, rocked with a secret force and heat swell. I want a shot. It's been days. And, Mommy, my bones feel improperly arranged. They're somehow creased and cold at their centers, deep inside where there once was marrow. And I want the coating of ice to fall off.

After a long time I said, "We grew up."

And it wasn't enough, not nearly. I sat up very straight in my chair. Francine was wondering if she had been a good mother. She wanted to know what she had given me. Was she in the red? The black?

"Did you notice the white-tipped mountains? It's kite season," Francine observed.

And I wanted to be a kite. I wanted to feel alive again, punched open, face wide, heart racing and feet moving, feet really moving again after all the limping and scraping. I wanted to feel my slow thick blood really and finally pumping. I wanted to learn how to breathe at last, how to do more than numbly gasp and force the air into my lungs painfully, out of duty. I wanted more, my cells dancing and assured, throbbing, real. God, I wanted a shot.

"I should go to Aspen," Francine said. "When this is over, we'll go skiing."

I shook my head no. Francine regarded me coldly, oddly. But no, she wasn't really looking at me. She was simply studying the thing that sat near her, the slow huddled cold numb slab, the impersonator.

"You keep sticking it to me." Francine banged her fist against the table. "Jesus. Right from the start. You never stopped crying. You were born trying to scratch out your eyes. They had to tie up your hands in the hospital with special silk mittens. You wouldn't eat right, wouldn't shit right." Francine lit a cigarette. "You refuse what I offer you. Then you act deprived and blame me."

"Come on, Francine. I'm damaged but not an amnesiac," I said. "Generosity isn't your strong suit. You're fueled entirely by guilt."

"But at least I move. You just drag your ass. You're a walking nervous breakdown. Year after year. You introjected my personality minus the guts. Look at your father up there," my mother cried. "That's guts. He's struggling just to live a few more months. You squandered your life." My mother stood up. "You better loosen up. Be eclectic. Get off that edge you're hanging on to. Do you follow me? I mean shit or get off the pot." I watched my mother walk out of the room.

❧ 22 ❧

My father was sitting up in bed. More of his head dressing had
been removed. His eyeglasses fit easily around his ears again.
He looked gray, worn and weary, a granite mountain being
ground down. He was reading the sports page.

THEY MADE ME WALK AGAIN.

"How did you do?"

I TRAILED THE FIELD. NEXT STOP CALIENTE.

"You'll have a long rest, Daddy. Come back fresh."

SAW PTLAND ON TV LAST NITE.

"How was the game?" I felt myself smile. In the beginning
my father had refused to watch television. He said the noise
made him dizzy, made his eyes hurt.

WALTON BEST EVER SAW. WORTH LIVING 4.

We considered this in silence. Francine had pulled the blinds open. It was still morning. I was thinking if I could just take one shot, I could wake up. If I could just have one shot, I would feel the train start to move through me. I could careen wildly down black tracks and stream through gullies, my fists and teeth grinding like engine parts and my body weaving, swaying with the motion, the sudden hard curves. If I could just have one shot my lungs would become steam and my heart would start pumping. The train would begin running through a day gigantic and borderless. My heart would pump painfully, insanely, providing the rhythm, the many sharp wheels. I could reel into noon and bellow down thin tracks, thin black metal grooves like twin rows of tiny black stitches.

If I could just take one shot, I could be riding that train. With one shot, I could be the train. I would wind around a ridge and plunge through a valley. The train. Yes. An express. Yes. A runaway with no one driving. A train that just kept going, going. Silence would be smashed by the black whistle shrill at some indifferent station where moths coughed in an arc of light. I would pass the familiar scattered bits, smoky magnetic ruins in their own riptide. I would glimpse them from the window, partial, drilled with neon, while steam curled like white fingers reaching out of a grave.

BAD SCARS. I LOOK LIKE A CRAZY QUILT.

"We'll find a way to cover them. They won't show when you're dressed."

WILL TELL PEOPLE AM VICTIM OF PLANE CRASH.

"Sure. You could do that," I said.

And I was a train reeling through noon. It was a train from my childhood. There was a train station near our house in Philadelphia. My bedroom windows faced the train station. I had starched yellow curtains. At dusk I would watch men climb the low hill to their houses, newspapers rolled up under their arms. A parade of men returning to make everyone safe and warm.

Our house is gray stone and brick surrounded by a low wire

fence. The Murphys live across the street. Their father is a drunk. Tommy wants to be a priest, he's sixteen. Then there is Teresa, Paul, Billy who talks funny, talks like he ate worms. And Caroline, the youngest, my friend.

Caroline wears a white dress and veil and goes to a different school. I tell Mommy I want a white dress and veil. "No dice," Mommy says. Caroline takes me with her to church. She baptizes my rag doll. We want to be nuns, black-gowned princesses promised to God with his glorious stained-glass eyes and chimes. I am going to name all my dolls after saints. Daddy sends me to bed without supper.

Then I am big in the soft snow, bundled up with a scarf and mittens in the center of the blizzard-sheeted street. The roofs are white, the whittled branches and buried cars. Even the train tracks below the hill are white. I won't let Caroline Murphy hold my doll. She says I stuck nails in God's hands. I tell her Billy talks funny because he eats worms. And Caroline says my father eats stones. She knows. She heard my mother tell her mother that my father had stones inside him, that he went away to get shot at by a big blue gun. His stones were growing like a bucket of big black worms.

It is dusk. We are watching the 5:57 train, impossibly black in the snow, nun black, briefcase-leather black, black as the felt around my father's wide-brimmed winter hat.

I leave Caroline standing alone on the corner. It's cold. The train is my signal, the time I must go home. And I'm running, the ground icy. Daddy has the first cancer then and can't talk or swallow. And Caroline Murphy is six years old. She is about to step off that curb above the train station. She is about to step into the icy dusk street, the world whitish. The truck. And later the driver will say he felt a small bump. He thought he had a flat tire. That's what made him stop.

My father is upstairs. He is lying under piles of covers. Everyone is screaming. Someone is pounding on the big wooden door, shouting, "Where's your girl? Where's your girl?" Mommy wraps me in her arms and rocks me, rocks me. And they are shouting, "There's a run-over girl. Get a blanket. Get a blanket. She's dead."

Daddy comes downstairs. He looks as if he's screaming but he can't talk then, coughs blood, lies under blankets in bed all day. His toolbox is getting dusty. Mommy brings him lunch on a tray and he throws the food down and calls it garbage, garbage. Now he's pulling me close to him, against his old wool bathrobe. He's crying. I never saw Daddy cry before.

Then it's kite season. And something terrible is happening. My bedroom windows faced the train station. I had yellow cotton curtains. Caroline Murphy was dead. Below, the backyard is numb gray. Mommy planned to plant it. Mommy wanted tulips. But something happened.

There were lilac trees on the street, maples, sycamores, elms. The houses were surrounded by low wire fences. And she was bringing Daddy lunch on a tray. I collect clay models and fossils. I study the transformation of a butterfly and think, how is it possible? That big man my father is turning back into a little boy.

"They're lighting candles up and down the street for him," my mother says into the telephone. "The superstitious bastards."

Why is everybody lighting candles? Is it some kind of birthday? Where is my father? Why does she leave me alone all day? And I am dragged screaming to neighbors, the ones who light candles. And where is the birthday cake? The food they eat smells funny and I'm yelling, no, no, I don't want any. I want Mommy and Daddy. They take a box out of the closet. It opens into a little bed. I am given a blanket that scratches. People are sleeping near me, I can hear them breathing. I stare into the night, terrified.

I know I am safe. But when I close my eyes I suddenly think of being beaten, eaten. And terrible things are crawling across the black circle inside my head. Should I tell Mommy? But

Daddy has gone to the hospital. Preparing for the inevitable, she cancels my piano lessons. I stamp my small feet and grow pale, the blood drains and what does it mean? What does it mean?

"Just sit nice and quiet," Mommy says. "Look out the window. Let Daddy try to sleep."

We are riding on a train. It cuts a path to the Pacific. I witness the breathless rage of sunset when the bridges were consumed, the maps and borders. And the train runs in a tight circle powered by atomic fuels, radium and cobalt. Blue jewels, radioactive beams like a stream of blue asters, clusters of blue agapanthus.

And the train is an express. No one is driving. It just keeps going. It is powered by atomic fuels. It can grind its clipped metal wings forever while I ride in my window seat, crisscrossing the childhood I carry with me like stage props in a trunk.

Maple leaves. My sled. My kite. The cool sense of birth before the first snow and Mommy standing me at a window, saying, see it now before the tire scars, see it spread over there, falling in the streetlamp glow, a golden halo, and you are my daughter, my angel. Flowers pulled from the yard of a priest who chased me halfway home in an August of fireflies dying in jam jars. The run-over girl, the stain in the street and my six-year-old heart already shut. I never cried, even though she crossed that dusk street to play with me. There is a train rumbling down thin metal grooves like fine rows of black stitches weaving through the edges of the wound, the contagion of my girlhood. The train is running in a tight circle powered by atomic fuels, radium, cobalt. Blue jewels and pansies pressed between the pages of a book. The train is running in a circle over and over past the hosed-down stain of Caroline Murphy, the red patch in the street, my heart already shut, the strange neighbors, the blankets that scratched, my father spending entire days in bed under woolen blankets in an August of fireflies dying in jam jars.

SAW DR.

"What did he say?" I needed a cigarette. I needed a shot. I was too cold, too hot, half asleep and jammed wide awake. My age was unsolid. The geography unsolid. The world was swaying, decaying.

TOM. TRY 2 EAT.

"They're going to put you on solid foods? The graft must be working, right? He looked under the bandages?"

PINK. NEW SKIN.

"I knew you would make it. Ever since you got up and shadowboxed death." My father looked at me oddly. "Do you remember?"

My father shook his head as if trying to clear it. He shrugged his shoulders, noncommittal.

R THEY SENDING ME HOME 2 DIE? I THINK OPER. WAS FLOP.

"You mean you think the doctors are lying?"

My father nodded his head. Nothing spurted in a red stream from the crevice in his neck. The sunlight was streaming thickly, silkily into the room.

"Do you think you're really dying and they're just jerking you off? Getting the room ready for another stiff? Pretending and hoping for a miracle?"

BINGO.

I wanted a shot. I wanted to feel strong, warm, capable. The day was a set of train tracks. With one shot I could be atomic fueled. I could steam through gullies. I could tunnel dry clutter from Philadelphia to Los Angeles, from Berkeley to Venice, the tight circles of my life, the black tracks like rows of tight new stitches.

My father was staring at me.

"You always said life was a grab bag, a race for cripples, a six-thousand-dollar claimer. But one of them has to cross the finish line. And you know what separates a hero from a bum? An inch. A nose under the wire."

I SAID THAT?

"Yes."

I LIED.

"It doesn't matter. The thing that matters is that you pulled it. The inside straight. You're going to live."

I HATE YOUR CARD METAPHORS. INACCURATE.

"You get the idea, though?" I could feel something beginning. It had power and warmth. I was pacing, staring out the window down to the lawn covered by lacy white flowers. It could have been a snowdrift. The hills to the north and east were snow-capped. It was the kind of day when one could consider the possibility of resurrecting the dead. All the dead. And if I counted Picasso as the first and the old man with the mandolin as the second, who would be third? My father? But what if I counted Caroline Murphy as the first? Then Picasso would be the second. Then Mr. Gordon would be the third and that would be enough.

U LOOK SICK.

"I've been sick, very sick. But I'm starting to get better."

TALK ABOUT SICK. SAW YOUR MOTHER THIS A.M.

"What happened?"

THOUGHT AFTER 20 YRS W/CANCER NEED SILVER STAKE 2 STOP ME. WAS WRONG. FRANCINE WORSE THAN CANCER.

It was an old joke. No matter what he was talking about— inflation, Dodger hitting, the county fair cripples they sent down for the Del Mar meet—Francine was worse. I took a deep breath.

"Daddy, I know you're going to live. You'll go home." Back to your perpetually balding ivy, your fruit trees, your patch of pastel sanity in the soft pinkish heart of West Los Angeles. "The doctor said you can drive your car. He said you might even talk again. But I've got to leave for a while."

U WANT 2 SPLIT NOW???

My father wrote the note quickly. It was a black scrawl. It was a kind of black track in white snow. And if I counted Caroline Murphy as the first and Picasso as the second, then Mr. Gordon would be the third and it would be over.

I stared at my father's note. I didn't say anything.

BAD TIMING DONT U THINK??

I nodded my head in agreement. And when was it ever the right moment to leave a father?

My father looked down at the floor. There were sun patterns now, spokes of sharp light, a kind of shadowy knife.

I looked at the man in the bed. I was the daughter. We formed a chain. We were letters in the original alphabet. In the beginning there was A as in Adam. A man. In the beginning there was man. He was given Eve later, an afterthought. And everything she did was wrong. She stumbled out the rib cradle wrong. She had an affinity for the forbidden. And she became rage and red, autumnal and partial as an x-ray. She became a dream thing and evil. She sang on rocks and made ships crash. Woman. I am not whole, never whole. The one with the hole. I am the daughter. And when is it ever a good time to leave a father?

DONT LEAVE ME NOW.

I walked to the window. I could see the red roofs of houses stuck like rows of red steps across the hills. It was the yawning mouth of spring, fists of red hibiscus, the sun punched open above ripening lemons. On the lawn below, white flowers were lacy, intricate, crocheted.

A nurse entered the room. She told my father it was time for his walk. I draped his bathrobe across his shoulders. He took small broken steps. His legs were weak, rubbery.

I matched his steps. Suddenly I thought of women hobbling on ruined feet. In China they bound the feet of women. It was the custom there for a millennium, quite a lasting tradition. At age three the soft girl flesh was sealed in special sheets. How they stank in summer! A necessary preparation for the woman stink later. The nights were torn by girl children screaming in their sleep as the bones caved in, as the flesh decayed, as the toes fell off.

The mother stumbling on her crippled stumps cautioned at

the crib be thankful the earth coughed crops that year or you would have been drowned. You must be tamed, carried on a litter like a trophy that breathes. You cannot trust her. The forests are filled with madwomen hiding in caves, eating grasshoppers and howling.

My father was leaning against my shoulder. He was gasping for breath. Sweat had broken out across his forehead. His knees were trembling. And what the hell was I mad about, mad about?

His face was flushed red with strain. We had walked halfway down the corridor. The nurse helped my father turn around. We began walking back.

I wanted to explain to my father that one day I had accidentally limped to a window. I saw the road below filled with refugees. It surprised at first, the sheer number of women hobbling. They were selling everything. The linen hooks. The porcelain hooks. The checkbook and children hooks. All the hard evidence, Daddy. They were chewing off their ankle chains with their teeth. They were willing to chew off their feet. Understand, Daddy. The women have been to the quarry. And scraped the mountain clean.

I helped my father back into his bed. He reached for his writing pad.

WHERE WILL U GO?

"I don't know, Daddy," I said. I thought of the white tequila sun to the south, creamy and stinging. Sun of the permanent noon and warm harbors, fish smell and gull shriek thickening into jungle and sky under green vines, a crawling grid. I will be windswept, windsong, wingborne, reborn and tossing starsick into shimmering yearning of new, of clean. I will be windchime, sublime in the struggle away from drumbell of loss, loss and pierce into the other, the greater.

"You spent years on the road, Daddy. You know how it works. Things happen." If you are without anchor, the wind matters.

If you are naked, implements of survival appear. Logs will float and stretched skins will catch the winds. I will invent fire, clans, names, boundaries.

My father's eyes had darkened. He lay back on his pillow, lay very still. He was gray. He was granite. He was the father, fundamental, the beginning. He was the dealer. He was the house. He made it all happen. He struck the first match and the world blazed and spun in circles around his great yellow eye, the sun.

HOW WILL U TAKE CARE OF YOURSELF?

"I'll trust the intangibles. The most important thing is balancing class and condition. I'll check times against tracks. I'll remember California tracks are always fast and cripples run six in one ten and change. Look for Kentucky breds, weight shifts, bandaged horses, hot jocks, the obvious. Try to differentiate between honest and artificial class slips. Remember it's always hard moving up. Check the past works but don't rely on them. They only run as fast as they have to." I looked at my father. "I'm going to try to go the distance."

U HAVENT SHOWED MUCH FORM. U R ERRATIC. CANT FIND THE WIRE.

"Condition has been a problem. I haven't been in good shape."

FACE IT. U R A CONFIRMED QUITTER.

"There have been some equipment changes. I'm racing without blinders. I've been away a long time. I'm fresh. And I'm carrying much less weight, Daddy. I'm an overlay."

LIFES GONE SO BAD. U. FRANCINE.

My father seemed to sigh. He was granite. He was the mountain with rocks falling down. He was lessening, chipped. Then he began to cry.

"What do you want?" I asked, my voice soft, a mere rustle.

I handed my father his pad. His pen had fallen to the gray enamel floor. I picked it up. I was his issue, both more and less

than chattel. I was his necessity, his step into unborn generations, the first rung on the ladder to the millennium. I was the
moment forced into form, the passion of his manhood, an intrinsic and overwhelming measurement.

WANT IT ALL BACK. YOUTH. DREAMS. CIGARS. WOMEN.
HORSES. START OVER.

"Doesn't everybody?" I asked. I realized that I did. Maybe
everyone wanted it all back. Maybe the only difference was
that a few really had a chance. And maybe once someone
realized that, it gave a certain edge. I am twenty-seven
years old and a pine tree my age knows more. Still, with
some equipment changes, the blinders off, the long rest, and
a lot less weight . . .

I walked down the corridor. I didn't look into the room where
they kept the morphine. I didn't look into the little green cubicles with their newly made beds, their empty nightstands, their
hunger to kill. That didn't matter anymore, either. I didn't look
to the side or behind me. I just kept going toward the sunlight.
There were a few last-minute details.

❧ 23 ❧

I stood near the bridge over Eastern Canal. I was thinking if I
stood there long enough, my entire life would drift by. The toys
from childhood would pop up, pulled by a slow tugging current.
Miniature pie tins and starched pink smocks with the ribbons
at the collar Mommy always ironed. Roller skates and sled. And
peaches eaten at seven in a Philadelphia August, wet and hot
and Daddy upstairs in bed coughing red stuff and shivering
under woolen blankets. Brass lamps and new china plates strangers took away from Mommy. And what's that sodden mass of
cotton? My rag doll, the one Mommy sewed red spots on when
I had measles. And look, there they are. Near the light green,
lime green algae, there near the shadowy bridge spokes brush-

ing beer cans and big black and brown ducks. All is returned, returned.

I looked across the canal. Spring was an undeniable eruption. I felt a sudden clarity. A light wind nipped at new branches, tasted buds, pronounced them in order and moved on, moved on. Yards exploded with pink lilies, stalks of lust and perfect tongues repeated in the water. And clusters of agapanthus, bushy-faced carnations, crepe-thin poppies, new strawberries crawling slow and pink on threadlike vines. A hummingbird churning in place, treading the air forever. Sunflowers nodded swollen balloon heads. And I wanted to shout, hey, sunflowers, your intensity has driven you mad. Your greed for sun, sun has poisoned you, gutted your brain, and you are insane now. Your unborn generations will be insane. And you will recede back into the earth. You will end as tubers, in hell, the sky sealed.

I could watch my childhood drift by in the dreamy yellow water. I could talk to sunflowers. But what could I say to Jason?

Listen.

There are possibilities. You say it's all a matter of shape and color. You could paint anywhere. Come with me. Be airborne, windsong, starwarmed. Let's get out of here. Venice, the canals, this city, boulevards, billboards, noise, dead ends, temptation, isolation and ruin intense and abominable. The madmen in their stucco burrows. The madmen on the boardwalk under the lame sun, that deranged turkey falling plop into the god-damned dying ocean. Can you remember when the bay still breathed fish? Before they tacked the Contaminated signs to the pier? Before they embroidered the Contaminated signs across our flesh? Once we had arms that moved surely and without blood grooves, without snakeskin imprints across our skin. And, Jason, can't you hear that strange hissing? Listen. It is the sound of an interminable sinking in. It is the long white siesta of a race. And this whole place is a terminal ward.

Listen.

I'm tired of being Scheherazade at 5 A.M. This is my last story.

Once upon a time there was a woman. Not a woman, really. A suggestion of woman, an approximation. I lived as a tree in winter, branches whittled and half asleep, willing to merely endure. My life was a perpetual 4 P.M. in a cold February. I was not yet blessed with coral orchid eyes and sea bells. I knew nothing of sailing past reefs on the sea's ribs, the sea's steel-girded spine, though I longed for this.

I was by madness wooed. I pretended there was a mystery. I called myself an explorer. It gave me the illusion of purpose and movement. I lived on the banks of a swollen river. I could watch the restless water inch closer. I piled sandbags in neat little rows. It gave me something to do. It even seemed important.

You took my girlhood as simply as one lifts back a sheet, revealing the naked longing and inadequacy. There wasn't much to take. But you took it. I accepted this. I thought birth is historically a scream, a curse, a burst of blood and the long torture of sun and solitude. And you taught me. I tunneled parched ground while winds howled and stars scratched my face before the first intimation of jade banks erupting with shade trees. In a way you made me strong. The clay began to breathe. I didn't mind being a prop. I lacked all reference points. You were a kind of compass. I learned which way led down. I learned which way broke. Understand. It is not without a certain gratitude I wish you slowly drawn and quartered.

Listen.

I understand your compulsive whittling of our life, your secret dog teeth, fear of your unknown wolf blood and your love of taking night alone like a test of strength, grace between the demonic black waves. But you will regret this. My eyes are crystal shells now and I see you as you will be, mistakes repeated. The dream part, that underbelly of invention, will dry without residue. You will be left with remnants to sift, details, objects. The hard evidence without context will prove inadequate. You will suffer. You will remember when we were black-winged through blazing dark concrete concentric whirlpools, ecstasies of spring night excesses and dancing spontaneous and naked. It will be rubble.

I stood on the bridge over Eastern Canal for a long time. Then I walked to Jason's studio.

Jason was sitting at the table my father gave me. His small boy's body was pale. It glistened like a certain kind of enamel. It occurred to me that the entire world was beginning to look like the underbelly of an abalone shell, a glazed white and turquoise. Blue and white. The sky with clouds. The waves with whitecaps now permanently embossed across their backs.

Jason was tying up his arm. And you know right away if you've hit it. Blood jumps in the needle. You let the tie drop. Halfway in and you know. You smell sweet Martian wind dancing in your ribs, behind your new plum-colored eyes. You sigh and it is moss smooth, glacier cooled. You walk on the moon as she once was young, green right to the feet of her slow lapping amber oceans. Her yellow tongues. Her just pushed up cliffs are soft under your feet. A wind unfurls. The air steams with jasmine, bewitched. The ground is moss and ferns. And you are the grand ecologist. Planet builder, what will you have? Thunder and volcanoes? A flock of singing sea birds? And icebergs, a blue-white? And always day? Or always night? Here. Take a canopy of lights, the night scalped, a kind of gauze.

Then you are memorizing the linoleum tiles. The rest is mechanical, is merely survival. Watch for air bubbles, take out the needle. You are beyond standard divisions. You wear a cosmic surgery, cloud skin. You whirl the black gulfs, the black grooves where planets come to feed.

Jason offered the needle to me.

I turned my head away. "I've quit."

"How long?" Jason asked. He was running alcohol through his needle.

"A couple of days." Was it? I stood in the deserted morphine room. Nurses scurried with their lunch trays. I held the bottles in my hand. Then I put the bottles back.

"You shake and sweat? Do you have to fight the temptation constantly?" Jason asked. He might have been taking a census.

"It's not as hard as it was," I said. Not hard compared to this kite season of private burials. My girlhood fossils stripped and packed into boxes. My father. My rooms breathless, sensing death. My plants in the backyard dropping leaves like severed fists. The trail of my sins.

"You take a bath yet today?" Jason asked.

I shook my head no. Outside it was late afternoon. Branches were waving, swaying sunlocked and enchanted.

"Good," Jason said. "Come sit on my face."

I followed him into the bedroom. I touched his shoulder lightly, the way one might touch a statue in a museum, guards watching. Jason, my rare one, skin white as porcelain. You must be kept absolutely protected, encased in a kind of glass. You are yourself the work of art. Rare as a robin building a nest in rain. Something I saw only once, will probably never see again. You are beautiful. But so expensive. And it's survival time now. I can't afford you anymore. I'm going the distance. I've got to carry less weight.

"Jason, I'm bored by my contempt for you. My rage has scraped itself thin." Thin as a gutted throat, my friend. Thin as my father's sculpted hands, gray scab of the IV and bones poking through. "I want something else."

"You always want something else. That's your theme." Jason looked at the ceiling.

I memorized the bones in his ribs, the curly reddish hairs on his thighs that seemed to be reaching out for something. Fragile man, emotional hemophiliac, too rare and delicate for this world. You must remain as you are, encased and oddly protected and exaggerated, exaggerated.

"I'm leaving."

Jason leaned on one elbow. Skin pale as porcelain. A kind of statue. The last piece of hard evidence. He lit a cigarette. "I thought those boxes were significant. You folded things. It wasn't like you." Jason stared at me. "Isn't this sudden?"

"I've been packed for weeks. My father has cancer. But he's going to make it. By the way, I killed Picasso. I strangled him on the boardwalk. The waves buried him. It was a rite of propitiation. If you had come back that night, I might have killed you."

"You better slow down," Jason said. He sat up.

"I'm just beginning." I walked to the door feeling absolutely sober and thinking, it's possible to start over. A few equipment changes, no blinders, no bandages, a lot less weight. It's possible. And madness is a storm like any other. It passes.

"You're strung out," Jason observed, somewhere behind me.

I was standing in his front room. His new paintings were hung on the walls. Floors disappeared into a tapestry of purple and yellow threads. Patches of skin were swallowed by patterns within shadows, their own dimension. The shadows looked as if they were moving, a kind of moth feeding, eating something at the edges. I heard the water in the fountain falling lazy, drunkenly, while goldfish flashed their fins, a series of swift orange fans, behind me.

"You'll never make it," Jason shouted.

I stood on his porch thinking, I have been loved by a madman. I am twenty-seven years old and know the best has already been. Then I closed the door behind me.

I zigzagged a path to my house. The Woman's House. A duck swam below me, slow but purposeful. A gull shrieked and rushed back to the sea. Soon the peninsula would be a slow floating seal, enormous and dark. Soon the sky would lay a pink claw across the land, the corally gray sand. And madness is a storm like any other. It passes.

The sea breeze grew stronger. And wasn't it talking? Wasn't it saying, go, go. We are with you. We are your arms, your fuel.

Go. Go. We are your sails, your current. If you decide to swim, we will be your gills.

I sensed the breeze tearing at the house like a chorus of voices, women's voices. Women with kerchiefs chattering at a stream while they pounded clothing clean against rocks. A chorus in Polish and Yiddish. A stream of klulles, of dark winding curses. But no. They are smiling. They are saying, go, go. Do what we would have done had we known the world was round, had we known it possible, had we maps, the power of navigation, a few equipment changes, hope and the key to the ball and chain.

It was night. I turned on the kitchen light. I found a pad of paper and a pen.

Early Spring

Dear Rachel,

There is much to say and time is a cymbal crashing. And time is a disk of brass banged periodically and forgotten. When we realize it's getting late, it's almost over.

I must tell you about our grandmother's apartment. It bears the ruin of unrepaired living, of paint that peels, of streaked windows, stains from faulty plumbing. All of this, yes. But within her limits she keeps her two small rooms spotless, immaculate. Everything is polished. Her imitation cut crystal ashtrays perch on her always waxed secondhand tables. Her bright bouquets of plastic flowers are dusted. Her threadbare rugs are vacuumed. From the front door I smelled a faint trace of ammonia.

One entire wall of her living room is covered with memorabilia concerning us. She has tacked to the plaster the announcements our mothers sent of their marriages. She has tacked newspaper clippings she chanced to find about our mothers, yellowing slices of their careers. All the bits and pieces that have somehow drifted toward her across the decades. One Mother's Day card, a bright red heart such as a child might make, hangs in the center of the wall surrounded by the announcements of my birth and yours.

A calendar with the dates of importance in our lives marked with black crayon is taped to her front door. A black X.

She explained that when she sees the day of a birth or an

anniversary approaching, she takes the bus to a department store. She shoplifts a gift for us. It is the only time she ever steals.

And time is a cymbal crashing, crashing. When we realize we are mortal, we are already old. When we realize it is getting late, it's nearly over.

The first thing Grandmother Rose did was give me my gifts. I noticed the piles of oddly wrapped objects stacked along the wall beneath the child's red heart. The paper heart was a kind of eye in the wall and the wrapped stack of gifts a kind of altar. There were four such stacks.

I cannot really call the gifts wrapped. You must understand that she stole these things. Often she simply tucked them away in strips of old newspaper with string tied in a bow around them. I sat at her tiny kitchen table and began unwrapping my gifts. They were stacked in order. I began with my baby gifts, a silk hat lined with lace ruffles, a pair of infant's sky-blue mittens, a pink starched-looking cotton pinafore.

I was sitting at the table in her tiny kitchen, in the same kitchen where our mothers sat when they came on subways from the orphanage on Sundays and showed her geography in books of maps they stole from libraries for her. I opened each gift slowly. A little girl's change purse, a compact with my initials carved on the glittery surface, a scarf with bluish flowers stamped onto the cheap cotton and an apron imprinted with strawberries and daisies that looked somehow fresh, impossibly sunny.

My fingers began to feel haunted. Everything I touched smelled of her, smelled somehow pink and perfumed and broken. And I know even now, completely crippled, when she notices the approach of a birthday she will manage to climb down her six steep flights of stairs and make her painful way to a department store to grab a scarf or compact. And if it is a good day, without ice or rain or wind, she will stop in a dime store and buy a sheet of birthday wrapping paper. Then the new object will join the others in one of the four waiting stacks.

I saw twenty years of birthdays on the table in front of me. A progression, a chronology, a complete history from infancy through girlhood, womanhood. The later gifts were tokens for a house. Place mats with dancing yellow flowers and matching napkins, potholders, a ladle with a long wooden handle. "For your house," Grandmother Rose said. "For your husband?"

We sat in silence after the opening of the gifts. She explained that the other gifts were for her daughters and you. And I breathed in her smell, something pink and somehow broken and tinged with ammonia.

"I have more things for you," Grandmother Rose said.

Night fell like a black fist. Even the sky seemed to be holding its breath. She sat near me, hunched up, yes, and almost blind, with a cane. I had a sense of something black dancing in her eyes. And I was afraid.

I started to speak. "Not yet," she cautioned. And I sat in my assigned seat in her tiny kitchen watching the darkness thickening in the room and waiting, my pile of gifts on the table in front of me and an aroma of grief radiating from the cotton threads of apron and potholders and kerchiefs.

But I was impatient. I wanted to ask her about the farm, the village in Poland, the Cossacks, her sea journey to America. I wanted to ask her about our mothers and the orphanage, the foster homes. I wanted my history all nice and complete, a series of answers filled in like the openings left in certain questionnaires, dates and places clearly designated, a matter of checking the appropriate boxes. I wanted the map colored in. Did I tell you I wanted warm-from-the-oven butter cookies in round printed tins?

The darkness spread like a wound in soft flesh. After a while she let me babble, let me ramble about what grew on the farm in Poland and did she pull water from a well and how did that city New York first seem to her startled eyes fifty years ago?

Suddenly she flicked on the light switch. For an old bent woman she moved with astonishing speed. She reached easily across the table to the wall and flicked on the light to cockroaches. Everywhere. Cockroaches crawling across her kitchen walls, hopping across the bread and sugar in their shined and polished tin containers.

I screamed. I tried to leave the room, the walls of curling black roach legs, curling red roach legs, waves of roaches, a sea of sickening insects making their tiny insect sounds, sounds like distant stars slowly sizzling and sinking in their own terrible bloated heat.

Grandmother Rose gripped my wrist. "Look," she commanded. Her voice was powerful and full as the imperatives shouted by the dead. "See them dance?" She smiled at the black walls. "All these years," she sighed. "My only friends. All these years when no one comes to see me. No one." She stared at me. "You wanted to know," she said softly. There was something sharp and cunning in her voice. "They say I'm crazy. They're afraid of me. But you came. You knew I had secrets. But you wanted to know about the farm. The times I carried the trays. The afternoons when the little girls came and sat here with me."

"Please let me go," I screamed.

My grandmother looked at me. She shook her head from side to side, sadly. "So afraid," she observed. "You're so afraid."

A cockroach crawled across my arm, the arm my grandmother was holding. She studied me. "See them dancing?" She was staring at the walls, measuring something. "The stragglers," she sighed. "The frightened black ones? The babies? See how they play, my little friends?"

I was still screaming. "You wanted to know about my life," she said again. She threw back her head and laughed. Then she let go of my arm.

I ran out through the living room, past the three stacks of wrapped gifts, past the calendar, the red paper heart and the altar. I ran into the dark tiled corridor where drums were beating behind closed doors and radios were blaring and her voice was ricocheting somewhere behind me like a bullet. "They dance," she was screaming. "Remember this."

Her voice followed me as I ran down the steep stairs. Her voice bounced and echoed across the tiles in some horrible and final benediction.

Rachel, I'm telling you this because I left my gifts there on the table in her kitchen. The same kitchen where our mothers came on the subway from the orphanage on Sundays and helped her trace the exact route from Krakow to New York while she studied the map and cursed half the world. I left my gifts there and I have always regretted it.

Time is a cymbal crashing, crashing. I'm sorry but I won't be able to write to you for a while. In part I am afraid you will one day tell me of becoming a college student, of discotheques and boys with beer and grass. I'm afraid you might develop a fascination for the succession of European kings, border disputes in the fifteenth century, Middle English or Mayan art. They all mean something. It just isn't enough. Not nearly.

There are crevices in the mural that is the world. There are moments when the individual times/time/cells open suddenly. Those are the moments that matter. When I sat with our grandmother in her kitchen and she suddenly flicked on the light switch, that was such a moment. If I could do it again, I would do it differently.

I am enclosing our grandmother's address.

May we both find fair winds and safe harbors.

I folded the letter into an envelope. What was left? Sofas and chairs? They were simply shells, substance removed, anonymous. Jason could keep them. After all, I hadn't even given him two weeks notice.

♜ 24 ♜

I drove north on the Pacific Coast Highway to Sunset Boulevard. It was the longer route. Waves beat their black backs below me, below the gouged rubble of coastal cliffs, those slow-falling terminal victims of windlash and mud slides. The cliffs would feed the sea in time, in time. The night was dark, clear and sharp. I wasn't in a hurry.

I followed Sunset Boulevard inland where it curved itself between hills and sudden gullies. I felt the sea beating behind me, waves curling on shore and withdrawing, waves clawing at the shore and leaking out spent. Crash and foamy silence. Crash and sudden silence. And if Caroline Murphy was the first and Picasso the second, the old man with the mandolin, wood reddish and fine like a stretched heart, was the third and it was enough. It was over.

I took the cardboard boxes out of my trunk, one by one. Francine took a long time to answer the door. She did a double take.

"It's after midnight." She pulled the folds of dark green silk close to her neck. She stared at the cardboard boxes as I dragged them through the living room.

A stiff-looking balding man sat on the tufted tan living room sofa. He was buttoning his shirt as I walked in. He tried not to look at me, tried to somehow disappear, blend in with the oyster grays and eggshell whites. He reached onto the wide cocktail table and picked up a glass. He held it tightly in his hand and stared into it as if trying to connect to something. I walked past him, pulling the boxes with me.

"Make it quick," Francine whispered. "What's wrong? Not your father?"

"No."

"Because I just called the hospital. They've taken him off the critical list. It's going to be like the other time, at Jefferson Hospital. You wouldn't remember. You were only three."

"I was six."

"Not so loud," Francine said quickly. "Anyway, he got better so fast last time. He used to grab the head nurse. He pinched her ass every time she walked in. They barred him from the hospital. They said no matter what ever happened, he could never be admitted to Jefferson Hospital again."

We were sitting in my mother's bedroom. The walls were tan. The lamplight made everything seem rose-tinged. The door was closed.

"Well?" Francine studied me out of the corner of her eye. She lit a cigarette. She placed her hands on her hips, graceful, formidable.

"I need money."

"Tell me something I don't already know."

Francine seemed relieved. Maybe it was something that could be handled simply, quickly. She had put in a big day. The hospital in the morning. A lunch conference. A budget session. There was the stiff balding man downstairs. And now me, still eight years old and helpless, afraid of everything, the thick slats of palm trees, the huge gouged sun, my afternoons alone.

My mother opened a drawer. She removed an envelope and sifted through a green stack. She extended a fifty-dollar bill in my direction. It was new and crisp. It made a small snapping sound between her fingers.

"I need more."

"How much more?" Francine looked as if she was starting to sober up.

"What am I worth?" I opened my purse. It appeared that we were going to play seven stud high. I extracted items from my pocketbook. It was my bet. "Here's the ring, the bracelets and the stock."

"What stock?"

"The Disney you coughed up when I married Gerald. The ring is five grand. I had it appraised," I said. I was holding the jewelry and stock certificates out to her. I felt good. A picture card.

"What am I? A bank? A pawnshop?" Francine was getting nervous. You had to bet your hand. I was high. And I had an ace in the hole.

The man coughed somewhere downstairs. A polite cough. Francine glanced at the door. I could sympathize with her. Her parallel worlds were colliding.

"Get rid of him," I suggested. I was high. Was she going to see me? It was her turn.

"He had a horrible flight from Atlanta. He came back and his house was burglarized. They even took the balls from the tennis court. He just got here. He's got a heart condition. He's going to Tokyo tomorrow." Francine stared at me, trying to read between the lines. Trying to check. Trying to buy time. Bluffing?

Was she going to throw in a chip or not?

"Could we talk then? Tomorrow? You could spend the whole day with me. I'll take you out for lunch."

"Put that asshole in a cab, Francine. He only feels comfortable in airports, anyway." I was still high. It was my bet. I tossed in a chip. "Get rid of that turkey before I give him a stroke."

Francine studied me in the pink lamplight. She lit another cigarette. Then she picked up the telephone and called a cab. The man left. So she was going to see me after all. She must have something in the hole, too.

I followed Francine into her den. She poured herself a shot of Scotch. I poured myself a glass of Scotch. We sat on low round cream-colored chairs facing one another. Were we going to put our cards on the table?

"What do you need money for?"

"I'm pregnant," I said and regretted it. A bad lie. The first thing that came to mind. But it didn't matter. I had a pair of aces underneath. Twin aces.

"Abortion?" Francine tilted her head. She looked as if she was sniffing the air. "That's a cheap item. Go to the Free Clinic. Tell them you're a hippie. Get the state to pick up the tab."

I said no.

"You're not pregnant," Francine said suddenly, accurately deciphering the air between us. She looked from my face to the cardboard boxes in the living room. "You're running," Francine realized. She seemed to relax. She was getting a lay of the land, all right. She was beginning to feel better about her hand. She might even toss in another chip. See me and raise.

"I'm running," I admitted. I had the ring, the stock, the cardboard boxes. I threw in another imaginary chip.

"You can't. What about your father? He needs you. He's dying."

"He's not dying," I yelled. I stood up. The round glass and

chrome table was between us. "Look at me, Mother. Concentrate. Pretend I have a cock, Mother. Pretend what I say is important. I'm telling you, he's not dying."

"I talked to the doctors, to specialists. You don't understand. The prognosis is—"

"Fuck the prognosis. What do they know?" I lit a cigarette. Why did Francine think she had a high hand? Was she raising on the prognosis?

"O.K.," Francine said. "O.K. But we need you. I'm lonely, don't you realize that? I'm terrified. And Father needs you. You owe him," she said, tossing in a big chip. A big black five-hundred-dollar number.

"No I don't," I said evenly, seeing her and throwing in another chip. A black one. "Daddy and I are even."

Francine scrambled. "We need some time to think. You want money and arrangements can be—"

"Don't jerk me off," I shouted. "I'm desperate." I was still standing up. I sat down.

Francine was staring at me through wide yellowish eyes. Her lower lip trembled. "I'm the desperate one," she said. "The old man is dying. I'll be all alone. You can't abandon me. You are the child of my longing, my hopes, my passion. I have no grandchildren. I'll have nothing," she said. Somewhere she tossed in another chip.

The pot was getting bigger. I began to wonder what we were really playing for.

"I'll be alone," Francine gasped. "I'll die," she assured me. "It's like when I was an orphan. It's like the time the mice fell on my head. Did you know they sicked a dog on me? A German shepherd? They were Irish, I remember. It was summer. The dog took a chunk out of my leg. I was only five when it happened. I needed nineteen stitches. Look." Francine pulled her silk bathrobe apart. There was a faint white circle engraved into her thigh. "I'll be alone." My mother began to cry.

"But you're not alone. You have your sister," I said, seeing her. My mother made an ugly face, as if she had just eaten something foul. Human flesh, perhaps. Was I still high? I took a deep breath.

"You have your own mother," I said carefully. It was my ace in the hole. I had the stuff. I knew I was going to win.

Francine jumped out of her chair. She seemed to leap up effortlessly. Could she defy gravity? "My mother?" she repeated. "You call that creature who abandoned me a mother?"

"But she's still alive!" What the hell was wrong? Didn't Francine see the ace, the pair of aces? "You knew her in childhood. She's still there in the same apartment. She refuses to move. She wants to stay there so you'll always know where she is if you need her. She has presents for you, Mommy."

I looked straight at my mother. I had a pair of aces. I searched her face. Francine didn't even blink.

"You knew," I realized slowly. "And your half-sisters and brothers all over the fucking country?"

Francine didn't say anything. The silence seemed to last a long time.

"Of course, you must have known. Always," I said.

Silence. So she had two aces underneath, too. I glanced at my mother. She was staring out the plate-glass window at the brick terrace jammed against the mountain, at a pine tree perched on the hill and sending spokes of black shadow into the darkness. Somewhere I threw in an imaginary chip. I had to call, even though I knew she had me beat.

"It was a million-to-one shot," Francine began. "A man comes up to me at the Regency. I'm eating breakfast. It's a business trip. I'm in a hurry. He says I look exactly like a woman he knows. Do I have a sister? And I realize he's not trying to hustle me. His wife is standing next to him. And I say I have a twin in Maine. And the man says no. The woman he's talking about lives in Seattle. I gave him a business card and the woman calls me. We started talking and bingo." Francine looked at me, looked into me. "Should I have told you?"

I thought about it. "No. It's O.K. You win. I give up."

"You can't do that."

"I already have. Just cash me in," I screamed.

Suddenly Francine sprung awake. She was on her feet. She was moving. "There's so much you don't know," she yelled. She grabbed the cut-crystal vase from the round table and threw it into the plate-glass window. The window seemed to shatter in slow motion, the glass soft and feathered, a flock of yellow birds. I noticed a long splinter of glass had fallen near my ankle. It stuck up from the carpet like a dagger.

"Do you think this crap means anything to me?" Francine demanded. She brought her face very close to mine. Her eyes were enormous, stormy, dangerous. "It's illusionary. Don't you think I know that?"

"Stop it," I yelled. I stood up. I didn't know what to do.

Francine was hurling whiskey bottles from the bar with the imported black marble surface against her tan and cream walls. The bottles broke and left ugly stains, like urine on alley walls. That's when I noticed the blood. Her foot was cut. She began hopping through the den, screaming, "It's nothing," her bleeding foot curled in the air.

I reached out for her but she hopped past me, hopped to the cardboard boxes I had brought with me. She grabbed a glass-framed poster from a painting exhibit in Rome and hurled it against the wall. It shattered.

"You wouldn't go into the world," Francine cried. "So I tried to bring the world to you."

A hand-painted vase from Barcelona broke. A delicate statue of a little girl combing her hair hit the wall. Decapitated.

Then as suddenly as it began, it stopped. Francine fell to the floor. She put her head into the crook of her left arm, the arm that can still bend, and wept, sobbed, her shoulders shaking. I wrapped a towel around the gash in her foot. I patted her head gently. "It's O.K., baby," I said over and over. "It's going to be O.K., baby." Her hair looked red in the lamplight. After a long time she lifted her head.

"I've made mistakes," Francine began. "Monumental mistakes. I was just reading the Harlow experiments. The deprived monkeys. They gave them surrogate wire mothers. Just like foster parents. And when the monkeys reached maturity they couldn't function." Francine looked at me with wide orbs of yellow eyes. "Do you think the Harlow experiments would have a wide popular appeal?"

I thought about it. I said no.

I helped my mother weave a path through the glass splinters back to the den. She finished her Scotch and poured another. I finished mine and poured another. I looked at the cut on her foot. I put a piece of gauze and adhesive tape around it.

"I broke my arm when I was six. It was the year after the dog bit off a mouthful of my thigh. I slipped on ice and they wouldn't take me to get it set. My arm doesn't bend. That's why I'm such a shitty tennis player," Francine said.

My mother finished her drink. I finished mine. I poured us both another.

"Remember when we snuck down the stairs in Philadelphia and I showed you the first snow of the year, before it got damaged?"

"I remember. It was beautiful. We drank hot chocolate."

"Chivas is better."

"Yes."

"You've never spent the night here before," Francine said. She seemed to search the air for something. "Are you really leaving Jason?"

"Yes."

"Good. Are you going to see your father first? Make sure the throat job works?"

"Yes," I said. "But I know it will work."

"You think I'm looking for a man?" Francine suddenly asked.

She seemed to be evaluating a pinkish slice of shadow near the light creamy wall. "I'm not. I know everything about men. I've known since I was eleven." Francine took a sip of Scotch. "I'm not looking for a man. I just try to keep busy. I keep punching. The bell rings and I get back in the ring swinging. I'm punch-drunk. But I'm not expecting anything from a man." Francine smiled. Her eyes looked lit from the inside the way they had when she told me she knew all along that the mice were in her room, in the sewing machine and ceiling. "Men always break in the end," Francine said. She was staring at me. "May I comb your hair? Like when you were a little girl and we used to play together all day?"

I said yes. My mother found a hairbrush. She hopped over to me. She knelt on the floor and began brushing my long tangled hair.

"I used to brush your hair when you were little," my mother told me. She brought her face very close to mine. "I put ribbons in your hair. I had a drawer of different-colored ribbons. I liked to make your ribbons and socks match."

I thanked my mother for combing my hair then, when I was an infant and when I was a girl, and now. Terminal now. Outside the night was deep, a solid black without a trace of dawn in it.

"You don't leave a mother in the middle of the night," Francine said. "That's how I left the foster homes. Just disappeared. But you don't leave a real mother that way. Not a mother who put the right-colored ribbons in your hair. You don't leave a real mother in the middle of the night, do you?"

I said no. I finished my Scotch. Francine poured me another. The gash on her foot had stopped bleeding.

"I can't go on," I said finally.

"I know. I'm exactly the same as you. There are no boundaries between us. It's just that I've gone through it more often." She was looking at the arc of pink light pushing into the night.

"Inside I'm unchanged. Your father loved me once. You loved me once. But despite it all, the core of who and what I am remains unchanged. The only time I was allowed in a kitchen was to clean it. If I wanted a glass of water I had to go to the bathroom and I was afraid of the men, the fathers, the uncles sleeping over drunk." Francine looked at me. What was she looking for? She refilled our glasses.

"Every time I went to a new foster home I changed my identity. You never knew when they were coming for you. A social worker would just appear and you'd pack your suitcase and be driven to a new foster home, a new school. I would pretend I had just arrived from Wyoming. Can you imagine? Wyoming?" Francine laughed. She touched my arm with her hand.

"Your father said I was too damaged to have a child. He was wrong, wasn't he?"

"Yes, Mommy." I held her hand. "He was wrong. Remember the robin building his nest in the rain?"

"Are you really going?"

"Yes."

"Maybe we can be adult about this," Francine began. "Don't you think leaving like this is merely a regression? A flight into fantasy? The romanticized childhood and idealized past?"

"Hardly."

Francine started to stand up. She remembered the cut on her foot. "It's been done, kid," she said. "The Woodstock trip is passé. The journey to the east, to the south. It's a standard convention, a cliché."

"That's irrelevant," I said.

"It's wall-to-wall redneck out there. The bathrooms are unclean. You won't like it," Francine assured me.

"I'm going beyond that," I told my mother, "into something greater. I am going to go the distance."

There was a long silence between us. A lonely wet robin built a nest in a low branch. We watched him struggle. Snow fell in an arc of lamplight, perfect, unmarked. A pansy was pressed between the pages of a book. A purplish imprint across the title page. A moment severed out of time and preserved.

"Go the distance?" Francine said finally. "I like that. I've been waiting for you to wake up. Connect. Open your eyes. Reach out your arms for something that matters. Only a fool stays at the same losing table. Get a new deck, a new game. Just go. Go while you've got momentum. There were doors I stood at," my mother whispered. "Train terminals. Corners. A few steps in either direction and your whole life is different. I could have been someone."

"You are someone."

Francine laughed. "I mean someone good."

"You are good, Mother."

"I fucked up bad."

"So did I."

"But you can do it over. You still have a chance," my mother said, her eyes large and glowing, pulsing with something.

"I know."

After a while Francine said, "Tell me about my mother."

I told her. The night grayed. Spokes of dawn shoved through. and night was a pair of charcoal wings parting. My mother and I sat together on her brick terrace and waited for the sun. The air began to sting.

"You better go," my mother said. Her voice was small, the voice of a little girl.

"I'm afraid," I said.

"There's nothing to be afraid of. There's nothing but mediocrity out there. It's a six-thousand-dollar claimer. Our father taught us that."

We were standing near her front door. The splinters of glass glistened in the early morning sunlight. Birds chirped. My mother tried to smile. Her lips twitched. It looked as if pieces of her skin were crumbling, falling off in big white blocks.

"Go now while you've got momentum," Francine said. "Go out and box smart, slug hard. Go out and do it better than I did. Do it cleaner. Do it without lies. Do it strong." Francine opened the front door.

"You surprise me," I began.

"You surprise easy, kid."

I started walking to my car. I knew I had to walk quickly, right then, or the waves would rise inside again, the sudden black riptide, the impossible current, the whirling and spinning in black concentric circles, useless, useless.

"Wait," Francine yelled behind me.

I turned around. Francine hopped into the street. She still had the big white gauze around her foot. She was carrying something. "For your trip," she said. She handed me a brown shopping bag. She leaned close to me. "You will come back?"

"Yes."

"Do you promise?"

I started driving. At the first traffic light I looked into the brown shopping bag. One small can of tuna fish, an onion, a box of crackers, a flashlight, a large can of lima beans, a butter knife, a fifty-dollar bill, some paper napkins and a gold American Express credit card. Jesus, Francine, what a crazy picnic. And then I started laughing.

I could still feel the laughter inside me as I walked down the hospital corridor, walked through the dim folds of shadow curled across tiles the color of enamel mud. My father was sitting up in his bed. He was watching the morning news. When he saw me he turned off the television. His movements were abrupt, sharp. His eyes commanded attention. Something had happened.

GOOD NEWS. SAW DR. ATE.

"You ate already?"

VANILLA CUSTARD.

"And it worked? You swallowed it?"

My father nodded his head. There was something different about him. The color of his skin, perhaps?

BOURBON?

"Maybe tomorrow." My father's blinds were wide open. Outside, the sky was a pale and dreamy blue. The sun seemed uniform, creamy and warm and possible, possible.

My father stood up by himself. He reached for his bathrobe. I helped him drape it across his shoulders. He motioned for me to go with him. We walked into the corridor. My father produced a pad and a pen from his bathrobe pocket.

1 STEP AT TIME. DO WHOLE LENGTH TODAY. AM OLD WAR HORSE. GOOD CAMPAIGNER. WILL COME BACK.

We walked the length of three hospital rooms. He motioned for me to stop. He leaned against the corridor wall. He took a deep breath. A nurse appeared. She asked if my father needed anything. My father took out his pad and pen.

DOES SHE HAVE A BOYFRIEND?

We started walking again. We reached the midpoint of the corridor, halfway to the elevators. My father stopped dead in his tracks. I thought he was going to collapse. He extended his arms. He rolled his hands into fists. What was happening? Should I get a wheelchair, a doctor? Then he started punching at the air. His feet were moving in a very slow shuffle and he was jabbing and dodging, finding combinations, turning his bandaged neck and hooking, swinging. And behind us in the nurses' station they all stopped what they were doing. They let the phones ring, let their clipboards lie in their hands and watched my father shadowbox. Then they clapped. I helped my father back to his bed.

After a while I said I was going.

U JUST GOT HERE.

"I mean out of the city. Away. I've got to try for it."

My father looked down at the floor. One tear formed in the center of his eye. He blinked his eyes and the tear disappeared.

LIFES GONE SO BAD.

"I know. I know." I was pacing. The hills outside were fine and firm, young bodies. I could almost smell them. I looked at my father. "It's not the world you planned on, right?"

My father nodded his head.

"I understand, Daddy. The changes, the disruptions, the disintegration of the nuclear family, the failure of marriage and religious institutions. The loss of human values. The collapse of tradition." I took a deep breath. I noticed that my father was studying me carefully. His expression seemed intense and puzzled.

"I can understand. I can imagine. Once the gray-haired man was sage. A dispenser of wisdom, revered. Once the cities were different. They were holy places, enclaves of knowledge. That was before the mutations and the long process of severing man from the ground and his animal heritage. That was before industrialization, decay, rot, drugs, free sex."

I WAS BORN 30 YRS TOO SOON. I WOULD HAVE BEEN A HIPPIE.

I stared at my father. He stared back at me. Then he pointed to his wrist. I went into the corridor and looked for a clock.

"It's eleven-thirty."

My father put on his eyeglasses. He opened the *TV Guide*.

GOLF AT 1:00.

I was still on my feet, pacing and looking at the mountains through the wide-open Venetian blinds. It occurred to me that the mountains were a kind of spine. I sat down on my father's bed. I held his hand.

"I know how it must seem. You feel deserted, abandoned, cast off. The world churns. You're sixty-five. You remember another kind of world, another kind of summer. You knew the Bronx as farmland, forests with trees and streams. And here you are, one of the last of your kind. It's like being the last of a tribe. All the skills have become scrambled, decayed. How to build canoes and trap fish."

TRAP FISH??

"Not fish. Forget the fish. I just mean the old days. You can remember when any six-footer could play basketball. You watched baseball evolve. You saw them all. The entire Hall of Fame. The Yankee dynasty of the twenties. The house that Ruth built. The immortal infield. Gehrig at first. Lazzeri at second. Mark Koenig at short. You saw the first All-Star game. You knew the world before instant replay. It's like you're one of the last of a vanishing species."

My father was staring at me. He shook his head slowly from side to side.

"I know you envisioned a different sort of future for me. For us. Me married with children. Grandchildren for you to take to games. To teach them how to be shortstops. To initiate them into the culturally determined forms of manhood."

KIDS BIG NUISANCE AT GAMES.

"Look, Daddy. I failed you in a lot of ways. Things happen. Think about Native Diver struck down without warning at seven. Things just happen. The world must seem so alien to you. The role reversals. The emergence of women. The fall of America. The rising of the Third World. You even hated expansion baseball."

PROVED GOOD 4 THE GAME.

"Daddy, I'm not talking about baseball," I said.

My father shook his head from side to side. Suddenly I realized what was different about my father. The red plastic feeding tube was gone from his nose. My father was staring at me. He picked up his pad and pen.

U R NUTS.

I laughed. The feeding tube was gone. I felt pure. I felt clear, blessed. A nurse brought my father a dish of green jello. He ate it slowly. He stared at me between spoonfuls. His face was registering some form of disbelief.

NUTS.

"Then you forgive me for failing you? I'm going to do better. You'll be surprised."

U R A LUNATIC. WE R SQUARE.

"I was hoping you'd say that."

WHERE IS THE OTHER NUT? 46 YR OLD TENNIS STAR?

"She hurt her foot. She'll be here later, Daddy." I looked at my father. "Will you take care of Francine?"

HAVE PUT UP W/HER ABOMINABLE SHIT SINCE SHE WAS 16.

"You're a good man, Daddy."

U KNOW WHAT HAPPENS 2 GOOD MEN?

"Durocher was wrong. You're finishing up like a champ."

WISH I COULD B SENT 2 STUD DUTY.

"I can't help you with that. Can I get you something? There's a gift shop downstairs."

My father seemed to consider his possibilities. He nodded his head.

GO DOWN & BRING UP A NEW FAMILY.

My father was somewhere smiling. I kissed his lips. He was pointing to something. He was pointing to the door. He made a kind of ripping motion with his fingers.

"You want me to tear off the door?"

My father shook his head violently from side to side. He looked at me as if I were the strangest sort of anomaly. He took a deep breath and pointed to the door again.

I studied the door. He didn't want me to break off the door. No, of course not. I didn't even have any tools with me. Just a door. A door with a piece of paper that said NO VISITORS. Yes, of course. He wanted me to remove the sign.

My father motioned for me to come back. I stood near his bed. Then he reached out and grabbed my hand and kissed my palm. I closed my fingers tight into a fist.

I was walking down the corridor past the green cubicles, the death chambers, the humming, the human aquariums. My fist was clenched around my father's kiss. When I was a child and frightened, my father would kiss my hand. He said if I closed my fingers fast enough, the kiss would be caught inside. My father told me the kiss would stay with me all night. I could put it carefully under my pillow. I could slide it into my pocket. And

I would have a piece of him with me always. And the kiss in my hand would warm me. He said it was a magic fire.

I was halfway to the elevator. I knew I could make it. I had a can of tuna fish, a box of crackers, a flashlight, a jumbo can of lima beans, a gold American Express credit card, napkins, an onion and my father's kiss stored in my change purse, instant fire. It was early afternoon. I got in my car. What more could a woman ask for?

❦ 25 ❦

Going, yes, past gray blocks of stone chips called Civic Center rising like cliffs. I tunnel through narrow channels, through sunswirls, liquid yellow whirlpools. I am blurfast past tortuous thin cement gorges, pale scars between concrete slabs and starched hiss of bombardments, asphalt, Minotaurs, cancer, futility. Green chambers scrubbed and waiting for death, human aquariums, fluids oozing, humming. And I am plunging beyond intricacies into the unknown, unpolished, undiminished, also nameless. I am driving. It slips behind me. Cloverleaf interchange of alternative poisonous hissing deadend pathways behind me. Los Angeles, brutal claustrophobic basin of delusion and ripoff, clutter, eerie, sticky, horrible. They came, they saw and went blind. O hallucination of urban gray slabs senseless and rotting behind me. Poor ruined sunsore and sadness for demented City of Angels, of white torment and hideous albino predator birds.

I will awaken.

I will awaken. I will begin again. Anything can be a mantra. Awaken. Begin again. There are precedents: Creation from nothing, water, fire, visionary quests, human sacrifice. I will pick one, invent one. In the beginning, lightning striking a primeval soup and forging amino acids, the original alphabet. In the beginning, black volcanic rock, gneiss, basalt. In the beginning, a Polish village. And out of chaos, ignorance, gangbang lame street follies and ceiling falling down, mice scampering. Something. An inspiration tattooed by lacerations self-inflicted. And Francine, I'm talking about you. Magna Marta, the original, celestial goddess of childbirth and weaving, burials, the unconscious and ancestors. I am surrendering my rage, my sins, contempt and grief. I am beyond and into a greater, older, an impulse, the lashed faces of certain rocks.

I am streaking past pastel boxes, squashed streets with raised chicken feet of television antennas, poultry scratches, sky mutilated by black electronic webs. I am a somnambulist stretching, trying to find the right distance, pushing beyond foundations, the hard evidence. I am released from the familiar grooves and black metal tracks of parallel worlds, insanity, desperation, numb and hot and gutted. And Jason, I tried to make myself small enough for you, kept hobbling and hacking off my limbs, but they kept growing back, growing back. And I am moving, strings cut and winds blowing and going, going. I had a kite in a bird's shape. It upended in a tree stump and I forgive, I forgive. I am the kite now and terrified as road reaches out fat and gray into a muted unforeseeable distance. Cars weave around me, bumperstickers of CARLSBAD-CAVERNSPETRIFIEDFORESTSGATORGROVESMAGICMOUN-TAINSCRYSTALCAVES. And I am aiming for the arched spine, the fundamental, the bone cradle. Before bedrock and reference points. Before prime and evil. I am windsong, glistening, talking in tongues. The road curves into raw desert, how it stretches, stretches. I am drilling past sand, skimming rocks, gray scorpions and bleached gravel. Yucca waving puffs of white fists. Joshua tree with arms spread in supplication, a sunblinded demented pilgrim.

I will shed intricacies.

I will shed intricacies for the not yet known. I am grace in action and moving fast. I am twenty-seven and a pine tree my age knows more. Rushing into and casting off. I will become lighter, naked. Stone canyons of useless winding steep-sided monster face of ambivalence and indecision behind me. White haze hissing in the city of snakeskin, the rattle at my back, behind me. I am plunging in windtime, bending into the road, the rhythm, the asphalt glistening. Are you listening, Daddy? Clock these times. Inches separate the hero from the bum. I keep going, the heat terrible, scratching my face with fingers of wiry brush. Sure there will be long brutal nights alone, blind into blind and dangerous. But already I sense an other, a morning punctuated by wormsong, ecstatic, exalted. I will run a mile and an eighth. A mile and a half, goddamn it.

Rushing into afternoon, the Mohave opening slightly purple. I will have drums. Boom! Boom! Into black hawks and out the needle's eye. How I burrowed covert, curled and unnatural. I am shedding the shell, oyster grays and stinging silences, the jars of dried blood unnecessary. I am transformation from molesmall cowering into wind currents, rockchimes, cactus blossoms red and hard and memory is painful. I am streaking through Victorville and I am crazy. I am red driving into walls of red, daze of red. I am Rose. There was struggle, disgrace, failure. I will shed this. I am windborne into airtight crosshatch of coming night, into big feet and drumbeat. Boom! Boom! I will go mad, then, but keep going. I will shed all I have ever known for what is not, what may never. And the sunswirl is behind me. Savage spent hideous sunsore of greed and ruin, Los Angeles most damned. I will shed this. Seventy-three miles from Barstow, last outpost. I won't stop the car. The road is mine. The wind is mine. I will let it tumble from my lips. I will have cymbals and drums.

I can almost remember.

I was younger. I said this is mine. Big Sur. Berkeley. Mine. Aspen.

Mine. I can almost remember. It was before the bayonets and war. Mendocino and Laguna Beach were a strand of exploding jewels I wore. I said this is my town, my land, my country. And I am going, gripping the wheel and not stopping, not stopping. Nineteen miles from Barstow, last littered urban beacon. Clouddance in desert sky, white wings flapping. Hello, clouds. Where are you going? West? Forget it. I'm rushing past Barstow and going. Pass go and keep going. No two hundred? Fuck it. I don't need it.

I can almost remember.

I was dormant, numb and stupid. I said I never tried to stop a war. I said if it was me, it was some other me, irrelevant. I said I subscribed to absolutely nothing. I said I accepted, submitted, was beaten, utterly broken, willing to slide into the white haze and long white siesta of a race. And I lied. Lied on purpose, yes. Hush of windbreath that I might become and aming, unfamiliar, severed, unique, cut out of time, both the first and the last of the line.

Rushing into slow falling tentative web of fragile velvety darkness halfway to the Arizona border, the possibilities, the fundamental and starwhirl. I am going farther. I will say it out loud and let it pour from my mouth. I am taking the goddamn bricks and thorns and plaster out. I remember when the world was mine. North to Mendocino, redwoods with a tapestry of moss and pine cone spokes at their feet. Holy. The path south a sacred gash into the liquid face, white tequila sun. Holy. The Arizona border at nightfall. Holy. I can say it. I can take the stinking bricks out of my mouth and say Salt Lake, say Taos. The earth shakes. It is mine. I will not tremble. I will grip the wheel and go the distance. I am driving, my face widening with the dusk coming down in sheets between spokes of sagebrush layered in dark chalks. Pale hills inching purple into night. Stubborn rocks curled tight while winds whip and ride.

Daddy, I'm afraid. The world is a six-thousand-dollar claimer for cripples who can't find the wire. But I can barely see straight. A wind is blowing cold and hot. I'm shaking, trembling, spinning and needing a shot. Soon I enter Navaho lands. They thought the hills carcasses of slain monsters and the black spongy-looking lavaflow cliffs to be congealed monster blood. I sense a certain residue, a part of a process. The stones have faces. Is that what you meant to tell me, Daddy? Then won't you be with me always, your face and torso chiseled into hills? In the beginning, the father. In the beginning, gneiss, granite, stormclouds, steam, lightning. A sudden invention. And you are the father, fire. You made the stars from quartz chips. You hollowed abalone shells for the sky. It is your face in the lavaflow.

I will awaken.

I will begin again.

I will shed intricacies for the not yet known.

Last vestiges of sun hanging above me, a clean dry pink, chalk soft and possible. The blackpure desert, concrete stopped. And flametips of stars, rings within rings, the glorious eyes of frenzied prophets. Possibilities, quartz chips a canopy blazing, dazzling and not turning back. Out of fire and bloodnights into black night surging forward lit by twin globe automobile eyes. Silvery arcs, channels into scorpions and small things that scurry and glow. Some other time, maybe. But I've got to keep going, cross the Arizona border, an edge clearly marked, symbolic. South the white sands spread into Mexico, into waterfalls moss smooth and choked with ferns above warm harbors. Tequila sun, absinthe and mescal sun and sand crabs, coconuts, Bogotá, Lima. And east is the painted desert and mesas, lands of sheer purples and magentas, fathers carved into plateaus. And north is the Grand Canyon, solved equation of windlash, water and time. And somewhere the great mountains where forests branch infinite fir and evergreens, alwaysgreens piercing granite, the spine, substantial and possible, possible.

FOR THE BEST IN PAPERBACKS, LOOK FOR THE

In every corner of the world, on every subject under the sun, Penguin represents quality and variety—the very best in publishing today.

For complete information about books available from Penguin—including Pelicans, Puffins, Peregrines, and Penguin Classics—and how to order them, write to us at the appropriate address below. Please note that for copyright reasons the selection of books varies from country to country.

In the United Kingdom: For a complete list of books available from Penguin in the U.K., please write to *Dept E.P., Penguin Books Ltd, Harmondsworth, Middlesex, UB7 0DA.*

In the United States: For a complete list of books available from Penguin in the U.S., please write to *Dept BA, Penguin*, Box 120, Bergenfield, New Jersey 07621-0120.

In Canada: For a complete list of books available from Penguin in Canada, please write to *Penguin Books Ltd, 2801 John Street, Markham, Ontario L3R 1B4.*

In Australia: For a complete list of books available from Penguin in Australia, please write to the *Marketing Department, Penguin Books Ltd, P.O. Box 257, Ringwood, Victoria 3134.*

In New Zealand: For a complete list of books available from Penguin in New Zealand, please write to the *Marketing Department, Penguin Books (NZ) Ltd, Private Bag, Takapuna, Auckland 9.*

In India: For a complete list of books available from Penguin, please write to *Penguin Overseas Ltd, 706 Eros Apartments, 56 Nehru Place, New Delhi, 110019.*

In Holland: For a complete list of books available from Penguin in Holland, please write to *Penguin Books Nederland B.V., Postbus 195, NL-1380AD Weesp, Netherlands.*

In Germany: For a complete list of books available from Penguin, please write to *Penguin Books Ltd, Friedrichstrasse 10-12, D-6000 Frankfurt Main 1, Federal Republic of Germany.*

In Spain: For a complete list of books available from Penguin in Spain, please write to *Longman, Penguin España, Calle San Nicolas 15, E-28013 Madrid, Spain.*

In Japan: For a complete list of books available from Penguin in Japan, please write to *Longman Penguin Japan Co Ltd, Yamaguchi Building, 2-12-9 Kanda Jimbocho, Chiyoda-Ku, Tokyo 101, Japan.*